CANOPY OF MYSTERY

Wayne Peterson

Jane,

I really enjoyed talking to you about writing. I hope you write your own story.

Wayne
1-9-19

Book 2

I dedicate this book to Colonel Andrew Hudson,
a good editor, a great writer, and a better friend.

I would like to thank Cap'n Lee Sneath and the members of the Writer's Roundtable for their encouragement, companionship, editing, and feedback. Fellow travelers make the journey sweeter.

To my beta readers Diane, James, Andrew, Melissa, and Lawrence, thank you for keeping me honest. You helped me find the story.

1

"I thought when we settled Canopy, and Inception went down, we were definitively starting over. Then, when the first child was born on Canopy, I knew the real transformation had begun."
— *From the memoir of Myoki Miles*

~~~

Myoki was quite proud of the desks and chairs in her classroom. There were only four of each, but they were well built, sturdy, and beautiful. Her husband, Choop, sanded them using the skin of a stickypede tendril and varnished them with juices from the plant he called the varnish vine.

The desks and chairs were crafted in Canopy's first wood mill, located five-hundred yards below Knot City. Choop's best friend, Kejuon Washington, a famous Scout and the second human to live permanently on Canopy, started the wood mill. The mill was powered by a huge waterwheel built to take advantage of the continuous flow of water down tree trunks deep in the Shadows of Canopy.

Saoirse Miller, the first human born on Canopy, came into the classroom that Myoki still thought of as a 'cave dug into the trunk of a massive tree', but Saoirse only thought of it as a room. Every room the child had ever entered was dug from a tree. The forest went from the water to the sky in every direction. How else would you have rooms unless you dug them out of a tree?

"Happy birthday, Saoirse." Myoki had been practicing her teacher voice. "How does it feel to be nine years old?"

"It feels the same as eight and a half except I'm in the third grade!" Saoirse was so excited her voice squeaked.

"I'm glad you're excited about school, Saoirse. I am, too. This is a historic day. You are Canopy's first third-grade student, and I am the first third-grade teacher. You're also the first student to use the new desks. Please sit at your desk. Do you like it?"

Saoirse sat tentatively. Compared to sitting cross-legged on a wide branch, which was normal for a little girl, it seemed stiff and formal. She said, "It feels funny."

Myoki laughed. "It's how people sat in school on Earth when I was little."

"Why?"

"Well, Saoirse, on Earth the forests weren't so tall they filled the whole world like on Canopy. There were open spaces where you could sit in the sun. We built buildings from the wood of trees to live in. Schoolhouses, too."

"Open spaces? You mean like in the Overhead?"

Myoki laughed again. "No, open spaces where you could stand in the dirt."

"What's dirt?"

Myoki sighed. This wasn't going as she had imagined. "Okay, let's start over. Saoirse, you know we, all people I mean, came here from Earth, right?"

"Yes."

"And you know we had to leave Earth because its sun was going to go nova, uh, I mean, uh …, explode, right?"

"That's what Momma said, but I don't really understand it."

Myoki laughed again. Saoirse was so intelligent, entertaining, and honest that she was a joy to be around. As Myoki laughed, the unborn baby in Myoki's belly wiggled and kicked.

"That's okay, Saoirse. Nobody really understands why it happened. It just did."

"But, what does that have to do with dirt?"

"Well, nothing, really. I was just trying to point out that Canopy is not like Earth. Canopy is covered with a twelve-thousand-foot-deep forest where Earth just had shallow, scattered forests. Canopy has three suns where Earth had only one. Canopy has no continents where Earth had seven. …"

"What's a continent?"

Myoki chuckled while her unborn infant squirmed again. "Well, Saoirse, it's … uh … it's where we kept the dirt." Myoki's chuckle deepened into an open-throated laugh.

"Is dirt funny?"

"Only when you try to describe it to someone born on Canopy. Let's switch gears …"

"What's a gear?"

"I'll show you some when we visit the wood mill on our first field trip. But, for now, it means let's talk about something called ecology."

Myoki stepped to the "blackboard". She didn't call it that, but that's how she thought of it in her mind. It was made of wood, stained very dark brown with juices from one of Canopy's plants. It had been sanded with sandpaper made from stickypede tendrils and was very smooth.

She thought of her writing instrument as "chalk" even though it was a stick of soft wood soaked in juices of a milk plant and dried in the sun high in the Overhead. It left a chalky-white line easy to see and easy to erase. She did not refer to it as chalk for the same reason she did not refer to the board as a blackboard, because the name would have confused Saoirse and caused unnecessary explanations.

She drew three circles on the board and began.

"These two circles represent Earth and this one represents Earth's sun."

"There are two Earths?"

"No, it is circling around the sun and these represent Earth at two different times in the trip. Like this."

She held up an appleberry and a limefruit. The appleberry was the size of a large apple and tasted like blueberry. The limefruit was the size of a lemon, bright green, and tasted similar to grapefruit. She moved the limefruit in a circle around the appleberry.

She drew a line in the smaller circles at a slant and said. "This represents the axis of the spin of the Earth."

She held the limefruit with its long axis matching the line on the board and spun it as she revolved it around the appleberry, and said, "Can you see what I mean?"

"I think so."

"Okay, good." She put down the fruits and picked up the chalk, drawing parallel lines from the sun to the Earths. "This represents the sunlight shining on Earth. You with me so far?"

"Yes"

"Now, here's the important part. If we were on the Earth at this point, not down at the middle but here, then when the Earth is like this one it is called summer. See how the sun would shine straight down on you? This one over here, the sun shines at an angle. This is called winter. The sunlight is less intense."

Saoirse looked confused and said, "So the dirt is hotter in

the summer?"

"Yes! Saoirse, you're so smart. That's exactly what happens, the dirt is hotter in the summer. The reason I'm showing you this is to try and explain what we called seasons. The winter was cold and the summer was hot, every year. The plants and animals adapted to this and developed to deal with it. This matters because I wanted to explain that on Canopy we don't have seasons."

"Because we don't have dirt?"

Myoki laughed softly and said, "No, because we have three suns."

She erased the circles and then drew another set of them, this time with three large circles and one smaller one in the middle.

Myoki said, "This drawing is not accurate because our three-sun system is very complex, but the principle is accurate. The large circles represent our suns and the smaller one represents Canopy. See how the suns shine on us about the same all over regardless of the axis of Canopy's spin?"

"I guess so."

"I know it's complicated, but trust me, we don't have seasons."

"I already knew that."

Myoki paused, thinking. "I'm sorry, Saoirse, I'm not doing a good job as a teacher. That explanation was overly complicated."

"It's okay. I'm just glad we don't have hot dirt."

Myoki smiled and said, "Let's keep things simple. We have forest over all of Canopy, extending thousands of feet into the air. The top part is more open with more light and everything is green."

"The trees are thousands of feet tall, I know. Were they like that on Earth, between the dirt, I mean?"

"No. And they are only that tall on Canopy because they connect. We think down below the water, the roots are all connected so the trees are really just a single organism. We do have trees like that on Earth, called aspen trees, but they don't connect above ground. Here on Canopy, the trees come out of the water at an angle. They rise to a point where three or more trunks join together in what we call Knots. The Knots are tree trunks wrapped around one another. The trunks rise from these Knots to other, smaller Knots. In this way the trees form a stable structure that can rise thousands of feet. The real boon for us are the parasitic plants in the Knots. They provide most of our food and hard woods."

"I don't know what boon means and I don't know what a parasticky is."

"Parasitic. It means the plants are rooted not in the soil but in the tree itself. The parasitic plants live on the tree. Boon just means it's good for us."

"Why didn't you just say it's good for us?"

"Well, I should have. I'm new to teaching a third grader, I'll get better at it, I promise. Where was I? Oh yes, the top part is more open, has more light, everything is green.

"I know. That's what Momma calls the Overhead. Tripods live there and spinners fly around."

"Yes, that's right. The tripods have three legs and are all eyes. The spinners puff their skin out and fly like a frisbee when they jump from tree to tree."

"What's a frisbee?"

It's a toy we had on Earth. A platter you could throw. Moving on, a little deeper into the forest, about eight-thousand-feet elevation, begins what we call the Jungle. The light is much dimmer and everything is darker green. Lots of water trickling down the tree trunks."

"That's where the panthers live. They'll eat you," Saoirse said with a very serious expression.

"Yes, they're dangerous. We call them that because they're black and have claws and long tails like an animal on Earth. But the ones on Earth didn't have six legs, only four. The Jungle also has spidermonkeys. We call them that because Earth had things called spiders that caught their food in webs, and spidermonkeys use webs to catch their dinner. We call them monkeys because they have long tails to hold onto their web and Earth monkeys had tails."

"Momma told me they're smart."

"Yes, we'll cover them in more depth in a minute. The Jungle also has treerats, which are delicious, like spinners. And it has the stickypedes. They have five body segments and move kinda like a worm except they have tendrils for legs, covered with a rough surface that can stick to the tree branches like velcro. Please don't ask me what velcro is, it's too complicated. Just know it sticks to things. There are many other animals, I'm just hitting the highpoints."

"I like spinner sandwiches."

"I do, too, Grasshopper."

"What's a grasshopper?"

"It's what I call someone whose mind jumps around." Myoki continued her lecture. "And then down at the bottom, from about four-thousand feet elevation to the water, we call the Shadows. It is very dark with lots of water. Everything is wet all the time. Panthers live down there, too, as well as raccoons. Those are the main ones, there are others, but panthers and raccoons are the most noteworthy."

"Noteworthy?"

"It just means, uh, important. Then, living in the water, are all kinds of fish. We don't have them all catalogued yet. The most noteworthy are the ones we call whales."

"Momma says they're really big, and really smart. They can make you float."

"Well, you're momma is right. They can control gravity

in a way we don't understand yet. They are the Canopians, the owners of Canopy."

Sarah, Saoirse's mother, entered the back of the classroom quietly.

Saoirse said, "They own Canopy?"

"Yes, just like we owned Earth. They were here first and are the dominant species."

"Momma says they're distribled."

"You mean distributed. That's true. They are made up of many creatures that communicate with gravity waves."

"Momma says they deserve our respect."

Sarah said, "Saoirse, who's teaching who? You should listen to Myoki, not be telling her what I say."

Saoirse spun around in her desk. "Momma! You're here. I've been learning a lot. I learned we don't have dirt. I learned we don't have seasons. I learned we don't have one sun."

Laughing, Myoki said, "Sarah, I promise you I have also been teaching her about things we do have."

Saoirse said, "We've been talking about things we do have, but so far, only things that are noteworthy."

~~~

Myoki groaned as she sat up in the bed.

Choop said, "You alright? If I remember right, you don't think the last month of pregnancy is much fun."

"I know I'm repeating myself, but with Ela, I really

thought Canopy's thirty-percent gravity would make it easier. With Bina, I knew it might not be easier, but hoped Ela was just a hard pregnancy. Niti's birth confirmed it; I now have no illusions. Pregnancy sucks." Myoki sat on the edge of the bed to gather her strength.

"Sucks? You never say sucks. You're really taking this one hard."

"I'm just trying to talk to a soldier in his own tongue."

"I'm not a soldier anymore."

"You will always be a soldier. You just don't have anyone to fight right now."

Choop sat up in bed as he watched Myoki struggle to get up. "Look on the bright side. Maybe our son will come out easier."

"Choop, we don't know it's a boy. Quit getting your hopes up. And what the hell makes you think a boy would come out easier?"

"It's a boy. I'm certain you are carrying our son. We'll name him Mose. And he'll come easier because he's going to be polite."

Myoki waddled toward the toilet closet carved into the far side of the room. "At least this cave has a toilet built in."

"Myoki, why do you insist on calling it a cave. It's a room. Just because it's carved out of a tree doesn't mean it's a cave. It's man-made. It's built of wood. It's an apartment."

"And you, by the way, are a male and you're are the furthest thing from polite it's possible to be. You are anti-polite. You are not just impolite, you are unmannerly, inconsiderate, discourteous, and, dare I say, callous."

"I like that you try so hard to teach Ela good vocabulary, but she's not awake."

"Yes, I am, Daddy. I've been laying here listening to you be unmannerdly."

"That's unmannerly, sweetie, no 'd' in it anywhere. And don't listen to your mother. She's got ninth-month-pregnancy-brain. She babbles."

"Momma told me what to call it when you do that. You're being sarcastical."

From the far bed, Niti's cries filled the room.

Choop glanced at the panther skin that served as a door to the toilet. He didn't want Myoki lecturing him about waking Niti. "Now we've done it. We woke Niti. It's not time to get up yet, Ela. Why don't you lay down with her and get her back to sleep."

Eight-year-old Ela got up and padded over to three-year-old Niti's bed and snuggled up next to her, murmuring quiet assurances.

Myoki exited the toilet, pulling the panther skin slowly to keep quiet. She spoke in a whisper. "I wish you would make a tank for the toilet. I know it's weird because I haven't heard it for nine years, but I miss the flushing sound."

Choop whispered as well. "Water just runs through it all the time. It doesn't need a tank. One thing Canopy has in spades is water."

"I know. I said it's weird. We've been here so long, but we still miss things from Earth. It sounds like Ela, Bina, and Niti are back asleep."

"Yeah. I tell you what's weird to me. I still can't get used to how the kids move. They can't jump like we can in this low gravity, but it's more than that. They move differently than Earth-born."

"Well, duh. They're not Earth-born."

"Now look who's being unmannerdly."

Myoki giggled softly as she got back into the bed and snuggled up to Choop. She continued to speak in a soft whisper. "You still going to Knot City in the morning?"

"Yes. I need to see if I can talk some sense into the leaders. We are making the same mistakes we made on Earth. For some reason, I thought starting over would be different."

"It's not different. Look at Knot City, the whole place is covered in nets to keep people out. You have to get clearance just to enter. It's so stupid."

"They're just afraid of other humans."

"Yeah, I know. I wish I could say they shouldn't be, but

Burl City has become a military base run by Generals, no elections. Knot City is probably right to be afraid of them."

"And further to the north, in Thicketown, they only allow Muslims to enter. It's like we learned nothing from what we did on Earth."

"Well, what can you say — people." Myoki meant it to be cute, but her voice sounded sad.

"That's not the worst of it. I've heard talk of attacking the whales! Can you believe that? If they had been there to see a whale explode Captain Chamber's head, they would know better. We must get along with the whales. They could easily snuff us out if they take a mind."

Myoki snuggled up to Choop, throwing her leg across his stomach in the position that took pressure off her lower back. "Do you think I can ever get you to stop calling them whales? They are the sentient species of this planet. They are Canopians."

"Well, they live underwater, and they're big as hell, what do you expect?"

"But, they're smart. If you spent time every day talking to them, like I do, you might call them Canopians, too. At least call them that when you go to Knot City."

"You're right, you're right, it is better if the leaders see them as the dominant species of the planet." Choop had his arm around Myoki and rubbed her lower back. "How are the sign language lessons with the Canopians, by the way?"

"Pretty good. They are up to around seven-hundred words, but it's mostly nouns and simple verbs. I still struggle when I try to discuss anything abstract. The good news is every time we start with a new whale, they have gotten the vocabulary from the last whale, so the sign language is spreading."

"You just called them whales twice."

Myoki lightly punched Choop in the chest. "The bad news is their culture is a mystery that must be solved if we are to survive on Canopy. We don't really understand how they think at all, and they are more powerful than we are. We are *not* at the top of the Canopian food chain, we are number two."

"Do we really need to solve this mystery, as you call it, to co-exist with them?"

"Well, yes, I think we do. For example, you could say to any human something like 'I had to choose the wrong that's most right' and they would get it. Our morality is part of our culture and it drives our decisions."

Myoki moaned in relief as Choop found a tight muscle in her lower back and massaged it.

"Choose the wrong that's most right? Myoki, that doesn't make sense."

"Really? Sarah has shared with me nightmares she has about watching Enrique's blood spurt from his neck after you slit his throat. You think that was right?"

"Well … okay, I get your point."

"My real point is this. I can't get the whales to understand most abstractions. Love, loyalty, morality, none of it seems to get across. If we don't learn how they think about such things so we can really understand them, we are at risk of extermination. This mystery of who they really are is critical."

"Well, thanks, now my trip tomorrow has life and death importance. The last thing we need is some city getting aggressive and attacking a whale."

~~~

Choop missed sunrises. On Canopy, there were no sunrises or sunsets. A day was only a day because humans kept time. Those planning the colonization knew technology would struggle on a new world and had shipped many watches in the cargo. Humans all had a watch with no battery, just a spring you had to wind once a day.

Even though one rotation of Canopy happens every twenty-five hours, the leaders agreed that a day would be twenty-four hours just as on Earth. Not because they were stubborn, but because the watches only count to twelve. Choop smiled at the irony as he sat in his favorite morning-meditation spot.

Every time his nomadic tribe of former Scouts moved, Choop would find a good place to meditate. Here, he had chosen a small branch about ten feet in diameter located beneath a massive branching of the main trunk. With the large trunk over him like a ceiling, he could only be seen from the sides. He could see anyone coming, but, if he remained still, no one ever noticed him. Old habits are hard to break.

Choop was tall, six-one, with brown eyes and sandy brown hair. He was rock hard all over due to being an exercise addict. He tried to exercise every day. He thought it was just habit from doing it on Inception during the long voyage to Canopy, but the truth was he was a warrior at heart and being out of shape was inconceivable.

He sat in a cross-legged pose with his back against the main trunk. He closed his eyes to still his mind, and he could feel the vibrations of Canopy surging through the tree trunk. He heard the distinctive scratching sound made by a panther not far away as it sharpened its claws in bark. He felt as one with his new world.

He smiled again as he thought Myoki would object to the name panther being used for something with six legs, but it was black, deadly, and had fangs and claws. How could they call it anything but panther?

This connection to the forest made him think of Bipin. His mentor on Earth had taught him to "listen to the forest" when Choop was a child.

Choop opened his eyes and stared at the tattoo on his right forearm. Bipin's name was stylistically embedded in the silhouette of a tree branch with a bird perched on it. He thought of Bipin demonstrating how to move only your head — "like a bird" — while otherwise remaining still in the forest, snapping his head quickly from side to side. Choop smiled at the memory as he lightly traced the tattoo with his finger.

He got the tattoo when he was sixteen years old, just before leaving to board the starship that would separate him from Bipin, the only father figure he ever had.

He thought of how much fun it would have been to explain to Bipin how the time-dilation effect of differing cryo-sleep schedules on the journey had allowed him to age faster than Myoki. How he gained towelve years on her and turned into a man before they reached Canopy. Bipin would have had some interesting comment.

He thought of his unborn son and wished Bipin were here to help Choop train him to understand the forest. His son Mose was going to be born in a three-dimensional forest that would fill his entire world. Choop was certain Mose would learn to listen to the forest at a young age and would be instrumental in helping mankind survive in it. The thought of Bipin watching Mose scramble around in the trees made Choop smile even more.

He looked at his watch. It was time. Choop planned a trip to Knot City today to speak with Congress. He jumped from the branch towards the next trunk, into which his local home was carved, to say goodbye to Myoki and the girls.

"There you are." Myoki was preparing breakfast for Ela, Bina, and Niti. As she sliced a tangerana into thin slices, she smiled at Choop. "You ready for your big meet?"

Her smile was genuine, but her eyes still carried worry. She was well aware of the importance of his discussion with Congress.

Choop said, "Ela? Bina? Niti? Are y'all going to be good today? Don't make Momma chase you around, her tummy's getting too big for that. Y'all stay close and help her, okay?"

"We know that, Daddy." Ela put her arm around Niti to emphasize her point. "I'll take care of everyone."

"Well, I guess I can go then, the family is in good hands."

~~~

The trip to Knot City gave Choop a good opportunity for exercise. Living near the Clearing for the Canopian they named Beluga suited Choop, but spending time taking care of children and assisting Myoki with her research didn't leave much time for serious exercise. He jumped many long jumps that weren't necessary but felt good.

He knew he was at the beginning of the suburbs when he saw the first streetlight, which was nothing more than the vine of a lamp plant. Acting like fiber optic cables, the plants brought light all the way from the Overhead. The vine would die without the plant itself, so the street light was a combination light and odd sort of planter box. The lamp plant grew wrapped around the pole of the light, which stood over a platform of the footbridge it illuminated.

The footbridge was another indicator he was entering a human settlement. The platform had a sign on it that read **Knot City: 2 miles**. He wondered if it was two miles to the Knot at the center of the city or two miles to the nets surrounding the city. Either way, a bridge that stretched for miles was impressive. He could see more streetlights in the distance.

The bridge was constructed from thick ropes made by Shorty Wanstedt. A prolific plant dubbed hemp, for obvious reasons, was used to make ropes, and the planks came from Kejuon's wood mill located beneath Knot City. The bridge was only four feet wide, but that was enough for people to walk side-by-side or pass going in opposite directions. Ropes braided into thick cables, attached to overhanging branches, suspended the footbridge. There were other ropes from the Overhead anchor points down to the center of each span, many of them, similar to suspension bridges everywhere on Earth. Choop thought they were beautiful.

The hemp plant was a godsend. It was used by many burgeoning industries, including makers of ropes, clothes, and paper. Knot City had many clothing shops that started with hemp, made it into thread with spinning wheels, then wove cloth with looms. Paper mills used hemp to create a beautiful and tough light-brown paper.

All equipment for these enterprises was made from wood.

The main trunks and branches of Canopy's massive forest were soft wood, but the various parasitic plants living in the Knots were another story. Some had stalks so dense it rivaled iron in hardness and strength. There were 'blacksmith' shops where enterprising owners created a wide variety of useful tools.

Choop did not use the footbridge except as a landmark. He continued his long jumps, paralleling the bridge. Occasionally, settlers using the bridge would look up at the 'old-timer' jumping through the forest like a monkey and smile and wave.

He began to encounter bridges at right angles to the one he was following. They circled the city outside of the nets with odd three-dimensional intersections. One intersection had six bridges leading from it: north, south, east, west, up at a forty-five-degree angle to the northwest and down at a forty-five-degree angle to the southeast. He was now officially in the suburbs and slowed his jumps, finally getting on the bridge and enjoying the sway of it as he walked.

He decided the two miles had been to the nets after all. He had been traveling quite a while before he encountered them. They were made of a combination of spidermonkey webbing and thick hemp ropes. He knew the official reason for the nets was to keep panthers out of the city. He also knew they were intended to control access by people.

No weapons were allowed in the city. This was enforced by having limited access points through the nets. There were six major gates at the cardinal points around the city: north, south, east, west, top, and bottom. Other, smaller gates were used only by the military.

He had to check his buck knife at the gate, but the guards didn't appear to know his slingshot was a weapon, so he left it in the pocket on his thigh. He did not want to go anywhere unarmed and was glad he got to keep it.

Once inside the netting, the city teemed with life. There were children everywhere he looked. There were many 'squares', huge platforms with many bridges connected to them. Shops were located around the edges of the squares, open for business selling clothes, fruit, nuts, tools, and everything one could imagine. He saw a fortune-teller and a blacksmith open for business side-by-side.

There were outdoor restaurants where customers could enjoy Canopy's version of coffee, made by boiling and crushing tangerina seeds. spinner sandwiches were popular.

All transactions were on a trade basis. Anyone willing to

work could thrive.

Earthborn moved differently than children born on Canopy. The native-born children were extremely thin with a fragile bone structure. They were taller than their Earthborn counterparts.

Choop found himself feeling hope for humanity's existence on Canopy. He saw industrious, honest people living simple, meaningful lives. He was proud and thought his uplifted mood was just what he needed to deal with Congress.

~~~

The large room, dubbed Congressional Chambers, had twenty people in it. Each of the nine human settlements of Canopy had two citizens present, the elected official and his aide. There was also a shorthand reporter with pencil and paper, ready to document everything for the official record.

Choop sat at a large table in front of a huge, raised dais where the Congressmen sat. Each Congressman had an aide behind him, seated on a large bench cut into the wall of the chambers. The setup reminded Choop of 'Congressional Hearings' he had seen on TV when he was young. The person sitting at the table was never in a good situation, he was on the 'hot seat'.

Behind Choop were six rows of benches that would hold twenty people each. All were empty.

On the back wall, to Choop's left, was a beautiful engraving of the brief text of the Constitution. The letters were carved deeply into the wood and each letter painted black. But, Choop was more interested in the board hanging to his right on the back wall. A hand painted sign had the most recent census information on it.

As he waited, Choop studied the board carefully. Not only was he interested in he numbers, but he wanted to make sure he had their names right.

City	Adult	Children	Total	Representative
Knot City	1678	327	2005	Anwar Pawar
Burl City	230	35	265	Dedric Krieger
Thicketown	303	74	377	Abisali Mahmoud
Woodstock	223	34	257	Ayden Mahoney
New Frisco	167	45	212	Allison Bramble
Utopia	178	56	234	Lynn Eschew
Shade	130	29	159	Jason Warheit
Threshold	167	24	191	Thomas Brandt
Daylight	650	243	893	Hye Jang
Rural areas	534	156	690	—
Total	4260	1023	5283	

Anwar Pawar, Majority Leader, said, "Mr. Miles, you

have the floor."

Since three of the leaders were women, Choop decided against the term 'Congressmen'. He said, "Leaders of Congress, I am a little disappointed you chose to have this be a closed meeting. The issues I wish to discuss concern all people on Canopy."

Seated in the middle of the dais, Anwar said, "We represent all the colonists on Canopy."

Even though Anwar, tall, striking, well-groomed, was dignified in every respect, his statement rankled Choop. "We have almost seven-hundred colonists who don't live in one of the cities. What about them?"

Dedric Krieger, Congressman from Burl City, said, "They should move into a city if they want to be represented."

Choop disliked Dedric immediately. He had the look of a bully. He was blond with a receding hairline, stocky and muscled, with beady brown eyes. Choop responded, "I don't live in a city. Are you saying I have no business here?"

"He could not say that because it is not true." This statement was made quietly. Choop noticed how the room grew still in order to hear the soft voice of Hye Jang, Minority Leader. Choop was reminded of how his former boss, Sergeant Stallman, had commanded a room by using the same tactic. To hear her, you had to be still and pay attention. "I apologize for Congressman Krieger. He has a tendency to blurt."

"Blurt?" Krieger's face was red and blotchy. "Why, you yellow witch…"

"Enough!" Ayden Mahoney's bellow reverberated in the large room. "I've told you to check your racism at the door to these chambers, Dedric. I'm not above coming over there and putting a knot on your head."

"Gentlemen, please!" Anwar raised both hands, palms out, facing the two Congressmen who were situated at opposite ends of the dais. "We're not here to discuss old feuds. We're assembled to hear what Mr. Miles has to say."

The room gradually grew quiet while Choop waited. The only person in the room who seemed calm was Hye Jang.

"I come to speak with you today because I have heard rumors that some of the settlements are saying they think we should attack the Canopians."

Abisali Mahmoud, Congressman from Thicketown, Canopy's Muslim settlement, said, "Canopians? You mean who, exactly?"

"I am referring to the native species of the planet. They are commonly called whales for obvious reasons, but they are the dominant sentient species of Canopy and should properly be called Canopians."

"It seems as though you're trying to put them on equal footing with humans, Mr. Miles. The Qur'an gives us dominion over animals."

"With all due respect, Sir, they are not animals. My wife, Inception's Xenobiologist, has been working to communicate with them using sign language. They are very intelligent."

"Dolphins were intelligent as well, but still animals."

"Congressman Mahmoud, all of you, there is one thing you need to understand. On Earth, humans climbed to the top of the food chain. Here, we are not at the top of the food chain, we are number two. The Canopians could wipe us out in a day if they chose. Aggression against them is suicide."

Allison Bramble, Congressperson from New Frisco, exclaimed, "What? You're surely exaggerating. That can't possibly be true."

"I assure you, Representative Bramble, I am not distorting the truth. I saw the Canopian that lives in the Clearing under this very city kill twenty Scouts. He first warned me to clear out in order to save myself. Later, he caused the head of Captain Chambers to explode when the Captain was threatening the life of a child. These actions show both the power and the intellect of the Canopians."

Jason Warheit, Congressman from Shade, the lowest city on Canopy and the closest to the whales, said, "We've all heard those fairy tales, Mr. Miles, let's stick to reality, please."

"I'm afraid he's telling the truth, Jason. I was there when Captain Chambers head exploded," Anwar said quietly.

This caused the room to grow quiet. Choop let the silence stretch. He wanted the reality of the situation to sink in.

Finally, Thomas Brandt, the Dean of the University of Canopy and the Congressman from Threshhold, said, "You speak of rumors of aggression against the whales, Mr. Miles. Could you be more specific?"

"Well, Dr. Brandt, the problem is they are just rumors. I can't speak of hearing anything firsthand, but I live in the boonies. The rumors I heard referenced people from Burl City stating they knew of plans to kill a Canopian in order to claim his Clearing for a new city. They want to live on the water, it seems."

All heads turned to look at Dedric Krieger. Lynn Eschew, Representative from Utopia, spoke first. Her curly blond afro bobbed as she exclaimed, "Well, Dedric, you want to clue us in?"

Dedric spoke in a subdued monotone dripping with malice. "First of all, they're animals, these whales. They are not intelligent and they are not powerful. Secondly, the myths that they can control gravity and explode heads are exactly that, myths. Last, and most importantly, this Congress does not have the authority to interfere in the internal affairs of Burl City. How we choose to expand our city limits is none of your business. Congress can't tell us what to do."

The entire dais erupted in exclamations and questions, everyone talking at once. Finally, Anwar took control by slamming his palms down on the dais loudly and repeatedly until everyone quit talking. Anwar said, "Everyone keep quit and let me speak. I'll give others a turn when I'm done. First, I have a statement, and then some questions for Mr. Miles."

All the representatives on the dais settled back in their seats. The aide behind Dedric Krieger leaned forward and whispered in his ear.

Anwar spoke evenly, not showing emotion. "I state, for the record, I witnessed the whale, er, Canopian, known as Moby, who occupies the Clearing beneath Knot City, control gravity by trapping Scouts and relieving them of their weapons. I also saw the head of Captain Chambers explode into mist. He was no more than fifty feet from me when it happened. I have no scientific proof the control of the Scouts or the death of Captain Chambers were the actions of the whale, but nothing else makes sense.

"I also state for the record, that the concerns presented by Choop Miles seem significant and real. Creatures with the power to control gravity and explode heads should be dealt with seriously and treated with caution.

"Now for my questions. Mr. Miles, you say further

efforts to communicate with the Canopians are ongoing, is that correct?"

"Yes, Sir, it is."

"You also have told me in the past that these creatures are a 'distributed being'. By that, I mean they are composed of different bodies that communicate wirelessly, for lack of a better term. Has this been confirmed?"

"Yes, Sir. We have even gotten a good understanding of their reproduction and the extent of the creatures which comprise each Canopian entity."

"I believe a part of that collection of 'creatures', as you say, are the animals we call raccoons, correct?"

"Yes, Sir. There are normally six raccoons, six spidermonkeys, and dozens of spider-looking things called tripods which comprise each whale, er, Canopian. New raccoons, when needed, transform from spidermonkeys. spidermonkeys transform from tripods."

"So, would it be correct to say that when raccoons, spidermonkeys, or, tripods in the case of Utopia, are around people, they can understand the speech of the humans due to you teaching them sign language."

"Well, yes, I guess that's correct. They understand a lot, but I think their ability to communicate without speech gives them the ability to understand us even better than with just speech. I think they pick up on emotions straight from our brains, although I have no scientific proof of this."

"So, would you agree it is likely that, if people are planning to kill a whale, the whales already know this?"

"Well, Sir, I have to admit the possibility, although I suspect people in favor of killing them don't hang around with raccoons and spidermonkeys."

Dedric roared from the end of the dais, "This is a waste of our time. Where are you going with this, Anwar?"

"I am trying to determine the danger we might be in, and appropriate actions to take."

Dedric and his aide were already on their feet as Dedric responded, "This is bullshit. Anyone with common sense knows they are just animals. We can and will treat them as animals. We're done here."

As Dedric stormed from the room, Anwar said to Dedric's retreating back, "Wait. Dedric. ... Aw, for God's sake."

2

"I remember learning about 'paradigm shifts' in school. I'm not sure I can shift my paradigm far enough to understand Canopians. They don't have gender, they don't have speech, and they are connected in a way humans can't fathom."

— From the memoir of Myoki Miles

~~~

"Good morning, Myoki." Danielle's greeting was genuine, her tone light.

"Is it? Morning I mean? I miss sunrises. It's only morning because the clock tells us it is and we agreed twenty-four hours make a day. Why are you in such a good mood?"

"Wow. Grumpy much?"

Danielle was the physical inverse of Myoki. Where Myoki was short, five-three, Danielle was tall, five-nine. Myoki's green eyes and alabaster skin were in stark contrast to Danielle's olive complexion and dark chocolate brown eyes. The only physical characteristic they shared was jet-black hair.

Adam raised his hand, palm-out, to Danielle. "Danielle, leave her alone. Sorry, Myoki, she's going hunting this morning, and you know how much she likes to kill things."

Danielle's husband, Adam, shared her dark complexion and dark features. With a closely-cropped black beard and receding hairline, his six-two frame made Danielle slightly less imposing, if you didn't know how deadly she was with slingshot, knife, hands, feet, and anything else she might have handy.

Myoki had a fleeting thought that made her smile. In this new world, on this new planet, the fact that he was of Pakistani descent and she was of Israeli descent mattered not one iota. Her own Irish-Japanese roots were inconsequential. Where you came from was Earth, period.

Danielle said, "You think he's funny? Please don't tell me you think he's funny."

"What? Oh, no, I just had a thought that made me smile. Here we are, standing on a thirty-foot diameter tree branch like it's normal. Don't you occasionally pause and realize how far we've come?"

Danielle and Adam looked at each other. Danielle asked, "Myoki, have you been having contractions? Is it time?"

"What? You think because I had a moment of introspection that I'm going into labor?"

"No, I think because you look like a watermelon that you might be going into labor."

"Well, I'm not. Why don't you go kill a woodland creature that's edible? I'm in the mood for some spinner chili."

Danielle said, "That's the spirit. There's the Myoki I know and love."

Myoki said, "Did Sarah whine about being the only one on daycare duty?"

Danielle said, "Her two are already a handful, but when you add my three boys and your three girls, she has more than enough to keep her busy. She hates it when I go hunting."

Danielle jumped towards a higher branch fifty feet away, calling, "I'll be back around lunch time. Adam can help deliver your baby if necessary."

Myoki turned to Adam and said, "I don't know how you live with that constant stream of sarcasm. Let's go talk to Beluga. She doesn't have a sarcastic bone in her bodies."

Adam replied, "I couldn't live without Danielle. And, I think it's odd you refer to Beluga as she when you know it's not female, yet you make it a point to use plural bodies to be accurate about the fact Beluga is a distributed being."

"Well, she's not male, and saying 'it' seems wrong."

Myoki jumped to a lower branch, nimble in spite of her girth. Adam followed. She continued descending into the

Shadows for several minutes, making long graceful jumps.

When they reached Beluga's Clearing, Myoki landed on one of the lowest horizontal branches and motioned to Adam by putting her index finger in front of her lips.

Adam said, "Why are you shushing me? It can read our minds."

Myoki frowned and said, "Adam! Here we are trying to teach an alien sign language and you can't even understand the universal signal to keep quiet."

"We don't sign to it since it can read our minds; it just signs to us. What good does it do to keep quiet when Beluga can read our minds? And why do you want to keep quiet anyway?"

Myoki just pointed down at the center of the water in the Clearing.

Adam turned, expecting to see open water surrounded by active raccoons as was normal. Instead, he saw six inert raccoons. Each was totally still, resting on one of the shelves carved into trunks surrounding the Clearing.

In the middle of the Clearing, he saw two eyes. Each at least two feet in diameter.

They weren't set in the head of a creature as one would expect when seeing two eyes. They were on the side of the biggest snake he had ever seen. The eyes weren't side-by-side: one was above the other vertically.

He knew it wasn't a snake, but a Canopian, called a

whale because it was large and stayed submerged.

He couldn't see how much was below the water but could sense it was massive. The Canopian was bowed into an arc with the body disappearing into the water in each direction. The part above water was shaped like a dark gray earthworm on its side, rolling over and over in the water. Adam smelled charcoal intensely.

Adam estimated the eyes were about ten feet apart. He could see only two eyes at a time as it rolled. One eye would disappear over the top, and another would rise from the water. The whale had to be at least twenty-five feet in diameter.

He knew it had six eyes, but hearing them described and seeing them were different matters. His mouth hung open, and Myoki got her wish for quiet.

The eyes had no pupils and looked like human eyes when totally dilated. They could rotate in the socket like human eyes and stayed focused on him while passing.

He snapped his mouth shut. He felt no danger, but inside his skull was a deep rumbling.

Myoki whispered, "I think she's giving birth. Stay here. Stay quiet." She jumped and landed next to one of the inert raccoons.

The raccoon lying at her feet stirred and stood up.

The whale stopped rolling.

The entire forest was eerily silent.

The rumbling, itching feeling in the humans' brains intensified.

Myoki said, "I am sorry we disturbed you, Beluga. It's the normal time for our sign language exercises."

Beluga's whale-body began to slowly roll again. It's raccoon-body stuck two arms in the air, two towards the water, and began to sign.

[*Birth. Soon. Imperative.*]

Seeing the sign for 'imperative' gave Myoki a sense of pride. It had taken two days of training before she was confident Beluga correctly understood the meaning.

Myoki said, "May we watch?"

[*Affirmative. No signing.*]

The raccoon settled onto the shelf and became completely inert. Myoki recognized this as a 'disconnection' from Beluga. Choop had described it, but this was the first time she witnessed it.

The whale resumed rolling. The sound of the water splashing as it rolled filled the air. The charcoal smell was overpowering.

Myoki and Adam sat where they were, watching, as the rolling increased in speed. This continued for several minutes. It was mesmerizing to watch. Myoki felt peaceful and calm, but her unborn child began to kick hard and frequently.

As the rolling became almost a blur, it felt like Myoki's

unborn baby was running in place. Suddenly the rolling stopped. As the splashing sounds died, her baby became still.

Myoki had both hands on her belly as she stared at Adam.

Adam said, "What? Are you okay? You're kinda pale."

"It's nothing."

Bubbles began to rise from the water. Hundreds of bubbles floated up into the forest over the Clearing.

The whale dived, disappearing into the depths. All the raccoons stood up and ascended into the foliage around the Clearing except for the one near Myoki. It stood and signed.

[*Birth complete. You have questions.*]

"Yes, I do. Were those bubbles your offspring?"

[*Affirmative.*]

"There were so many of them!"

[*Most not survive. Tripods food source for others.*]

"So a normal part of your experience is watching through the eyes of tripods as they die?"

[*Not die. Beluga continues.*]

"Beluga, I know you see into me. I know you see I am carrying an unborn child. Is it the same for you? Is there a gestation period?"

[*Not same.*]

Myoki learned early in the process of communicating

with Canopians just how literal and succinct they were. She knew it was partly due to the limited vocabulary of the sign language, but suspected it was also just the way they thought.

"So, you pass only your own genetic material when you give birth?"

[*Negative.*]

"You have mated with another Canopian?"

[*No signs.*]

This was a single sign which Beluga used often. Myoki knew it meant 'I do have an answer to your question, but don't know signs to convey the answer.' She used her normal tactic of simple, direct yes-no questions.

"Did the bubbles contain DNA from another Canopian?"

[*Affirmative.*]

"But there was no mating with this Canopian?"

[*Affirmative.*]

"Have I met this other Canopian?"

[*Myoki met all Canopians.*]

"Your statement confuses me, Beluga. According to my records, you are the twentieth Canopian I have taught sign language to, and yet you have told me there are thousands of you."

[*One Canopian. Many Canopians. Same.*]

"That again. It still confuses me when you say things like that."

[*Offspring will understand.*]

"What does that mean? The spidermonkeys and raccoons resulting from the newest tripods will be able to explain it to me?"

[*Myoki's offspring.*]

Myoki caught her breath and grabbed her stomach. She closed her eyes and lowered her head.

Adam said, "Myoki? Are you alright?"

"My baby kicked just as she signed that. I'm a little freaked out."

Adam said, "Just close your eyes and lay back, Myoki. Let me talk to Beluga."

Myoki complied. She lay on her side with her knees drawn up, head resting on her forearms. She closed her eyes and became still.

The raccoon turned to Adam as only a raccoon can. Its body did not pivot as there was no reason due to its symmetrical build. It just used a different set of eyestalks and the four hands nearest Adam to sign.

[*You have question. Ask.*]

"We heard a disturbing report that one of the human settlements might be planning aggression towards a Canopian. Are you aware of this?"

[*Affirmative.*]

"I apologize for this. The sentiments of this colony do not represent the feelings of all the humans."

[*Confused.*]

"Uh, … , well, the rest of the settlements bear no ill will toward Canopians."

[*Query? Humans not whole?*]

"Not whole? Uh, well." Adam looked at Myoki but found no help. She appeared to be asleep. "Sometimes humans disagree on what is appropriate. Sometimes we disagree strongly, like when religion comes into the picture."

[*Not comprehend.*]

"Don't Canopians have the concept of God? You know, believe there is a higher power?"

[*Confusion.*]

"Well, we do, and not all humans believe in the same God."

[*Humans not whole. Confirmed.*]

"I wish I could argue that point, but I don't know enough about what you mean exactly. I just wanted to warn you of the danger."

[*No danger.*]

"But there might be. Humans are sadly very clever at attacking things."

[*Danger to humans. Warning.*]

Myoki sat up suddenly, gasping, holding her belly.

"Myoki? You okay?"

"I must have been having a nightmare. It felt like my

baby was pitching a fit."

~~~

Using her teacher voice, Myoki said, "Okay kids, everyone pick a desk and sit down, please."

Saoirse, Sarah's nine-year-old daughter and the first child born on Canopy, sat down immediately in the desk she thought of as 'hers' since she always sat in it during the third-grade lessons.

Ela, Myoki's eight-year-old daughter, sat quickly as well. She worshiped Saoirse and did everything Saoirse did.

But, Ben, Danielle's eight-year-old son, didn't sit immediately. "I thought we were going on a field trip?"

Myoki responded, "We are. But, first, I am going to teach you how we draw 3D maps for navigating Canopy. The route for our field trip will be a good example of how it works."

"Can't we just go?"

"No, Ben, we can't just go. We need to know where we are going and the best way to get there. Please sit."

Ben harrumphed and sat at a desk. Myoki knew him to be willful, but she was normally able to keep him in line. As a last resort, she would use what she called 'putting the fear of Danielle' into him. He knew going home with a report of bad behavior from Myoki was not something he wanted to experience again. His mother did not allow such to pass without significant punishment.

Myoki stepped to her chalkboard and began to draw.

"This domed circle symbol is what we use to represent one of the whale's Clearings. This double-connected line represents a footbridge. This circle of short arcs we used to call a cloud symbol on Earth. I know you've never seen a cloud, and the word means nothing to you, but you might hear me call it that sometimes. It represents a Knot or, at the very least, a large trunk intersection with parasitic plants."

"I already know all this."

"I know you've seen maps, Ben, but to really understand the 3D nature of them takes a little effort. Bear with me."

Ben crossed his arms and slumped in his desk.

"So, here's the 3D trick: if you draw something with thick double lines it is in the foreground, or closest to you. The drawing is from the top down so that means it is the highest in the forest. If you draw something with light dashed lines, that means it is farthest from you, or deepest in the forest. For objects in the middle, in between those two extremes, use just single lines."

"So, if I draw a domed circle with thick double lines, that means a whale's Clearing is in the top of the forest?" asked Ben.

"No, that means whoever is reading the map will think, 'This must have been drawn by Ben. It makes no sense'," responded Myoki.

Saoirse giggled, and Ben glared at her.

"Now, here is the real trick that allows for these 3D maps to be detailed enough to be really useful," said Myoki, as she continued to draw. "When you want to show the relative depth of objects at the same level, you just break the lines. So these two footbridges cross, but you know it's not an intersection. They are just one above the other. You can tell because the lower one has the lines broken to make it look like it's in the background."

"Couldn't you just draw the lower one with dashed lines?"

"Yes, Ben, you could. Valid observation, thank you. It becomes a sort of art. One map artist might use broken lines only if the vertical distance between bridges is large, while another wouldn't. It's not an exact science, but it's very useful. You pointed out something worth understanding."

Ben smiled and sat up straighter in his seat.

"This symbol represents a human construct. Before you ask, a construct just means we built it rather than digging it out of a tree. This symbol represents a dwelling carved out of a trunk, as most of our homes are."

Myoki continued to draw without speaking.

Ela asked, "What is that squiggly line?"

"That is a large, sloping tree trunk which is used for travel when there is no footbridge. We Earth-born just jump over distance, but y'all can't so sometimes a certain trunk is used like a highway to get where you need to go."

Saoirse giggled and said, "Momma thinks it's funny when you say that."

"When I say what?"

"Y'all."

"Oh. Yes, I know she does. But I'm married to a Texan and lived in Texas for a long time so I use it to mean multiple people."

Ela perked up. Her mother seldom talked about life on Earth. She asked, "Texas was the country you lived in?"

This caused Myoki to smile. "Oh, Ela, if you only knew how right you are. But, we are getting sidetracked. Where was I? Oh, yes, the squiggly lines."

Ela frowned. She had hoped she could hear more about the country of Texas. Earth fascinated her.

"These squiggly lines usually appear when the map is near the edge of our civilized area. It just so happens the line you asked about is that tree just to the south of us. This symbol here is our classroom."

"So, you've been drawing a real map!" The astonishment on Ben's face as he said this made Myoki laugh.

"Yes, Ben, I have. This is where we are. This is the University of Canopy. This is Kejuon's wood mill down below Knot City. This is the path we are going to take."

All three kids murmured excitedly.

"On the way back, we go here and here, deeper into the Shadows. We are going to stop at this Clearing for a real treat. Y'all are going to get to meet some raccoons and learn a little sign language. We're going to visit Beluga."

Ben said, "Wow! Why are we still sitting here?"

From the back of the classroom came Danielle's voice, "Because you were waiting on me. I'm coming along as Scout in case of panthers and such. Your teacher is too big around to defend you. Plus, I have to deliver Sarah's research to the University."

~~~

The kids were well behaved during the entire trip. Not only because Danielle's presence caused Ben to toe the line, but because they were awed by the sights. They were used to living on the fringes of human civilization, so they were in a constant state of amazement most of the trip.

The University fascinated Ela. She was full of questions but didn't ask them. She would ask later at home.

Saoirse was enamored with the markets in Knot City. Danielle had to drag her away from a cloth shop as they prepared to descend towards the mill.

The wood mill was Ben's favorite. The huge water wheel was impressive. Kejuon even let him pull the lever that engaged the clutch so the kids could watch the huge saw-chain spin. Myoki thought the chain made of spidermonkey webbing, hemp, and panther teeth was remarkable and asked about its construction.

Myoki was glad she was with native-born children by the time they headed for Beluga's Clearing. She was getting close to her delivery date, and the children's inability to leap to distant trees was welcome. Myoki was getting tired and didn't feel like doing it.

Ben said, "Wow, this bridge is four times as wide as the footbridges in Knot City, maybe five."

Danielle, seeing Myoki struggle to walk along, decided to answer. "That's because this is used to bring logs to the mill and finished boards back to the settlements. There are five of these lumber bridges. That's how the settlements get their wood."

Ela asked, "But why don't people use them to travel, too. They are very sturdy and don't sway hardly at all."

"Well, for two reasons. One, all the people live higher up near the city. These bridges go to depots below most of the settlements, so they don't go where the people want to go. Second, most people don't even know they're down here, just like the tunnel system in New York, where I grew up."

Ela said, "So you grew up in the country of New York? How far was it from Texas?"

Danielle was temporarily confused by Ela's phrasing until she saw Myoki hiding a smile. "Your mother told you Texas was a country?"

"Wasn't it?"

"Well, some think so. But, New York was better."

Myoki couldn't keep quiet at that statement. "Yeah, better for the rats that lived in your tunnels."

Ela said, "What's a rat? Was it like our treerats?"

Danielle, seeing that their friendly repartee was lost on the kids, switched subjects. "Yes, but with fewer tails and legs. The point is, this bridge is used by wheeled trailers to haul wood, so we need to pay attention. Some of them are very wide so we may have to move to the side and stand still to let them pass."

When they got to the end of the lumber bridge, Ben was fascinated with the depot's cantilevered loading cranes. The movable counterweights allowed the operator to lift massive loads. Ben wanted the operator to let him turn the crank and move a counterweight, but the operator was not interested.

"It's okay, Ben. It's not that exciting anyway," said Saoirse. "I remember the map. This is where we start walking the squiggles."

The large trunks descended at a steep angle, and Myoki struggled, waddling down them with noticeable grunting. All the kids noticed and began taking turns climbing just in front of her, in case of a fall, and following her closely to offer support. She was embarrassed but appreciated that these were good, caring children. None of them said a word about what they were doing.

The trunk they were descending had a shelf for a raccoon next to the Clearing. As the group arrived. The raccoon stood and signed.

[*Welcome. Sit. Rest.*]

Myoki felt embarrassed once again, but, oddly, with more intensity. She knew that the Canopian could see into her mind and the total exhaustion she was feeling was obvious to Beluga.

[*I am honored your warrior comes near.*]

Ben said, "What's it saying?"

Myoki answered, "She's glad to see your mother. Your mom doesn't come down here much. Ben, you can't keep asking me to translate each time Beluga signs. I will translate occasionally and even discuss some of the signs, but you need to let me visit with her, okay? I won't be signing, of course, since she can read our minds. The more English she has learned, the better she gets at it."

Ben crossed his arms and said, "Aw, okay, sorry."

"No, it's alright. I'm glad you're interested. Maybe learning Canopian sign language is something that would interest you. I could make that happen."

[*Query? Offspring male?*]

When Myoki brought others for these sessions, it was sometimes disconcerting that Beluga would comment on things which were in the minds of the other humans. She was glad the kids didn't know the signs at all, and Danielle was not very proficient. She might have to edit her translations to keep the others from feeling intimidated. Myoki had grown accustomed to it, but people usually did not like the inability to keep secrets.

"Yes. His name is Ben. He is Danielle's child. This is Ela, my oldest daughter, and this is Saoirse. The first human child born on Canopy."

[*Oldest aware.*]

"I don't know what you mean. Aware of what?"

[*No signs.*]

Myoki turned to look at the kids. "That last sign she made you will see all too frequently. It means she has not learned the signs necessary to convey what she would like to say. Beluga could you make that sign again for the kids?"

Beluga complied, making the three-armed sign slowly.

Ben said, "Why do you call it she?"

"It's just a habit I developed. She can have offspring, so she just seems better than it."

[*Male offspring thinks gender critical.*]

"Yes, that's true. It's a normal part of the way our minds work."

[*Beluga proud you witness bubble ceremony. Will share at 'No signs'.*]

"No signs? Okay, let's play the game of 'close enough' I taught you. What's a sign you've already learned that is close to the thing you're trying to say?"

[*Event.*]

"Okay. Have you learned another sign that might be close?"

[*Ceremony.*]

"An event that is a ceremony? Okay, is there a sign you know that might be considered opposite?"

[*Alone.*]

"So this event is the opposite of alone? Will there be other Canopians there? Will they be the ones with whom you're sharing the news of my seeing the bubbles?"

[*Not one question.*]

"Sorry, will there be other Canopians there?"

[*Affirmative.*]

"And you will share the news with them?"

[*Negative. Truth.*]

"I don't understand. You won't share at all, or you won't share this particular information?"

[*Truth not information.*]

"Oh, I think I see. You're not just telling the story, you're sharing in a way we can't understand?"

[*Affirmative.*]

"What else occurs at this, uh, ceremony?"

[*Whole.*]

"Wow. I'm not sure how to take your meaning. How about this. Is this ceremony important?"

[*Affirmative. Affirmative.*]

Myoki had never seen Beluga repeat a sign for emphasis. She sensed she was on to something important.

"Okay. Let's create a new sign for this event. Show me a new one you would like to use."

Beluga put three arms in the air with all fingers extended. She stuck the other three arms, alternating ones, straight down with all fingers extended. This was the first time Myoki had seen Beluga suggest a sign using all of her arms.

Myoki pulled out her Canopian vocabulary notebook and drew the sign. "Beluga, when I refer to this in the future, I will use the word 'Gathering'. Do you see what I mean? Is it clear to you what you see in my mind when I say Gathering?"

[*You and warrior see different.*]

"I know our uniqueness confuses you, but at least now I can talk to you about your Gathering. Is there mating at the Gathering? Is this where you exchange genetic material for propagation?"

[*Not same. Yes and No.*] … [*Male amused.*]

~~~

After saying bye to the family, Choop traveled only a mile before stopping. He found a spot to meditate straddling a three-foot branch from which he could look straight down at two-hundred feet of open jungle. From above he could not be seen.

As he tried to empty his mind, he rubbed the tattoo on his right forearm. Thoughts of his unborn son intruded on his attempt to reach a quiet mind. He felt certain of the positive impact Mose would have on Canopy, so he used those thoughts as his mantra to become still.

After thirty minutes of meditation, he pulled a pad and pencil from his pocket and started his map. Each time he scouted for new whales that had not yet encountered humans, he drew a detailed map. His scouting trips served the double purpose of finding whales and mapping territory.

The 3D nature of this mapping exercise caused travel to be slow. As he progressed, he purposefully went up and down, from Overhead to Shadows, to try and get a complete picture of the terrain.

Myoki had come up with a clever idea. She taught the whales a sign to use in greeting. When he saw raccoons or spidermonkeys on his scouting trips, they would sign recognition, and he knew the local Canopian had already received the knowledge transfer from his neighbor. The Canopians agreed to spread this both forward, to prepare new students for further training, and back, to transfer new teachings to past whale-students.

Choop would travel as far as it took to encounter a Canopian who did not give the sign. He would then map the area around the new whale and locate a site for new homes. Each time Choop's exploration team left a home for the next, they left a cache of tools. The dwellings served as way-stations for future human travelers.

They had learned that the larger the Clearing, the older the Canopian. Working on the assumption that more mature Canopians would have more influence in their culture, he would always carefully measure the Clearing of any whale he encountered. The Canopian culture was still a huge mystery, and Choop knew human assumptions might be wrong, but they had to try.

Choop, Myoki, Danielle, Adam, Sarah, and Larry had decided to stick to an easterly exploration course for the time being. Eventually, they would return to human-occupied territory and head north. Mapping an entire planet was a big job, he would sometimes skip sleep periods to continue the work, losing track of his days and nights.

After mapping the Clearings of three Canopians who signed recognition, the fourth surprised him. As he was drawing the location of the spidermonkey web for the new Canopian, one of the spidermonkeys signed, but not with the recognition signal.

[*Stop. Talk.*]

Choop put away his pad and pencil, jumped to the branch the spidermonkey occupied, and said, "Hello. So, I guess it's pretty obvious you've learned our sign language. I'm

Choop."

[*Hello. First use of signs. Must talk.*]

Choop thought the spidermonkeys were a little creepy. They looked like raccoons except smaller, with wrinkly leather in place of fur. No eyestalks, just big eyes ringing the dome on top of their platter-shaped body. But, it was the tails that creeped him out. This one had the tails folded between his arms, but Choop knew they were very long. He was eight feet from the creature but knew he was within reach of those tails.

"Of course. Something important?"

[*Human settlement plans aggression. Must stop. Danger to humans.*]

"Yes, Burl City. I've known of this, but my pleas for peace have been unwelcome."

[*Danger to humans.*]

Myoki had shared the significance of a Canopian repeating itself. This suddenly had the feel of a threat. The itching in Choop's skull intensified. He knew there was no point in pretending he wasn't frightened since it could read his thoughts.

"Please, take no actions. I will stop my mapping and return immediately to talk with our leaders."

[*Hurry.*]

3

*"Even as new life arrives, we try to destroy that which
exists."*

— From the memoir of Myoki Miles

~~~

Before hearing the Canopian's implied threat, Choop had
never cared about Canopy's lack of metals. About how
electronics did not exist. No computers, no TVs, and more
importantly in the current context, no phones. No long
distance communications of any type.

Even in the 1800's on Earth, there was telegraph.
Canopy's communication technology was closer to the of
Earth in the 1700s. Choop had grown used to it, even
embraced it — until now. He needed to talk to the leaders
of Congress, and he needed to do it as soon as possible.

As he took long jumps towards Knot City, he worried
about getting an audience with Congress. The Congressmen
all lived in their own cities. Calling them together would
take days of planning and travel. He decided to go directly

to the home of Anwar Pawar to impress upon Anwar the critical nature of his message.

But, he didn't know exactly where Anwar lived. He looked at his watch. It was 3:15 am. He estimated he would take two hours to get to Knot City. He would be dealing with guards on night duty who would not be pleased when he insisted they let him enter and tell him where Anwar lives.

He slowed his pace. An hour or two wouldn't make a critical difference and arriving exhausted would be counter productive. For the first time in years, he felt the adrenaline rush of battle. The foe was time and logistics rather than a human, but the stakes were high. He needed to think like the warrior Myoki kept telling him he was.

His overall objective: to inform leadership of the serious threat to humanity. His first action: get to Anwar. The obstacles: guards at the gates who would make the process take hours and ignorance of Anwar's location. His main weakness: time was short, and he was alone.

He couldn't do anything about the urgency except hurry. But he thought of a course of action that would help with all the other obstacles — Kejuon. Someone he had been in battle with and trusted with his life. Kejuon lived below Knot City, and Choop was willing to bet Kejuon did not go through the gates as he traveled between his mill and the city. He might also know where Anwar lived.

He went lower, into the Shadows, to continue his journey. It would get him to Kejuon sooner while avoiding being seen by other travelers who might be out early. He had no real need to keep his arrival secret, but old habits were kicking in. Arriving without being seen seemed the right thing to do.

When Choop got to the mill, it was 6:20. Kejuon was sitting in his office at the mill, drinking coffee and going over paperwork. Kejuon would occasionally look out the open window of his office at the loading dock and the beautiful forest. This deep in the Shadows, the colors were all dark green, so he had put lamp plants on all the support posts, not just for the light but the color. Their leaves were brighter green, and he thought the scene was not only beautiful, but it calmed him.

Choop purposefully made his final jump a long one. He seemed to appear out of nowhere on the loading platform outside Kejuon's office.

"Ahoy the office! Permission to enter?" Choop couldn't help smiling at his old friend in spite of the serious circumstances causing his arrival.

"Choop, what the hell? You scared the crap outta me."

"How are you old friend? I would rather visit, catch up, and see how big your kids have gotten, but I'm here for something important."

Kejuon's face became solemn, his expression guarded.

"What have you done?"

"I didn't do anything. I'm trying to fix it."

"I've heard that tune before."

"Give me two minutes to explain and you'll be singing the tune with me."

As he prepared to explained the situation, Choop saw Kejuon's wife, Latesha, come in the rear door of the office wearing just a robe. She stopped, looked surprised, gathered the robe, turned and went back inside.

Choop sat in the only other chair. It was a nice chair, a fine example of Kejuon's workmanship. Choop put his elbows on Kejuon's desk and stared, waiting.

Kejuon said, "Well, what are you waiting for? Tell me."

"I'm searching for the right words."

"It's me you're talking to, Choop. You don't need to put a nice face on anything, you know that."

"We will soon be at war with the Canopians."

"Wait … What? Please put a nice face on it."

"Okay. I am trying to prevent the Canopians from wiping us off this planet, and my odds of success are greater than zero."

"I forgot how bad you are at pep talks. Let me ask what really matters. Why did you come to see me? How can I help?"

"I need to talk to Congress, but to get them all here would take days. The next best thing is to talk with Anwar.

I need to talk to him in a hurry, and I mean like right now. I was hoping you know where he lives and could get me through the nets without the normal bureaucratic delay."

Latesha appeared, dressed in a beautiful dark green jumpsuit. Choop had seen the design sold in one of the markets in Knot City.

"Choop! It's been a long time. Tell me you didn't come to get my husband into trouble."

Choop looked at Kejuon. Kejuon nodded. Choop said, "I'm sorry to say I *am* getting him involved in a mess, but I need his help."

She frowned. "What are you not telling me?"

Kejuon said, "Yeah, what are you not telling us? Give me details. She can take it. She's tougher than I am."

Choop took a deep breath. "Dedric and his faithful followers over in Burl City are planning to attack a whale so they can use his Clearing. I talked to Congress about it, but they can't control him with words. I spoke with a new whale who surprised me with the news that the whales — yes, plural, they have a culture and talk to each other — know about his plans. The whale didn't threaten me exactly, he just shared that 'humans are in danger', but he scratched on my skull a little harder as he signed and I got the message. So now I need to talk to Anwar to see if I can get Congress to control Dedric with more than words."

Latesha put her hand on Kejuon's shoulder and said, "I

can run the mill for a couple of days without you. Go. Be my hero." She then turned and walked back into her home.

"K, what did you do to deserve her?"

"I don't deserve her. Give me a couple of minutes to put some things in my backpack. The guards at the commercial supply gate will need some bribes."

~~~

When Anwar heard Choop's message, he immediately sent aides to inform and fetch Congressmen. Only four had arrived by 3 pm — Abisali Mahmoud, Hye Jang, Lynn Eschew, and Thomas Brandt. The aide sent to fetch Dedric Krueger from Burl City returned with a terse and rude message declining participation. When the shorthand reporter arrived, Anwar decided to start the formal session of Congress since, with five congressmen present, they had a quorum as defined by the constitution. Anwar, Hye, and Abisali represented the three largest settlements, so Choop's hopes were raised that meaningful decisions might be possible.

Unlike the first time he had spoken in this room, there was an audience. Kejuon and the five returned runners sat on the benches behind Choop.

Anwar's voice was solemn. "Let the record show that we are convening this emergency session of Congress at the request of Mr. Choop Miles, who assists the colonies in mapping new territory and training Canopians in sign language. Mr. Miles, you have the floor."

"Thank you, Congressman Pawar. I regret the need to inform Congress that the situation I spoke of in an earlier session has become quite serious. When communicating with a previously unknown Canopian many miles to the east, it informed me of its knowledge of Burl City's plans to attack a Canopian. This Canopian used the phrase 'danger to humans' and repeated itself, indicating emphasis. My perception of the strength of its sentiment was also accentuated by a very strong *brain-itch*, as we call it. Put more succinctly, I felt seriously threatened. I am here because I honestly believe humanity's existence on this planet is in jeopardy."

All four congressmen began talking at once.

"Order, order!" Anwar banged his gavel on the bench as he shouted. "One at a time! We all have questions. I would like Representative Jang, minority leader, to have the first shot at asking them."

Choop marveled at Anwar's political acumen in choosing her. Hye's tendency to speak softly quieted the room as people leaned forward to hear her questions.

"Mr. Miles, you say many miles to the east? How did this creature become informed? Did you relay the information?"

"The Canopians communicate among themselves as a matter of course. As I map territory and look for new

Canopians to teach sign language, I find that many I encounter will already know sign language. I keep going each time we move until I find one that has not learned the language. This time I passed five Canopians before I was hailed by one that wanted to talk. It informed me of the situation."

"So, you're saying it was told about Burl City's plans by another whale?"

"Yes, Ma'am."

"Please, Mr. Miles, bear with me in my ignorance. How far apart are the whale Clearings, on average?"

"Three to four miles."

"So the whales cannot communicate with each other at that distance? They must travel to relay information, is that correct?"

Thomas Brandt yelled, "What has this got to do with anything? We should be talking about how to stop those idiots in Burl City!"

The entire dais erupted into babble again. Each leader speaking into the chaos. Only Hye Jang, from Daylight, and Lynn Eschew, from Utopia, restrained themselves. Even a couple of the runners behind Choop were yelling.

Anwar banged his gavel repeatedly, bellowing for order.

Choop had never seen Anwar so angry. When the room quieted, he said through gritted teeth, "Please continue, Hye."

Her voice had a sing-song lilt to it Choop had not noticed before. "I am trying to approach this problem for what it really is. We may soon be at war with a formidable foe. I feel unprepared for this and wish to understand what we are up against. I feel the need to know my enemy."

Thomas Brandt spoke calmly this time. "They won't be our enemy if we don't attack them."

Hye turned to him, leaning forward to look past Anwar. "And how do you know that? After nine years on this planet, we still know almost nothing about them."

Abisali Mahmoud said, "Surely that is an overstatement."

Hye Jang said, "I think if I am allowed to continue my questions, it will become obvious."

"Sorry, please continue."

"Well, Mr. Miles? You say the Clearings are about three miles apart and they must travel in order to relay the knowledge of sign language. So, they can't communicate brain-to-brain over a distance of three miles, correct?"

The warrior in Choop understood what she was thinking. He said, "We believe their Clearings are spaced intentionally to allow them privacy, if that's even the right word. Having someone else connected directly to your consciousness seems like something you would want to limit, but I'm probably projecting my own views onto something I don't understand."

"And how often do they travel to communicate with a neighbor?" Her lilt was less pronounced.

"We don't know. We stay for a while with one Canopian, teaching it sign language and trying to understand more about them. Usually we stay put for many months before moving on. By the time we do, several of its neighbors will already know the signs."

"So is it safe to assume that if this distant whale knows of Burl City's plans, then they all do? At least in the region of human settlements, I mean?"

"Yes. That seems probable."

"Now, about this ability to cause us harm, to explode heads. At what distance can they do that?"

"I only have one data point for that, thank God. Moby, the first Canopian humans talked to, warned Kejuon and I to leave a Clearing where humans were threatening its breeding ground. We went about seven-thousand feet up before it killed the Scouts. At that distance it still affected us. We both passed out. I had headaches for days afterward."

"Mr. Miles, I find it interesting that you phrase your answer to that question such that it's obvious we were aggressors, and the whale was justified. I wonder where your allegiances lie?"

Kejuon jumped to his feet. "Just a damn minute! How dare you! You have got to be out of your ever-loving mind!"

Choop spun around, facing Kejuon, and bellowed, "Scout! Stand down!" He was so loud all of the aides cringed and scooted away on the benches. He remained standing as the room became silent. He turned back to address the leaders.

"Representative Jang, I take no offense at your ignorance. You don't really know me. As a warrior, I understand your thought process, your attempt to understand the threat and evaluate your options. I cannot stress strongly enough the danger humanity is facing. These creatures are alien in every sense of the word. They don't even have a face."

Hye asked, "Mr. Miles, what does their lack of a face have to do with anything?"

Choop spread both hands, palms up. "If I asked a human artist to draw a spidermonkey, a raccoon, or a whale, and he had never seen one, the first thing he would ask is what does its face look like. They are so alien they don't even have a face. We cannot pretend we understand them at all. Their motivations, their culture, their understanding of who we are, all mysteries. Do they think of us like we think of ants? Do they …"

"Oh my God! They did it! They killed one!" Three people rushed into the room. Brice Evans was yelling at the top of his lungs.

Everyone in the room was on their feet, asking questions. But, Brice's voice could be heard clearly.

"Over in the Clearing beneath Burl City. All the raccoons are floating in the water. A big thing like a giant gray snake is floating in the middle. Blood everywhere. Lots of humans with no heads! I can't believe they did it!"

~~~

After passing through the supply gate, they stopped on a huge branch at right angles to one of the main trunks leading to the Knot that gave Knot City its name. The branch was over sixty yards in diameter, so Choop and Kejuon were squatting on a level surface of dark brown bark.

Staying concealed and covering each other was second nature to them; they had been the only two humans living on Canopy for the better part of a year. They had foliage on both sides, but they could look over each other's shoulder to see anyone approaching from the open areas.

"Choop, what are you gonna do? Myoki is about to pop any day, right? You need to stay near Knot City to get her to the hospital when the time comes."

"Well, K, humans have been giving birth without hospitals for centuries. I may just have to be a midwife. I think it's too dangerous to stay as low as Knot City, but I've been married to her long enough to know this ain't gonna be all my decision."

"You gotta do what you gotta do, but I'm shuttin' down the mill and taking the wife and kids up high, at least into the Overhead. You remember how high we were when Moby killed those Scouts? I wanna be at least that high."

"But the further you go into the Overhead the harder it is on your kids to move around. They can't jump across gaps like we can. They're dependent on civilization. They need the bridges. You should take'em to Daylight. It ain't as big as Knot City, but it's growing. Y'all could do okay there until we get this mess straightened out."

"I don't think you can just 'straighten this mess out', Choop. I know Anwar asked you to talk to the Canopians about it, but I don't think it's gonna be that simple. We killed one of 'em."

"I gotta try, K. If they decide all men are their enemy, we won't survive on this planet."

"I know, I know. You just remember what Moby did to those Scouts. And they weren't even attacking him, they just wanted his Clearing."

"Oh, I'll never forget that day."

"Have you thought about this, Choop? Maybe they don't know yet about the dead whale, and you'll be tippin' 'em off. I don't know how impulsive they are, but it might just pop your head by reflex, like a hiccup."

"My first decision is whether to head straight to Beluga or go see Myoki first. I'm afraid if she knows about all this, she'll want to talk to Beluga with me, and I don't want to put her and Mose at risk."

"Sounds like you already figured out what you're gonna do. She might be pissed, but you gotta do it that way."

"Yeah. So, y'all going to Daylight?"

"Yes, I think that's the right place for us. When you need me — and you know you will — look me up."

With no further goodbyes, Choop's best friend and most trusted ally ran to the edge of the branch and jumped down towards his family.

Choop headed along the branch gradually gaining speed. He had made his decision. It was to be full speed all the way to Beluga's Clearing.

It took him almost three hours. As he sped along, making huge jumps, he thought hard about what he was going to say to Beluga.

Since Beluga could read his mind, this was tricky. Myoki had a theory that the reason verbalizing your thoughts when talking to whales helped was because it was necessary. The whale couldn't pick out your thoughts against your will, you had to sort of 'project' them and verbalizing them was the best way.

Choop prayed that was true as he slowed his approach. His last jump onto one of the raccoon shelves by Beluga's Clearing was executed in near silence.

He had considered talking to one of the spidermonkeys

since it was several thousand feet further from Beluga. That seemed safer, but Choop figured he should do what he and Myoki always did, which was to go to the Clearing when they wanted to talk with Beluga.

As he was pondering whether this was a mistake, a raccoon came out of the opening above the shelf.

It signed, [*hello*], and did not pop his head, so Choop breathed easier.

"Hello, Beluga, I was hoping you would be home."

[*Gathering time has not yet arrived.*]

"Yes, well, uh, there is something I need to speak with you about."

[*You are emotional.*] [*Hot.*]

"Remind me not to play poker with you."

[*Confusion.*]

"Sorry, ignore that. I might as well get right to it. You know how we humans are 'disconnected' as you like to say? Some of us do things the others disagree with. I know this always seems to confuse you when we bring it up, but it's important for what I am about to tell you."

[*Query. Circle talk? Confusion.*]

Choop almost laughed. He usually thought it was funny when Beluga accused him of 'circle talk', but it wasn't funny now. Beluga's mind was very organized and logical, so sometimes human thought processes seemed irrational and 'talking in circles' was Beluga's response. Choop took a deep breath to steady his nerves. He was sweating profusely.

"The folks who live in Burl City don't like Canopians. They believe y'all are dumb animals and that we have what we call dominion over you. This is how we thought when we were on Earth, and they continue these beliefs. I want you to understand this before I tell you the bad news."

[*Circle talk.*]

"I know, sorry. It's just vital that you understand how strongly I disagree with their philosophies. In fact, most humans do, the majority of us."

[*Circle talk.*] [*Circle talk.*] [*You hot. Explain.*]

"Okay, okay. Don't get worked up."

[*You hot. Explain.*]

Choop wiped sweat from his brow. It was dripping into his eyes.

"The humans at Burl City killed the Canopian living in the Clearing below that city. The one we called Bottlenose. He's dead."

Sudden pressure inside Choop's skull became unbearable. He dropped to his knees screaming. Loud splashing sounds filled the Clearing as Beluga rose above the surface of the water. A small tidal wave washed up onto the shelf where Choop knelt, soaking his pants up to his groin as he knelt helplessly. The charcoal smell filled his nose. He felt like he was buried in sand up to his neck as an invisible force held him in a crushing grip.

~~~

Albert Beumers was nervous. He was finally going to meet Dedric Krieger. Albert, the bastard son of Simon Goetsch, was used to dealing with powerful men. His father Goetsch was the ranking officer who took over Inception on the trip from Earth and attempted to set up his own dictatorship on Canopy.

Albert was a "star-baby", born on Inception during the voyage. He was one of the Scouts trained by Choop Miles on methods for moving through Canopy's forest without detection.

He was very good at it, and it was this skill that allowed him to play an essential part in killing the whale. He knew he was only getting to meet Dedric because of this, but was also aware that making himself valuable to Dedric was the path to success.

He had been told to wait in the raccoon's cave. After killing the whale, many things were learned about the whales. One of the surprises was that each raccoon had a cave that had been chewed into one of the trees surrounding the whale's Clearing.

It had two entrances, one was an opening high on the wall leading from a tunnel through the tree. The other was from the water. The cave had been designed with an underwater entrance on the side nearest the Clearing. He sat with his back to the wall of the cave facing the high opening on the opposite wall, subconsciously clicking his tongue as he waited for Dedric.

He was startled by splashing as Dedric and two Scouts rose from the water to his right. He jumped to his feet and stood at attention.

Dedric stood for a moment looking closely at the cave and at Albert. The two Scouts spread out and made sure there were no hidden spaces in the cave. Then they stood, dripping. One faced the water and the other faced the opening on the wall.

"At ease, Scout."

Albert relaxed his posture but said nothing. He knew about men of power. Dedric was not interested in Albert as anything other than a useful tool.

"I understand it was your idea to observe the raccoons to determine by their behavior when the whale was absent from the Clearing?"

"Yes, Sir."

Dedric chuckled. "Not much for small talk, eh. I like that. Tell me, how did you know from their behavior that the whale was not home?"

"Well, Sir, since they all share the whale's brain when it's here, their movements would be very coordinated. They would all move as if they were a single entity. But, the best we can figure, when the whale is absent, they kind of go on 'automatic'. They still tend to the duties of trimming the branches around the Clearing and such, but it appears a lot more disjointed, as though they are now individuals. It's subtle, but we were able to figure it out."

"Were you a part of actually killing the whale?"

"Yes, Sir. Once we knew it was gone we killed the raccoons and then set up the three harpoon cannons. I didn't actually shoot it, I was higher in the trees, observing. But you already knew that, since all the trigger men died in the beast's final convulsive brain waves. I still have a lingering headache."

"I think it's funny that we call something powered by rubber bands a cannon."

Albert knew they weren't rubber bands, but spidermonkey's webbing, but also knew to keep his mouth shut rather than correct the most powerful man on the planet. He said nothing.

"Were you the one who came up with idea of the diving corps?"

"No, Sir. Shamar Neita was a pearl diver on Earth. He thought of it. Not to use in an attack on a whale, but just to explore the underwater parts of Canopy."

"I understand they can hold their breath eight minutes?"

"Well, Sir, that's a bit of an exaggeration. Shamar can hold his for over five, but most can't even match that. But, four minutes is a long time for exploring if you aren't going very deep."

"I'm told, using what they've learned, you've come up with a plan to secure the Clearing so whales can't attack us if we build a town here?"

"Yes, Sir. It turns out Canopy's water is filled with tree roots. Massive tangles of tree roots everywhere. The seas are not open and clear at all, but full of roots of all sizes. Even our divers have trouble fitting through the openings. There are huge 'underwater Knots'. It's completely impassable."

"Then how the hell do the whales leave and return?"

Albert knew Dedric knew the answer to his own question, but was just allowing Albert to share his plan. *This is a good sign*, he thought.

"It turns out raccoons have duties other than keeping the Clearing free of branches. They also spend a lot of time keeping roots out of 'tunnels' they created through the roots. They made tunnels connecting Clearings. The whales use these tunnels to move around Canopy. This particular Clearing has five such tunnels connecting it to other Clearings."

"So whales just jump from Clearing to Clearing to move long distances?"

"We believe that there must be wider paths, highways if you will, but we have yet to find one. But the point is that — simply by guarding or blocking five underwater tunnels

— we can keep whales farther away than their brains can reach to attack us."

"You make it sound so simple."

"It's not. It will take many men, many more trained divers to guard this Clearing, but it can be done. We are working on the best ways to do it. Then we just move on to the next Clearing and repeat the process. We should be able to gradually eradicate these hateful creatures and inhabit all of Canopy."

~~~

When Myoki finally caught her breath, she said, "I'm too old for this."

Sarah held a damp rag to Myoki's forehead. "You're doing fine."

"Myoki, this is your fourth kid. You should have it down pat," said Danielle.

As her next contraction started, Myoki responded, "Kiss my ass, Danielle."

Sarah giggled as she said, "Ooh, we must be getting closer, the potty mouth is starting."

"You can kiss my ass, too. You can each take a cheek."

Danielle said, "You should save your strength for pushing, girl. Just think about how this is your last one. You're over forty, you gotta quit doing this."

Larry stuck his head through the door. "How's it going?"

Myoki screamed, "get the hell out of here!" Then she

screamed at the universe.

Larry jerked his head back, and Sarah said, "My husband doesn't have a lick of sense. What's he thinking, sticking his head in here?"

Danielle answered, "Maybe he's thinking what I'm thinking. We should have taken her to Knot City's hospital as soon as she started labor."

Sarah glanced sharply at Myoki and said, "Shh, she'll hear you."

"She's in the middle of a contraction, she's not processing external input at all. I'm getting worried about her. She's right, she *is* too old for this."

Larry yelled, "Choop, what the hell happened to you?"

Choop burst though the door covering and stumbled, falling to his knees. He had caked blood on his lips and chin from a nosebleed. He said, "Myoki," and then looked pleadingly at Danielle.

Danielle spun and knelt in front of him.

She said, "Choop, what in the world happened to you?"

"I'm fine. It's a long story. Is she okay? How long has she been in labor? Is the baby breach? Niti was breach at first. How far apart are the contractions? Why didn't y'all take her to the hospital? Is she okay?"

Myoki said, "Choop, you're here. Where the hell have you been? I should kick your ass, leaving me to do this alone."

A grinning Danielle said, "As you can hear, she's just fine. Let me help you up."

By the time they got Choop settled into a chair by her bedside, Myoki's contraction had subsided. She noticed the blood on his face.

"Choop, what happened? You're bloody,"

"I'm fine. How far apart are the contractions, Sarah?"

"That last one was seven minutes, but it was a strong one. She's started with the potty mouth."

"So, we could move her then? We should move higher for the birth."

"Choop, what the hell are you talking about? We decided she would have it here, remember?"

"Sarah, trust me, things have changed. Danielle, get the guys in here."

The authoritative sound of Choop's voice as he gave Danielle what was obviously a direct order caught everyone's attention. Danielle didn't argue with her normal flippancy. She just spun to the door and yelled, "Larry, go get Adam, then bring him back and get in here."

Larry responded, "What about the kids?"

"Have Saoirse watch 'em. Choop says he needs you and Adam in here — now."

"She can't watch seven kids by herself. She's just nine years old."

"Larry, now. Did you hear what I said? Now. Why are

you arguing with me like a civilian? NOW."

Larry said, "Civilian? ... Oh, crap." He then turned and jumped toward the nursery.

Myoki said, "Choop, you're scaring me."

Choop answered, "There ain't nothing to be scared of. There's just no time to waste."

Sarah and Choop locked eyes. Sarah said, "Myoki, you should lay back and work on your breathing."

"Breathing? My husband comes home covered in blood, and then he puts on his military attitude. I've seen this attitude before, you know. Bad stuff happens when he gets this way. I don't need to work on my breathing, I need to know what the hell is happening."

Larry and Adam entered the room and stood stiffly, looking at Choop. Everyone waited for his lead, even Myoki was silent, staring at her husband.

Choop said, "Battle stations. This is not a drill. Burl City killed Bottlenose. I spoke with Beluga about it." He touched the blood on his face. "She was not happy."

It made Choop proud that no one said a word. He thought how glad he was to be with these people. They were all warriors in every sense of the word.

"We will move quickly. We will go vertically to the Overhead to get far from the whales, then northwest to Daylight. Kejuon is there and will help us find a place to settle in. Adam and Larry will take turns carrying Myoki while the other carries Saoirse. I can carry the three youngest. That leaves two kids each for Danielle and Sarah. If you can work out some kind of sling where the two of you can carry all four, do that. We head out in one hour. We take nothing but our children and our weapons."

~~~

"Choop must have a rash. He just sits there scratching his forearm and staring into space," Adam said.

Kejuon grunted as he turned in the uncomfortable chair. "Didn't you ever hear him talk about his tattoo? He's rubbing it because it reminds him of Bipin, and Bipin reminds him of being a father. He's sure it's a boy and he thinks of what Bipin meant to him. Choop didn't have a father, but he had Bipin."

"These damn chairs are uncomfortable." Larry squirmed around, looking for the best angle to keep his legs from going to sleep in the waiting room at Daylight's clinic. "Adam, you've heard him talk about Bipin. I know you have."

"But I didn't know the tattoo made him think of Bipin, Larry"

"Yeah, it's hard to figure, since the tattoo says Bipin right on it," Kejuon joked. "And he's not staring into space; he's staring into the corner."

"You guys know I can hear you, right?" Choop didn't bother to turn and look at them. "I'm right here."

Kejuon said, "I can't believe she wouldn't let you in there. That's cold, man."

"I'll ask her about it if she ever starts speaking to me again."

Larry said, "Let's talk about something else. Did anyone ride on a Daylight elevator? Ingenious."

"They just use water for ballast. What's so ingenious about that?" asked Adam.

"You're kiddin' right?" Larry turned, searching for a comfortable position, faced Adam. "Not only does each elevator have a large tank for ballast, but there are reservoirs at top and bottom to refill them if necessary. They have ropes connecting two operators, one at each reservoir. They yank on the ropes to signal whether to fill or release water. It's ingenious, I say."

"Okay, but have you been down below one of the elevators? Both elevators are pissin' water all over everything."

"Come on, Adam. This is Canopy. When's the last time you were dry? Every surface is damp if it's not wet." Larry was really getting into the debate as he changed his position in the chair again, drawing both legs under himself. "You gotta at least appreciate the pulley at the top. That's the biggest pulley I ever saw."

"I got bigger ones at the mill," Kejuon said. "Y'all should come and visit. Bring the kids. They'd get a kick out of watching the band saw."

"Are you people out of your minds?" Choop yelled.

All three men turned and stared at Choop.

"We're at war with a species that can kill you by simply thinking about it, and do it from almost a mile. We're here in Daylight because it's the only settlement high enough to be safe. The mill is for damned sure too close to Moby's Clearing to be safe. So, we're gonna sit around and discuss Daylight's architecture?"

There was silence after Choop ran out of breath. Kejuon spoke softly.

"Your baby is gonna be alright, Choop. And Myoki is gonna get over it."

"How's she gonna get over it? She believes that if I had let her tell Beluga about Bottlenose, then things would have turned out different. As long as we're at war with the Canopians, she's gonna think it's partly my fault. How the hell is she gonna get over that?"

The door from the hallway leading to the delivery rooms opened and the nurse stepped out.

"Mr. Miles?"

"That's me."

"You have a son."

All three men whooped with joy, but Choop was watching the nurse's face.

"What are you not telling me, Nurse?"

"Come and see your son, Mr. Miles. This way."

As Choop followed the nurse down the narrow hall, he noticed the swaying movement of the entire clinic. This high in the forest, everything was in constant motion, but that was not what was on his mind. His heart was hammering as he thought of the look on the nurse's face. Even her gait seemed strained.

She opened the door to Myoki's room, held it wide for him, and stared at the floor.

He stepped into the room to see Myoki's tear-stained face staring at him. She wasn't smiling. Choop thought, *she should be smiling.*

He stepped closer to get a look at his son. He said, "hello, Mose," and leaned closer.

The baby squirmed and the swaddling fell back from his lower torso. Where there should have been legs there was, instead, just more torso. There were no feet at the bottom, and no legs. Choop lost his balance and staggered back. He found himself falling into a chair and staring at Myoki.

Her face turned cold. "Aren't you going to hug your son, Choop? Don't you want to hold him?"

Choop couldn't breathe. His mouth opened and closed like a fish out of water. He finally managed to squeak out a reply.

"Where's the doctor? They need to separate his legs, that's all."

"The doctor's already looked at him. It's not just two legs fused together. There's no leg bones in there. It's all torso, full of organs, intestines and other stuff they're not even sure of."

The last thing Choop heard as he stumbled out the door was Myoki's voice coldly saying, "You should hold your son, Choop, or there's no hope for us. Choop? … Choop, I mean it. I'm not …"

4

"Humans are a mess. How can the Canopians hope to understand us even a little? We don't even understand ourselves."

— From the memoir of Myoki Miles

~~~

"I know what you're doing, K. You might as well go back."

Kejuon's face looked as innocent as a five-year-old with his hand in the cookie jar. "What? You're scouting for new settlement sites as high in the Overhead as possible, and I'm helping. This is a two-man job. You might get lost."

Choop responded by leaping fifty feet to the next good-sized branch and immediately launching towards another. But Kejuon was as nimble a forty-something as there was on Canopy. He followed closely.

Choop landed on a branch eight feet in diameter. He stopped, turned, and stared at Kejuon. "I know what you're doing. I don't want to talk about it." He turned and jumped to a slightly lower branch forty feet farther to the east.

Kejuon landed beside him. Choop turned to confront him, and Kejuon said, "The further we get from the South Pole the more likely the winds in the upper atmosphere are going to be felt down in the Overhead. This was a good idea. We need to know that as we create new settlements up here."

"K, quit pretending like you're scouting for new territory. I know why you won't let me go alone." Choop then jumped off the branch, going straight down.

"Choop? What the … "

Kejuon could not even tell which branch Choop had aimed at with his jump straight down towards the Jungle. It looked like Choop had just chosen the widest open section so he would fall for a few hundred feet before encountering a large tree trunk or branch. Even in just thirty-percent gravity, this was dangerous. Kejuon hesitated only slightly before following. He jumped in the exact path Choop had as he thought *serves him right if I land on him.*

Choop fell two hundred feet before encountering a small Knot formed by three ten-foot trunks wrapped around each other. The foliage covering the Knot was mostly hemp plants. Kejuon watched tree rats scatter as Choop smacked into the plants. He missed Choop by a couple of feet. The wind was knocked from him, and he hoped Choop didn't jump again quickly, but a glance showed him Choop was also having trouble catching his breath.

"Choop, you know we shouldn't go too low. We're not sure exactly how high the whale's brain waves can injure us. And …"

Kejuon didn't have to explain further as Choop pointed to several tripods which were on the branches extending out from the Knot. If the whale controlling these tripods could see through their eyes this high, then the question wasn't whether he knew they were here, but whether they were high enough he couldn't control gravity around them or turn their brains to jelly.

"Great, more company. I just want to be alone."

Choop gathered his feet and jumped up at an angle to a branch thirty feet higher. He quickly leapt from it to another, then another, gaining altitude as he went. The tripods didn't follow. Kejuon did.

After several minutes of strenuous jumps, Choop finally stopped on a short, narrow branch with only room for one person. So, when Kejuon landed beside him, he almost knocked them both off the branch.

"Get off me, you lunatic!"

"You need to land on wider branches. You're not getting rid of me that easy."

"How about I just kick your ass. Would that get rid of you?"

"Nope."

Choop put his elbows on his knees and his head in his

hands. All the air whooshed from him, and he grew still. Kejuon just waited.

"I swear to God, K, if you tell me you know how I feel, I'll punch a hole in your head."

"I don't know how you feel. I can't imagine how you're coping as well as you are. I just know you're screwing the pooch."

"What's that supposed to mean?"

"You got a wife who loves you, and you won't talk to her. You got a son that needs you, and you won't even hold him. You're being an asshole."

Kejuon put his hands up in defense as Choop balled his fists.

"K, we live on a world where cripples are doomed. There ain't no wheelchair ramps in trees. And Myoki won't talk to me, so how am I gonna talk to her?"

"Choop, he's nine months old. He grins at me and grabs my finger and squeezes so hard you wouldn't believe it. He's smart as a whip; he's already started saying stuff. He calls me KayJou. And Myoki loves you. She just don't love you bein' an asshole."

"Would you please just leave me alone?"

"Nope. I told Latesha I was gonna be gone as long as it takes. I'll go home when you go home."

Choop pushed Kejuon off the branch, and as he fell, Choop jumped up and away from him.

~~~

"Are you sure you wanna do this, Myoki?"

"Sarah, for the tenth time, yes. I have to do this."

"At least leave Mose here with us. There's no need putting him in danger, too."

"He's nursing, Sarah. Where I go, he goes. And if Beluga kills me, he wouldn't survive anyway."

"Nonsense. We could find a nursing mother to share milk, and he's getting close to solid food. Plus, look how happy it makes Saoirse to take care of him. We really don't need you, you know."

"Oh, this is a new tact. If you can't keep me from going using logic, you'll just give the old reverse psychology a try."

"Saoirse's only eleven, and she's ready to replace you. I'm just sayin'. Mose won't even miss you."

"Wow, now guilt. You're pullin' out all stops."

Saoirse walked up the foot bridge towards them with Mose strapped to her chest in his panther-skin baby carrier. "What you guys talking about. You look awful serious."

"Let me have him, Sweetie. I'm goin' on a trip."

Saoirse stopped in her tracks, making no move to give Mose to Myoki. "Where are you going?"

She hugged Mose tightly as she stared at Myoki. He was in his favored facing-out position with his back to Saoirse. He swung his arms back and forth and squealed, grinning.

As Saoirse hugged him, he said her name in his own fashion, "Shsh."

"Saoirse, I just said I'm going on a trip, and I'm taking Mose. What does it matter where I go? Come on, hand him over."

Saoirse took a small step back. She looked from Myoki to Sarah and back. She said, "I'm old enough. You can tell me."

Mose became still. He stared at Myoki with a serious, solemn expression.

Sarah said, "It's like she can read our minds. I'm her mother, and I'll never get used to it. And your son is giving you his thousand-yard stare. Oh for God's sake, Saoirse. Can't you ever just do what we ask?"

Saoirse took another small step backwards. "I keep him safe. It's my responsibility."

"Saoirse, give him to Myoki. Now."

As Saoirse stepped forward, she said, "At least tell me the truth."

Myoki said, "You're right, Saoirse. I'm sorry, but I didn't want you to worry. I have decided I'm going to talk to Beluga. It's been months since any communication with the Canopians. They haven't killed anyone, but they've sure given a lot of folks headaches. We need to talk to them."

Saoirse stopped advancing and said, "Why didn't you

just say so? I'll come along and help take care of Mose.
Let's go."

Sarah said, "Saoirse, you are not going to put yourself in
danger!"

"Beluga won't hurt me."

"You don't know that."

"Yes, I do. The Canopians won't hurt Mose either. You
would understand if you could see clearly. I'm almost
twelve years old. I'm beginning to understand things. Mose
and I need to come along to protect Myoki, not the other
way round."

Sarah took Myoki by the hand and turned her away from
Saoirse.

"Myoki, I know this sounds weird, but Saoirse knows
things she has no business knowing. We've all seen it. I
think you should take her with you."

"I'm right here, Mom. I can hear you."

~~~

When Myoki first saw the spidermonkey, she was nervous.
She froze in place and stared. She was on a trunk that
descended at an angle to Beluga's Clearing. The
spidermonkey was fifty feet away on a large branch. Now
that she knew where to look, she could see the
spidermonkey's web in the background above and beyond
it.

From behind her, Saoirse said, "It's okay. That's Beluga.

She wants us to come down to the Clearing."

"Maybe. Or maybe she's thinking about exploding my brain."

The spidermonkey signed.

[*Descend to Clearing.*]

"How did you know that, Saoirse?"

"Can't explain it. It's obvious, right?"

Mose squealed with delight and began to jabber.

As they climbed down, the trunks became steeper, and Myoki worried about Saoirse carrying Mose. When she looked back to check on her, Saoirse was scrambling sideways, gripping the tree with the stickypede pads on her jumpsuit at the knees and elbows. She was at home in the forest. Mose was waving his arms and grinning, enjoying his big adventure.

When Myoki got to the Clearing, raccoons were waiting. Three were at the raccoon shelf nearest her, and the others were in the water. She looked back and discovered Saoirse had gone to the next shelf, on the tree to Myoki's left.

Myoki was very tense and decided to wait for the raccoons to start the conversation. The three near her were spread out in a defensive formation. They made no signs. The three in the water swam to the shelf occupied by Saoirse and Mose. Myoki was worried for only a second, until she saw Saoirse and Mose grinning as Mose windmilled his arms.

A look of pure awe filled Saoirse's face, accompanied by loud splashing. Mose became still and assumed his 'stare into infinity' pose.

Myoki turned and watched as Beluga, a huge worm-shaped creature, arced out of the water. Half the whale's width cleared the lapping waves created by her arrival. Myoki could feel the charcoal smell overpower her senses. Beluga was very close to Myoki's side of the Clearing, towering over her. Myoki could see two eyes, one at least twelve feet above the water, and the other level with her shelf. An intense rumbling-itching feeling filled Myoki's skull.

A sound brought Myoki's gaze down to the raccoons. One had been signing and was slapping its foot on the shelf to get her attention.

[*Offspring is welcome.*]

"I hope I am welcome, too, Beluga. I traveled a long way to talk to you. Humans and Canopians need to talk and quit hurting each other."

[*Offspring is welcome.*]

"Well, okay, subtlety never was your strong suit. But we need to talk. We need to find a way to stop fighting."

[*Humans kill Canopian. Humans approach another Clearing. Human activity does not match talk.*]

"We are approaching another Clearing? See, I didn't know that. The people doing that are not doing it with the approval of the rest of us. Most of us don't want to hurt you."

[*Words not actions. Dead is dead.*]

"All I'm asking is to give us some time. If humans living within range of your power are not attacking you, leave them alone. We are trying to deal with the people doing this to you, but it takes time."

[*Gathering soon. I go. Represent area. Others stay to guard Clearings. Your empty words will be shared. Humans should go back to own world. Now. Warning. Danger to all humans.*]

Mose began to cry.

~~~

Albert said, "Shamar, did you hear that Dedric is going to talk to Congress today?"

"Yeah, he's going to tell them we're seceding from their stupid country."

"Country? They don't even have a country. They never even bothered to name their country. That's how dumb they are. They thought they would just rule the whole planet because no one else was here."

"I never thought of that, Albert. That is dumb not to have a name for your country."

"Don't just stare at me while you talk, Scout. Continue observing. We need to know when this whale is not home."

Shamar turned his eyes back to the raccoons four

hundred feet beneath the branch he and Albert were hiding on. "Sorry, Sir. It's just that this duty gets really boring."

"It won't be boring once the whale makes the mistake of wandering away."

"Sir, do you know what we are going to name our new country?"

"Dedric said it's gonna be called the Republic of Humanity."

"Republic of Humanity … I like that."

"Did you see that, Shamar. All six raccoons froze for a second."

"No, I missed it. That means the whale probably just disconnected from them, right?"

"Yes. Keep your voice down. I'm gonna signal the others."

Albert whistled a distinctive bird call. He got responses from six teams, indicating their awareness of the operation's start. He then whistled the command to position themselves to shoot the raccoons. Four hundred feet was extreme range for their bows, so they had to move closer.

Killing the first whale had taught them a lot. They knew by eliminating all the raccoons at once, they could prevent any from diving into the water to escape. They could then signal the Scouts four thousand feet above them surrounding the spidermonkey net. The spidermonkeys were easier to kill since they would not stray far from their net.

As each team whistled to signal arrival at a predetermined position, Albert's heart began to pound. Each team was now within one hundred yards of the raccoons. It was time.

Albert noticed something weird. All the raccoons had stopped moving altogether and were staring up at the Scouts. Albert knew something was wrong. As he puckered his lips to whistle an abort signal, his head exploded.

~~~

Dedric slammed his fist down on the desk. "Explain to me what the hell went wrong!"

Colonel Bobby Monroe wiped sweat from behind his ear. It was trickling down his neck and distracting him. He needed to focus.

"Sir, the reports from the Scouts near the spidermonkey web were a little unclear as to the details. It appears the whale managed to fool Albert and his attack teams into believing it had left. Obviously it didn't. These things may be smarter than we think."

"Smart? They're animals. They can't be very smart." President Dedric took a deep breath to calm himself. "How many men did we lose?"

"Thirteen total, Sir. Six two-man teams, Sir, plus Albert, Sir. All the lower attack teams …"

"Quit sir-ing me, dammit."

"Sorry, Sir, uh, I mean, uh, all the attack teams high in the forest survived. The ones meant to kill the spidermonkeys weren't hurt. Apparently, the creatures need to have eyes-on to kill one of us, and since the men watching the spidermonkeys never received the go-ahead to attack, they stayed hidden."

"This is unacceptable, Colonel. New Venice is crowded. We need to expand to another Clearing to keep the promises I made. I assume you have been working on a solution?"

"Yes, Sir, uh, we have been testing our spear cannons underwater. We think it's possible to get close enough to attack the whale underwater."

"I like that, Colonel. It eliminates the long delay waiting for the whale to leave its Clearing."

Rather than say what he was thinking, *the delay is more important to you than the lives of the men we lose,* the Colonel said, "It will still be a slow process. To move a team through the roots with one of the cannons, and doing it quietly will take a long time. If the whale becomes aware of them, they're dead."

"Isn't it possible the whale's final convulsive brain waves kill them anyway?"

"Yes, Sir, not just possible but likely. We'll have to consider it a suicide mission and ask for volunteers willing to sacrifice their lives."

"Ask? Are you kidding me? You're their commanding officer. You pick the men and order them to go. ... Do you have a problem with that?"

"... Uh, no Sir."

"Make it happen as soon as possible."

~~~

Delmont felt his brother's hand on his leg. All was calm. There were no animals around Delmont could see, so he flexed his leg with the signal to surface. Pervis rose silently from the water. He came up only until his mouth cleared the water.

The brothers floated silently for several seconds, back to back, to make certain the forest above had normal sounds.

Pervis whispered, "Floyd would have loved this mission."

"Floyd is dead, Pervis. He'll never enjoy anything again. But we can make these demons pay for what they did to him."

"Yes, it will be a glorious death. I have no regrets as long as the monster dies while I watch."

"Perhaps if we shoot it through the heart, it will die instantly, and we will live to kill others. Alonso will be waiting, I'd better go."

"We got the cannon about thirty yards farther east."

After Delmont submerged, Pervis swam quietly to the east about forty yards. He felt Alonso's hand on his leg. All was normal. The forest above was full of the growls, squeals, and grunts. Pervis flexed his leg.

Alonso surfaced and assumed the back-to-back position with Pervis.

Alonso said, "We're making good time. Less than half a mile to go. We need to stay sharp, or those beasts will hear us."

Pervis had no respect for Alonso. Someone who would assist in preparation and positioning of the cannon, but then withdraw to survive the actual battle didn't deserve respect. Delmont, Otto, and Pervis would be heroes, martyrs for the Republic of Humanity, while Alonso would live on to sacrifice others.

Pervis kept the disdain from his voice. "How far has the cannon moved?"

"About another twenty-five yards east."

Pervis took three deep breaths and submerged to join Delmont and relieve Otto.

~~~

Alonso could see the raccoons clearly, five-hundred feet below him. The six bowmen under his command were hidden lower, close enough for good shots.

They were unsure of what would happen when the whale died while still connected to the raccoons. When they killed the beast comically referred to as Bottlenose, they had already killed its disconnected raccoons and spidermonkeys. This would be different. If Delmont's Squad succeeded, the raccoons might drop dead in place, they might dive into the sea to aid the whale, they might go berserk, no one was sure.

Each bowman had a raccoon in his sights, ready to shoot.

The cannon was anchored thirty feet underwater with many ropes to keep it steady when they released the harpoon. It was pointing into the underwater clearing just as planned. Delmont, Pervis, and Otto were rotating their duties. One of them had a finger on the trigger, while another was swimming stealthily down to become triggerman or back up to breathe, and the other had his head above the water, breathing.

They had practiced this many times. They called it their 'death dance'. The one moving had to be totally silent or they would die. The one with his finger on the trigger had to be constantly focused to recognize the opportunity to kill the whale as it moved around.

Visibility in the water was only sixty feet, so they would do the dance until the whale moved close enough to the cannon for a good shot.

They had been dancing for more than two hours when all the raccoons suddenly dropped. Two fell onto the shelves where they stood, and the other four fell from Overhead branches into the water.

Alonso felt intense pain in his skull and almost passed

out. His vision was blurry, and he thought he might puke. He managed to watch through squinting eyes as the whale's dead body floated to the surface of water red with blood. He was certain the blood was not all whale's blood. There was no possible way Delmont's attack team had survived.

He smiled at the excellent result. Now they knew they could kill one of these evil creatures even when it knew they were coming. They would conquer this world one whale at a time until the aliens were extinguished.

~~~

Anwar pounded his gavel and shouted, "Order! Order!"

It did no good. Shouting continued.

"Shade? Everybody? Oh, my God!"

"What are we going to do? I thought these aliens were friendly …"

"How many? One-hundred-fifty? All the children, too?"

"This has got to stop! Anwar, something has got to be done!"

Neither Choop nor Myoki added their voices to the noisy ruckus.

The runner had entered just seconds after the session had started and announced that the Canopians had attacked Shade. All one-hundred-fifty-nine residents of Shade, the lowest of the human settlements, had been killed. The headless bodies strewn about the city left no doubt as to the perpetrator.

"Order! Order!"

Finally, people stopped shouting. Gradually the noise subsided.

The representative from Shade, Jason Warheit, was slumped with his face on the dais, his head buried in his hands. Behind him, Warheit's aide was openly weeping. The other seven representatives couldn't bear to look at either of them.

The absence of representation from Burl City was glaring, but expected after Dedric had announced, at the last session, Burl City's intent to withdraw from Congress. Dedric had used the word *secede* and had threatened war if any of the other cities intervened in his attacks on the Canopians. He even had the audacity to welcome people at the well-attended session to move to New Venice if they wished to share in the coming prosperity and glory of the Republic of Humanity.

This emergency session was also well attended. It had been called to discuss what to do about Burl City's secession. The standing-room-only crowd numbered one-hundred-twenty with more gathered around the door, straining to hear.

Anwar spotted Choop sitting in the middle of the crowd next to Myoki.

"Mr. Miles, would you mind standing to answer some questions?"

Choop stood and responded, "Of course not, Congressman Pawar."

"Mr. Miles, you have testified before us in the past. For the benefit of those who were not present, you told us you had witnessed an event where the Canopians killed two squads of Scouts. You testified the raccoons warned you to go higher in the forest to be safe and experienced pain so severe you passed out. My question is this: what was the approximate elevation where you were when you survived this attack?"

Choop thought for a second. "I was above Moby's spider web a little, so I would estimate about seven thousand feet."

"I am sure you, as the early colony's main Scout mapping new territory, can also answer this: what is the elevation of Shade?"

"At its lowest point, about two thousand feet. At its highest, two thousand three hundred."

"And what is the highest elevation here in Knot City?"

Choop did not like where this was going, but it was too late to avoid stating it publicly. "About four thousand three hundred, give or take."

The room was silent. Choop heard his own stomach churn. He knew everyone was doing the math and would never feel safe in Knot City again. He tasted bile and felt sick, but continued to stand stoically.

"If I'm not mistaken, Mr. Miles, isn't it true that there is no Clearing below Shade?"

"Let me save you some time from asking the series of questions I'm sure you're about to ask, Sir. There is not a whale Clearing beneath Shade. The Clearing closest to Shade is over two miles to the southwest. The obvious explanation is that a whale had its raccoons clean out a new tunnel through the roots for the express purpose of allowing the whale to position itself under Shade for an attack."

The room erupted into a confused babble. Anwar slammed his gavel twice and the room quieted.

"Mr. Miles, we have no standing army, but you are our most accomplished warrior, so I have a very important question. After spending the last decade building this fine city, are we going to have to abandon it to stay safe?"

Choop turned to look at Myoki. His expression was unreadable.

He turned back to face the dais and said, "I think it's obvious that Dedric Krieger's stupidity has changed things. I've heard that they keep New Venice safe with teams of divers trained to hold their breath for long periods. They booby trap and monitor the water around New Venice to prevent whales approaching. Each settlement, needs to either do that or move into the Overhead out of the reach of the whales. I am willing to volunteer to help form, train, and then lead a standing force for Knot City to try and protect it. Daylight, New Frisco, and Utopia are all high enough to be safe, but the other cities will have a decision to make."

"I have a more comprehensive proposal, Mr. Miles. I suggest you lead a standing military composed of volunteers from all the settlements. We need your expertise, Sir. We need to have a good plan that works for all of us."

Ayden Mahoney shouted, "I agree. It's possible, God forbid, that we end up fighting this Republic of Humanity."

5

"Numbness is a mixed blessing. It's great to avoid feeling constant pain after an injury, but when it causes us to accept years of war, it's a bad thing. We've grown numb to the fear and the killing."

— *From the memoir of Myoki Miles*

~~~

I expected almost everything, but not the wheelchair. I can move around a tree faster than any of the other kids, but they make me sit in a wheelchair just because I have no legs. Apparently it's a rule, and mindless rule following seems easier to them than actually thinking through the realities of the situation.

The name of the school makes me cringe: Threshold Advanced Development Academy. I think about saying *TA-DA* a lot, and they wonder why I'm smiling. Well, at least most of them. Some of them can't seem to think of anything else except why I have a blanket hiding my lower torso. Shows how advanced they are; they think I'm hiding legs, but there are no legs to hide. I want to throw the blanket aside and shout *TA-DA*.

Mom and I had our first serious argument about coming here. I explained to her that going with her to visit Beluga was much more beneficial to me learning what really matters on Canopy than attending this awful place. She said she *put her foot down,* but she was thinking *adolescence is starting a little too soon.*

I looked up adolescence at the library the first day I got here. I thought I knew what she meant, but I wanted to be sure. I'm only ten, but apparently I am about to become emotionally unstable and have constant urges to rut with females. If the person who wrote that could see what the girls think about my blanket-covered lower torso, he would know I'll not be doing much rutting.

Mom wanted me to come here because she feels like I'm so advanced and she thinks TADA is advanced. She thinks her teaching me at home will hold me back because I'm a genius. I know I'm smart, but the truth is I can usually see the answers to her questions in her mind, so of course I always get them right. But I can't tell her that. I can't tell anybody that.

TADA is so advanced that today we are studying the nineteen-year history of Canopy. To be advanced I need to know that we killed Bottlenose in Year Nine, or that Moby fought back in Year Eleven, or that we killed Moby in Year

Twelve, or that every time we kill a Canopian it is followed immediately by the establishment of a new water-level City.

Knowing that the United Colonies Military was formally established in Year Thirteen doesn't make me progressive. Knowing that before Year Thirteen my Dad just told everyone what to do isn't very enlightening either. I'm not sure these *advanced* teachers know what *advanced* means.

They should call it the Threshhold Egotistical Asshole Machine. Go, *TEAM*. They think the nineteen years we've been here is history. Beluga's memories go back centuries. No wonder Beluga thinks we're nuts.

I'm homesick, but home isn't really there anymore, so I might as well be here. When Saoirse was drafted, they took the only person who understands me.

~~~

"Good morning, recruits. I'm Sergeant Charles 'Cooter' Holliston. My friends call me Cooter. You do not. My boss calls me Sergeant Holliston. You do not. You will call me Sergeant Cooter for the simple reason that I like the sound of it, and I can tell you what to do."

Ela was one of the recruits. She was both excited and scared. She knew her dad was a big deal in the military but expected it would work against her rather than benefit. She intended to keep a low profile.

"I know you know you must serve full duty from the

start of the year you turn eighteen until the end of the year you turn twenty, followed by reserve duty with monthly assignments once a year during your twenties. But, what you may not know is this system of military service is copied from an Earth nation known as Switzerland."

Ela looked around the huge room. She saw her entire high school graduating class along with many from other schools. There were at least a hundred recruits packed into the auditorium in the sky. The building looked almost like any other she had ever seen, except that it was huge and hung in the sky on massive ropes strung between trees. Some of the kids looked a little pale, but she found the constant motion of the building soothing.

"Switzerland was a very mountainous country on Earth, but that isn't why it should interest you. It should interest you because it was politically neutral. Just as the United Colonies are neutral. We will never attack a whale except in defense. We will never battle the Republic of Humanity except in defense. I gare-on-tee you that."

Ela's heart raced a little. He had an accent like her Dad's.

"On Earth, I was in the Air Force. I flew a plane known as the Hornet. All you need to know about the Hornet is that it was very fast and very deadly. The point is that I know how to fight, and can teach *you* how to fight, even though I look ancient to you."

Cooter had silver-gray hair. Ela didn't know he was only

fifty-seven years old and the hair was prematurely gray, she just knew he looked older than anyone she had ever seen. She also knew she didn't want to fight him.

"Before we move on, one more personal detail. Y'all might think I talk funny. That is because I grew up in a place called Texas ..."

Ela exclaimed, "I knew it! You're from the country of Texas. So is my dad," then she slapped her hand over her mouth and looked at the floor, trying to be invisible.

Cooter walked over to stand directly in front of her.

"And your name is?"

"Ela Miles, Sir."

"Who?"

Ela Miles, Sir."

"WHO?"

"Ela ... oh ... uh ... Ela Miles, Sergeant Cooter."

Cooter knew who she was and, if she had the same grit as her father, knew she could take it if he made her an example.

Turning away from Ela, he said, "There are two types of people in the military, first stringers and second stringers. There's a quick way to tell the difference." He spun back to face her. "Second stringers ask questions!"

Ela's face turned red, and she looked at the floor. She was glad her curly brown hair fell to cover her eyes.

"Now, where wuz I? Oh, yeah, I wuz just gettin' to the

topic of how each of you is now a soldier. This group of recruits is the biggest we've had so far since y'all are the oldest teenagers on the planet. So, we have dee-zigned things a little different, just fer you."

Cooter walked back to the center of the room and stood next to a large model of Canopy's human-occupied region. It was over ten feet tall and twenty-by-thirty, made from wood, and had well-trimmed lamp plants included on most of the model trees.

Cooter pulled on one of the lamp vines, and a light high in the model illuminated a small building hanging from strings.

Cotter said, "That is our present location. This model is not to scale but is accurate in layout. This building we are in is not only the largest man-made structure on Canopy but also the highest in elevation. We are at twelve-thousand-four-hundred feet elevation. You will leave this building after your orientation by jumping from it to land approximately here."

He pulled on another vine, and a platform beneath the model building lit up.

"Yep, you heard me. You'll jump from this building to …"

"What? I thought we get to choose whether we want to be Gliders, Scouts, or Divers?" said a young man near Ela.

Cooter froze, and the entire room seemed to gasp as one.

The sergeant walked slowly to stand in front of the boy.

"And your name is?"

"Crap. Liam Mahoney, Sergeant Cooter."

"Well, Crap Liam, you will be the first to jump when the time comes. Do you have any other observations you'd like to share with us?"

"No, Sergeant Cooter."

"As I wuz sayin', you will each be given a Gliders jumpsuit and take your first jump from the back porch, yonder. Don't worry, the platform you'll aim at is surrounded by nets. Most of you will survive. If Crap Liam don't make it, we'll call off the exercise."

Ela felt sorry for Liam but got excited thinking about jumping. *Maybe I'm meant to be a Glider*, she thought.

"It's a common misconception of civilians that United Colonies military is comprised of three different branches. We do have three major divisions but make no mistake about it, Gliders learn to swim as well as glide and Divers learn to glide as well as swim. All three divisions train and learn to excel at each skill set. Flexibility is the order of the day."

Ela was confused. She remembered Saoirse telling about gliding and showing off her Glider jumpsuit when home on leave.

"Each of you will, in fact, be assigned to one of the three divisions, Gliders, Scouts, or Divers, but you will have a specialty. There are Special Operations, Medics, Construction Engineers, Communication Specialists, etc. The list is quite long, but understand this: ever one of 'em can shoot a bow and arrow. Durin' trainin', you'll be given an opportunity to apply for the position you want, then we'll put you in the position we need. You get one vote, we get two."

Cooter pinched the vines again, and the lights went off in the display. He walked slowly around to the other side, hoping one of the impatient youngsters would ask a question. None did. He pulled on a different lamp vine, and the lower right-hand side of the display lit up.

"This east end down near the water and up to Burl City is the Republic of Humanity. Them rascals got us into this mess."

Cooter then pinched another vine; a large settlement at the bottom of the display lit up in a red glow. It was the floor of the display, or water level.

"What you see illuminated in red is where this all started. This is New Venice, the first island settlement."

Ela had never seen a lamp plant that glowed red. *How do they do that?* She wanted to ask about it but knew better than to interrupt Sergeant Cooter. He pinched and pulled on several more vines. The display glowed red on most of its floor.

"All you see in red is the Republic of Humanity. That

includes Burl City and its four water-level cities."

He walked a couple of steps and pinched more vines.

"What you see illuminated in blue is the United Colonies. The widely-spread lighter-blue area at the top is Daylight. It's now our biggest city. More of a suburban area really. Lots of folks don't want to live anywhere close to the Canopians."

Sergeant Cooter walked to the opposite end of the display where it had empty territory that was neither red nor blue. He pinched vines, and the empty area filled with lights like an inverted Christmas tree.

"And this is why we are here. These lights represent a Canopian. The yellow light at the bottom is the whale. The green lights in the Shadows are the raccoons. The orange lights in the Jungle are the spidermonkeys. The many white lights up high are the tripods."

Cooter paused to let the recruits absorb what they were seeing. He remembered the first time he saw it and the intimidating effect it had on him.

"As I said, the display is not to strict scale but is accurate in showing that all but two of our original cities are within reach of the tripods. To phrase it better, they are under observation by the enemy. And now for the grand finale."

He pinched a vine and a purple glow surrounding the whale appeared. It was a globe extending almost to the bottom of the Overhead.

"The violet area represents the region in which the whale can pop your skull. The smaller, darker maroon globe shows the area where the whale can kill you without a raccoon seeing you to focus the energy. The whales know about the Divers, so they just randomly pulse in case one is near.

"We need Gliders to observe the tripods, helping us know the approximate location of a whale. We need Scouts in the Jungle to observe the spidermonkeys and raccoons. We need Divers to monitor the whale's movement when it moves around. We've recently discovered that sometimes a whale will disconnect from its other critters and take just a single raccoon and spidermonkey as it moves around. We think it is looking for humans to kill when it does this."

He paused again. No one made noise.

"We regularly observe them for two reasons. First, they are trying to kill us. Second, we have learned a lot about their body language so we can actually discern their intent, at least to a limited extent. We are learning more every day."

Cooter walked in front of the display and stepped close to the recruits, pausing for emphasis.

"I saw the looks on your faces when I told you about jumping from this building. Get used to that feeling. You will be trained to observe the spidermonkeys and raccoons without being seen yourself. If they see you, you die."

He paused again. No one was breathing.

"And think about this: we can't simulate a raccoon. To train you to observe it, you have to go observe a real one. The difference between training and combat is really just semantics.

"There are jumpsuits in the back, don't be modest. Each of you find one that fits, and we can all watch Crap Liam fly.

"Are there any questions?"

~~~

"Saoirse, it's good to see you. You're so big. How far along?"

"Myoki! I've really missed you. I'm due in two months."

Kejuon walked into his living room. When he saw Saoirse, a big smile lit up his face.

"So the guest of honor has arrived. Wow, you're huge!"

"Uncle K, that is just what every girl wants to hear."

She enveloped Kejuon in a big hug. Her unborn child began kicking vigorously.

As they parted, Kejuon said, "I could feel him kicking me in the stomach. Or, is he running in place?"

Myoki said, "I wanna feel!" She stepped forward and put both hands on Saoirse's swollen belly.

Kejuon saw Choop approaching on the bridge that connected his living room to the main footbridge of Daylight. He walked towards the door to greet him.

"Howdy, stranger."

"K, I'm not strange. You're the one that's strange."

The two hugged and slapped each other on the back.

"K, this is one impressive house. It is the biggest tree house I've ever seen."

"Tree house? Choop, every house on Canopy is a tree house, by definition."

"But this one has, what, seven different buildings connected by footbridges? You should put some swinging ropes and fireman's poles."

"Eight buildings, and you ain't been around the back of the kids' bedrooms. There are some swinging ropes back there."

"Uncle Choop, you gonna hug me or just yap about architecture?"

"Take that beach ball out from under your shirt, and I'll give you a hug."

"What's a beach ball?"

All three adults broke out laughing. Before Choop could hug Saoirse, a thirteen-year-old human blur named Niti entered the room and moved between him and Saoirse.

"Saoirse! You made it! Ooh, can I feel?"

Saoirse laughed and hugged Niti close. Her baby resumed kicking, which caused Niti to giggle.

As she looked at Myoki over the top of Niti's head, Saoirse said, "Is Ela gonna make it?"

"No, she couldn't get leave. Mose won't be here either, he has midterms, but Bina is around here somewhere. There's a pack of kids out back. You should go say 'Hi'. Expect a lot of tummy rubs."

Saoirse and Niti went to find the kids, which left Kejuon standing between Choop and Myoki.

Kejuon said, "Uh, I'm gonna go find Latesha," and followed Saoirse.

Myoki said, "Hey."

"Hey." Choop shuffled his feet and put his hands in his pockets. "K has a nice house. I like the way they build houses in Daylight."

"I haven't seen you in three months, and that's what you want to talk about? Really? Are we going to discuss the weather next?"

Sarah entered the living room. "Enough of that, you two. We are here to celebrate the fact that I'm gonna be a grandmother soon."

She hugged Choop close and whispered in his ear. "I've missed you, Soldier."

Fifteen-year-old Bina came into the room. "Oh, hey, Dad. I didn't know you were here."

Choop stepped away from Sarah and approached Bina. "Hey, Pumpkin, you're a sight for sore eyes."

"You can see me anytime you want, Dad, if you'd just come home."

"There's a war going. I've been on active duty."

"Yeah, right."

"Okay, that's enough of that. How come no one seems interested in celebrating me becoming a grandmother?"

Bina said, "I was coming to tell y'all that Saoirse is going to tell us a war story. She's on the back porch." She spun and exited the room.

The three adults looked at each other sheepishly and followed her.

Kejuon's back porch was a huge platform that connected three of the buildings. The kitchen was in the middle on the long side of the platform. On one end was Kejuon and Latesha's bedroom. The other end was Kejuon's workroom, referred to by Latesha as his 'man-cave'.

When Choop, Myoki, and Sarah came from the kitchen onto the porch, they found quite a scene. Saoirse was surrounded by kids and teenagers sitting cross-legged. Besides Bina and Niti, there were Kejuon's two sons, Saoirse's two younger sisters, and Danielle's three boys. The adults sat in chairs along the wall of the kitchen.

"How did I get roped into this? I don't want to talk about the war."

Saoirse's fifteen-year-old sister, Alana, said, "Quit whining, Saoirse, and tell us about the war. Did you see any whales?"

"You wanna hear about the war? You think war is a

romantic adventure of some kind?"

Saoirse looked over the kids' heads at the adults. She paused, intentionally allowing them the opportunity to object. No one did.

"Okay, I'll tell you about the war, but everyone has to keep your mouth shut. No questions or interruptions." She waited. The room was very still.

"First I should tell you about my friend, Beasley. He's the father of my child. He and I met during Glider training."

The room stirred as people squirmed around. Sarah stepped forward, holding her hands over the lower half of her face.

Saoirse avoided eye contact by staring at the floor in front of the kids.

"One day Beasley and I were teamed together on a simple scouting run. He spotted a tripod. A single tripod, all by itself, crawled along a branch at seven thousand feet. Tripods don't travel by themselves. When you see one, you see a dozen."

Saoirse's voice was quiet. "The thing is, we had learned that the whales would sometimes go on what we call swim-abouts. They swim around in their tunnels accompanied by a single raccoon, spidermonkey, and tripod. When they do this, they are hunting humans."

Saoirse looked up. She stared straight at Choop.

"Some things you can't unsee."

She looked back at the floor.

"You want to know what I can't unsee? I can't quit seeing Beasley signal me that the Scouts below us were making too much noise. They obviously hadn't seen a spidermonkey yet and were in extreme danger. He signaled me he was going down to warn them."

A tear flowed down Saoirse's cheek. She made no move to wipe it away.

"He was at least a thousand feet below me when his head exploded. I can't quit seeing the red mist. I can't quit seeing his limp body falling out of sight."

Saoirse looked up at the kids.

"I still get headaches that remind me. I still dream of his head exploding. I can't unsee it. You want to hear an appealing, thrilling war story then you need to talk to someone else."

~~~

Sarah and Myoki sat on Latesha's back porch.

The deck chairs were the style Kejuon made famous when he first started the wood mill. He traded his mill for lifetime access to unlimited lumber. Enough lumber to build this house and start a business making these beautiful chairs. Free wood meant no one could match his price, but they were still the best craftsmanship of any made on Canopy.

The mill was now in the Republic of Humanity. It was supposedly protected from whale attack due to the killing of Moby, but Kejuon would take no chances with the lives of his family. He preferred Daylight where a Canopians' brain couldn't reach them.

The kids could be heard around the corner of their bedroom, squealing with laughter as they swung on ropes and wrestled and did what kids do.

Sarah said, "I'm so sorry about Saoirse's war story. I didn't think she was ever gonna tell me who the father was. Now I know why."

Myoki reached over and put her hand on Sarah's. "You have nothing to apologize for. I'm kinda glad, really. Those kids won't be romanticizing war anytime soon."

"Yeah, I found Alana crying in the bathroom. But whether she romanticizes war or not, she'll have to serve. It's how they set things up. Maybe it'll be over soon."

Myoki squirmed around in her seat and turned to face Sarah. "I have something I need to tell you."

Saoirse walked onto the porch from the kitchen and sat across from them on the bench at the edge of the porch. Her experience as a Glider left her fearless to the drop behind her.

Looking at Myoki, Sarah said, "What?"

"Nothing."

"But you just said …"

Myoki interrupted, "So, Saoirse, have you picked out names yet?"

"No, not yet. Mom, you okay? You look upset."

"What? No, I'm okay. Your war story was a little unsettling, though."

"Sorry about that. I just couldn't stand watching Alana eager to hear a war story. She thinks it's like some kind of game. I hope it's over before she turns eighteen."

Myoki said, "We all hope so. Ben and Ela are in harms way, too."

Sarah sighed, leaned forward in her chair, and put her elbows on her knees. "Latesha is the only mother here without a child fighting. Part of me is jealous of her. She's got five years before Sentell starts his service. Maybe it will end before then. At least one of us shouldn't have to go through this."

Nine-year-old Jayden, Latesha's youngest, came running around the corner with twelve-year-old Samuel, Danielle's youngest, chasing him. As he passed in front of Saoirse, she grabbed Jayden around the waist and upended him across her lap. She tickled him and Sam helped. Saoirse then stood up, carrying Jayden over her shoulder, and walked back towards the kids porch. Sam followed, still trying to tickle Jayden.

Sarah pulled her leg under her and turned in her chair to face Myoki. "What is that you were going to tell me, but wouldn't tell me in front of Saoirse?"

"You'll understand when I tell you why I couldn't say anything in front of her. Or anyone, but especially her."

"Myoki, I'm not big on drama. Would you just say it?"

"I can't *just say it* without first making sure you understand it stays private. Just us. I could get in trouble. I couldn't tell Saoirse because I want to protect her."

"Myoki, I didn't fly halfway across the galaxy to find a best friend only to have her think I can't keep a secret. You're kinda pissing me off." She just stared and waited.

Myoki lowered her voice. "I've been going to visit Beluga."

"What!"

"Shh, Sarah, keep your voice down."

Sarah spoke in a rough 'stage whisper' louder than her normal voice. "Okay, I'll whisper if that's what you want. I can't believe..."

"Sarah, stop!" Myoki lowered her voice even more. "If you're trying to be funny, well, it isn't funny. I knew I shoulda kept my mouth shut. This is serious. My bet is that I'm considered a traitor and Saoirse would be honor-bound to turn me in."

Sarah's voice was now so quiet Myoki strained to hear it over the noise from the kids. "She would never do that."

"Yeah, well, I'm not going to put Saoirse in that position. You know the Republic of Humanity has killed another whale. This was the first one with no name. I never visited it and taught it sign language."

"What does that have to do with Saoirse? You lost me."

"Since then, whale-swim-abouts have increased significantly. whales are on swim-abouts completely surrounding the borders of the Republic of Humanity."

"Still lost."

"The swim-abouts are a danger to the colonies of Woodstock and Thicketown. Those colonies are low enough to be at risk. Ela and Ben are risking their lives to locate a Canopian and provide early warning so the colonies can evacuate. Don't you get it? United Colonies citizens are having regular evacuation drills. This war is at the front of their minds and the whales are the enemy. My visiting Beluga is sure to be seen as treason."

"Aren't you scared of Beluga? You're risking your life, and for what? How can you have any impact on this madness?"

"I wanted to try and get Beluga to understand that all humans are not trying to kill the whales. I thought I might even suggest the United Colonies could fight the Republic of Humanity. You know, form an alliance with the Canopians or something."

"You just said *wanted*, past tense. I don't like the sound of that."

"Yes. It turns out the Canopians don't understand us any

better than we understand them."

"You'll need to explain that. You lost me again."

"The discussion of us fighting ourselves, *her words*, confused the crap out of Beluga. It's a completely foreign concept to her. I think she first thought I was lying to her, trying to trick her somehow."

"How can you trick it? It can read your mind."

"Thank God. I think that's the only reason she let me live. But it's what she told me next that's kept me from getting a good night's sleep since."

Sarah said nothing. She tilted her head to the side and raised her eyebrows.

Myoki said, "She told me that Choop and our families, especially Mose and Saoirse, get to live. But that's all."

"Wait. It singled out Saoirse and Mose for some reason? Why?"

"She always has. She says *they understand*."

"What does that mean?"

"Sarah, you're missing the point of what I'm telling you."

"Okay, simplify it for me."

"The Canopians plan genocide. All humans must die. They intend to cleanse their planet of the *disease* of humanity. She said they have a plan."

6

"Desperation leads to mistakes."
— *From the memoir of Myoki Miles*

~~~

Ela thought about Glider training. She had grown accustomed to hearing the instructor say, "See how she does that? She pulls up just before contact with the branch and lands like a feather. That's how I want you all to do it."

Setting aside the fact none of the trainees had ever seen a feather, Ela appreciated the compliments but not the resentment and jealousy of the other Gliders.

But as she landed on the branch, she was certainly glad for her ability to land quietly. The last jump had been a long one. She had descended several hundred feet and was in range of a whale's brainwaves. She saw no tripods or spidermonkeys, but recent reports had been pointing out that the Canopians had apparently been learning from the humans and would 'freeze' for long periods of time.

She thought of her dad. He was the one who had taught

the first Scouts how to move unnoticed in the forest. It was all about patience. Freezing in place most of the time, followed by spurts of movement allowed humans to see the Canopians before being seen.

Except the Canopians had learned the trick. They would freeze in place for long periods, especially when the whale was on a swim-about. A motionless tripod was very hard to spot.

In the last letter from her mom, she learned of Saoirse's revelation that Beasley was the father of Saoirse's baby. Beasley's death had put them all on high alert in this region. It took the fun out of something she enjoyed a great deal. She was happiest when gliding in the openness of the Overhead. She had learned there were some places with steady updrafts, and she could stay aloft for as long as she wanted. Gliding down into the Jungle with Canopians on the attack was stressful.

She was exhausted. They had been looking for Canopians on the current mission for ten days. She was at home in the forest, so sleeping in trees with a safety rope was no problem. The constant stress was a different issue. She wasn't sure she could move quietly in her current state.

Besides the exhaustion, she was sad and homesick. She had been upset at missing Saoirse's party. Myoki's letter had told of Saoirse's war story, and Ela wished she had been there to help slap some sense into teenagers who thought this was a thrilling adventure.

She checked her altimeter that was cleverly constructed from the clear and hollow rib of a spidermonkey. It was filled with fluid from a vine. The fluid would expand as it went higher in the Forest. It was very accurate and had proved valuable on these missions.

She whistle-clicked in the language they had developed. There weren't many words but enough to cover altitude, position, movement, and status. Her signal would allow the next Glider to move into position. Only one Glider moved at a time.

As soon as she whistled, she saw movement about two hundred yards below her and one hundred yards to the east. She froze. She struggled to make out what had moved enough to catch her eye. Whatever it was had quit moving.

Then she managed to interpret what she was seeing. A single motionless tripod. It had pivoted to stare in her direction when she whistled.

Ela thought through her options. She could whistle the piercing warning signal meaning a Canopian had been spotted. This would most likely mean her death.

The next Glider's position would not be in range of the whale's killing pulse, even if the tripod could see the Glider to focus the whale's aim. Their instructions were that only one Glider at a time was to be low enough to be in danger of being killed.

The instantaneous communication of the Canopian meant that the whale already knew she had been spotted. It would undoubtedly execute its short-range, unfocused pulse in the water below, hoping to kill any Divers without having to know their exact location. That pulse would occur even if she kept silent.

Her fellow Glider, Glenda, flew into sight thirty yards above the tripod. It swiveled to look up. Glenda was too low! She was supposed to stay at least four hundred yards higher than Ela.

Ela lunged into foliage to her left and whistled the piercing warning signal. It would be audible all the way to the water. Both Divers and Scouts would know a Canopian had been spotted.

She felt the effects of the pulse aimed at Glenda. Her head felt like she had been punched. She barely held onto consciousness as a headache began. She knew she would have this headache for days.

Squinting through a small gap in the foliage, she saw Glenda's headless body falling slowly out of sight. It was trailed by a light red mist.

~~~

Ben had not yet felt the telltale vibration of a passing whale when he heard the warning whistle. He immediately took a huge breath and submerged.

They had learned that the whale's brain pulses did less

damage underwater. They had no explanation for it, but underwater Divers — near Divers with heads exposed above the water — had survived. This was especially true of the weaker, unfocused pulses.

Ben had just surfaced a few seconds before hearing the whistle. This meant that Lawrence and Aiko should be able to stay under long enough to take the pulse while submerged. Certainly Aiko, who had just gone under as Ben took her place in the rotation.

Ben experienced the pulse as a mild irritation. The whale was not close enough for the unfocused pulse to do damage underwater.

He felt Aiko's hand on his ankle. They both surfaced and found roots to hold onto so they could stay up while completely motionless. Lawrence surfaced a few seconds later. None of them moved. Stillness meant life.

Aiko was the communication specialist. She was within five feet of the lamp plant which could be used to send Morse code to the Scouts above. It may as well have been a mile. She made no move toward it. She knew the Glider whistle was sufficient to warn the Scouts.

They felt the vibrations of the whale passing below, moving fast. It would swim a few hundred yards one way and pulse, then back the way it came and pulse. Fortunately, they were not directly above its tunnel. They had learned the hard way — through loss of lives — that vibrations from its swimming could be felt seventy-five yards away from the tunnel, so a Diver would only be killed by unfocused waves if the whale pulsed while at the closest position in the tunnel.

They knew the real danger was from above. A whale on a swim-about would have a raccoon in the Shadows Overhead. It would be looking for them, and if it saw them, the whale could focus and bring death.

Another thing that had been learned is humans are more patient than Canopians. Whether being stationary made the whale uncomfortable, or the creatures above objected to the prolonged stillness, was not known. Humans could wait them out. Unfortunately, it took a very long time.

All three Divers did as they were trained. They closed their eyes so not even the movement of a blink could betray them. They opened their mouths so they could breathe with long, slow, silent breaths. They prepared to spend the next hour refusing to succumb to the impulse to scratch an itch.

~~~

Diego thinks I have weak bones in my legs. That's why he's in a wheelchair, so he thinks that's why I'm in a wheelchair. What I like about Diego is that if he knew I have no legs, he wouldn't care. If he knew I can hear his thoughts, he wouldn't care. He's kind and intelligent, and I'm glad he's my friend.

"The doctors are trying to develop some braces for my

legs, but since Canopy has no metals, they aren't having much luck."

"I know, Diego, but I bet they come up with something. Some of the woods are as strong as iron."

"Yeah, they'll probably figure it out."

This is the hard part of being inside another person's head. Diego thinks in words like we all do, and when they match what he says it's just kind of an echo. But when they don't match, it can get a little confusing. *Probably figure it out*, when overlaid with *are as clueless as hell* makes my head ache.

"Diego, I gotta go to calculus class. See ya later."

He doesn't notice how easy it is for me to flip from the bed into my wheelchair. Most people don't. The few times anyone has, they just think I have amazing upper body strength. Control of gravity is not something most people would think of to explain it.

When I was little, I used gravity control to make army-crawling around trees easier, but I didn't recognize it for what it was. Now I do. Another damn secret I gotta keep.

The Knot Threshold was built on is the largest of any of the colonies, even Knot City. I am always amazed as I push my wheelchair along the bridges connecting TADA's *buildings*. I know the adults call them buildings because they have some idea in their head from Earth. But I've never seen one of these *buildings*. I think we should call a room dug from a tree a nest rather than a building no matter how big it is.

As I travel along the bridge connecting my dorm to the Math Nest, I tune out the noise from the thoughts of the other students. For a while, I had trouble with that, but now it is just a pervasive background noise. Sometimes it's almost soothing, but mostly I can't wait to get back into the forest where it's quiet.

I think of Saoirse and feel a pang of homesickness. She is the only other human who ever exchanged thoughts with me. They weren't clear, just whispers really, and I'm not sure she was even aware they happened, but it was nice knowing another person thought my deformity was not just okay but beautiful. She thought I am made just the way I should be but was reluctant to say that to dad because she was afraid of how he would take it.

"Whoa, Mr. Miles, calculus class is this way."

"Oh, good morning, Dr. Hilbert. I guess I was daydreaming. Almost rolled right past."

"How on Earth could you forget about calculus?"

"Well, Dr. Hilbert, I'm not on Earth, and you know what they say, *Calculus has its Limits*."

"Ouch. Mr. Miles, you're pun to be around."

I like Dr. Hilbert. He thinks about math almost all the time. Others think he is absent-minded, but if they could see the proof he is doing in his head they would understand.

He sub-vocalizes almost constantly. Most folks do it, but only during a conversation or when they're nervous or concentrating. He does it all the time. If people knew it let me hear their thoughts, they might try not to do it.

I'm not learning any calculus in calculus class, as usual. I learn that Cindy hates Della and that Della hates her back, because they are both subvocalizing like crazy. I learn that Jose thinks I'm a real freak and get preferential treatment. I learn that Dr. Hilbert is as bored as I am.

As I roll along to the gym, I am getting excited about my next class. I decided to sign up for swimming. I had mom make me a custom swimsuit that covers my lower torso. I've never been in a swimming pool, but for some reason, I think I'll like it.

I surprise the other kids when we change into our suits. I'm wearing mine under my normal wrap. Most of them think it's weird. One thinks it's funny. They all laugh.

They quit laughing when I launch myself from my chair into the water. I succumb to the impulse to take advantage of gravity control. The coach's thoughts are so loud I can hear them underwater. *Oh, no, he's going to drown. Oh, wait, he can swim. Holy crap, look at him go. What the hell? No one can swim that fast.*

~~~

Choop told no one of his decision. He knew it was wrong, but he felt it was necessary. He thought he could put a stop to the madness.

He sat motionless, surrounded by slingshot vines. Below him and to his left at ten o'clock was the memorial amphitheater of Shade. It had been built following the massacre of the residents of Shade. After the responsible whale had been killed and the tunnel it used was blocked, the location was safe from Canopian attack. But, nobody wanted to live there, so they had built this beautiful memorial.

Then Dedric had decided to defame the tasteful memorial with his amphitheater. It was designed for his speeches and served no useful purpose other than feeding his narcissism. He thought the sadness and reverence the audience felt when they saw this place would give his message power.

The podium was one hundred yards from Choop with a drop of thirty yards. The auditorium seats began on the branch just below Choop. The branches had been cleared and seats installed on them to form a huge semi-circular audience to watch Dedric preen and pontificate.

Choop had arrived early. Dedric was due to give his speech at noon tomorrow. Choop would be in his hide for fourteen hours. It had taken him three days to get to this location without being seen by the troops guarding and prepping the auditorium.

It had only been possible because there was no tactical awareness in the Republic of Humanity soldiers. They couldn't conceive of a credible threat existing in the heart of their country. The number of men on duty would increase tomorrow, but those would mostly be for crowd control.

Choop slept fitfully. He knew he didn't snore, which might compromise his position, but still woke regularly in a heightened state of awareness.

Two hours before the scheduled speech, more men began to arrive. They placed chairs behind the podium, strung a banner in front of it that read *Canopy's Greatest Fisherman,* and took positions all around the perimeter of the auditorium. A teenager with platinum blond hair was stationed on the branch in front of Choop. He sat in the end seat and lay his bow and quiver on the adjacent seat.

When the crowd began to arrive, it depressed Choop. They all seemed excited and happy to hear Dedric pontificate. They must all believe his rhetoric about how God had mandated that man destroy the Canopians. He hoped that was not true and they acted as if they believed to avoid the consequences of speaking out.

When Dedric walked on the stage, loud cheering began. He paced back and forth, strutting and preening. Choop felt nauseous.

Dedric stood at the podium and puffed his chest. "Today is a great day. On this, the tenth anniversary of the establishment of the Republic of Humanity, we celebrate another glorious victory. Another fish has been killed, and another Clearing is open for settlers."

The crowd cheered loudly. Many stood and pumped their arms. One in the last row danced a jig.

Choop smiled to himself at the irony of the tenth birthday party being the setting.

He loaded his slingshot with a tangerina seed and took a deep breath to calm himself. He aimed through a gap in the leaves. He stilled himself and expelled the air from his lungs as he stretched the bands to their limits. When Dedric assumed his famous cross-armed pose, Choop knew he would be still for a few seconds. He took the shot.

His aimed for Dedic's left eye. He missed by four inches. The heavy seed entered Dedric's forehead above his right eye. Dedric still had his arms crossed as he collapsed on the stage.

Many of the more observant soldiers turned to stare in the direction from which the shot had come. Being Canopian born, they were unused to seeing how an Earth-born can jump, and looked on with astonishment as Choop leapt fifty feet to a branch above him and then again to another branch, disappearing from sight.

Two of the men on the stage were Earth-born. They jumped across the branches of the auditorium to give chase.

~~~

"Choop, you know you can come over anytime and stay as

long as you want, but you gotta stop doin' this."

"Can't a guy just eat his breakfast in peace, K? I came out on the porch so I wouldn't bother Latesha and Jayden. Shouldn't you be in there with your family?"

"You're family, too, Choop. I think we need to talk."

Choop pushed his food away and stood. He walked across the porch and stood next to the railing looking down into the openness of the Overhead.

"I swear if you run from me again, I'll chase you. You're probably the toughest man I know, but you can't seem to have a simple, honest conversation."

"I know what you want to talk about, K. There ain't nothing simple about it."

"So now you can read my mind?"

"I know you're gonna ask about Myoki and why she kicked me out again. But what you don't know is she didn't kick me out this time. I just walked."

"Don't tell me, let me guess. The subject of Mose came up?"

Choop sat back at the table and resumed eating. Kejuon folded his hands in his lap and waited.

"K, it seems the other kids are starting to call him freak-fish-boy. He's on the swim team and breaking all the records."

"Yeah, I heard about that. He's becomin' quite the legend. But Mose ain't what you need to talk about. Not

Myoki either."

Choop took the last bite of his spinner bacon and pushed the plate away. He just stared at Kejuon.

"Choop, there's a few of us who've seen what you can do with a slingshot. You think we don't know it was you?"

"What are you talking about?"

"Don't act stupid. It don't play well. I've heard Danielle rave about some of the shots she saw you make in practice. You think she don't know either? She knows. I know. Larry knows. Sarah knows. Adam …"

"K, why are we having this conversation?"

"All kinds of reasons. First of all, if we hear about a tangerina seed being used as a bullet from over a hundred yards and we can figure it out, there have got to be people in R of H that know, too. That means you're puttin' everyone you love in danger."

"You give those idiots too much credit."

"Second of all, it's wrong, Choop. You're losing your moral compass. I know you. You believe in right and wrong. It'll eat you up. It *is* eating you up."

Choop stood and turned away. He paused, then walked to the porch railing. Kejuon scooted his chair back noisily and stood as well. He went and stood by Choop. They both stared at nothing for a full minute. Kejuon broke the silence.

"Am I gonna have to chase you? I really don't wanna

chase you. I'm gettin' too old for that. Cut me some slack."

"Are you done lecturing me?"

"Third of all, the new President of the Republic of Humanity, Bobby Monroe, is just as bad as Dedric. He took over with no election and has the full support of the military. He might actually be worse because he seems reasonable by comparison."

"Reasonable?"

"Yeah, he says no one could throw a tangerina seed and kill someone. He's saying those are just hysterical rumors and what really happened is a whale did it. A really big one with more range popped Dedric's brain. So, the obvious response is to go kill more whales."

"So, I didn't make it worse. It's just as bad as ever."

"Oh, no, you didn't hear fourth of all."

"God help me. I'm livin' a nightmare."

"Fourth of all, behind closed doors Bobby knows what really happened. He's talking about war on the United Colonies as well as war on the whales."

"What!?"

"Yeah, fourth of all's a bitch ain't it? So far, his military leadership is resisting, but that might not last."

"How do you know all this?"

"I can't tell you that. You're the traitor."

Choop turned swiftly to face Kejuon with fists clenched at his sides. "This ain't funny, K."

"Whoa! No sense of humor anymore? Good. Means you're taking this seriously."

"Please, tell me you're done bein' high and mighty, and this lecture is over."

"Fifth of all …"

Choop screamed and lunged toward the railing, but Kejuon had hold of his bicep. "Let me go!"

"Fifth of all, Mose is one of the smartest people I know. I ain't sure he can read minds, but he's so smart that don't matter. If I know, he knows."

Choop sagged to his knees at the railing and put his head in his hands.

"Choop, you're my best friend. Please talk to Mose. You gotta talk to him, or you're gonna lose him."

Choop was silent.

"I ain't stupid. I know what a nightmare it'll be. But you gotta or you'll lose him, I'm tellin' ya."

Choop said nothing.

"Choop, the only thing you got that'll work is the truth. You know he knows everything. He knows you did it. He knows you're embarrassed by him. He also knows you love him. Go talk to him, Choop. Tell him nothing but the truth. It's all you got left."

7

"I thought we had hit rock-bottom, but we kept digging the hole deeper."

—From the memoir of Myoki Miles

~~~

"Come on, Diego, we're gonna be late."

"Mose, we got plenty of time."

"It takes longer when we wait till just before class 'cause of the crowds. Get your ass in your chair and let's go. At TADA you could get away with being late all the time, but the university don't put up with it."

Professor Carson is just closing his door when we roll into view. "You just made it, boys. Was there a traffic jam?"

Diego almost skids as he comes to a stop by the door. "I couldn't get Mose in gear. He wanted to sleep in."

"That's it. Blame me. He knows you're fibbin'."

"Boys, please. Come in and let me get started. I have a lot to cover today."

I know he's pissed because 'I have a lot to cover today' doesn't merge well with *cocky little shit thinks he's remarkable.*

When we get seated, he starts right in on me. "So, Mr. Miles decided to grace us with his presence today."

But he's thinking, *a fourteen-year-old shouldn't be in college no matter how bright he is.* The disparity between his words and his thoughts sometimes gives me tired-head. But, my major is Canopian Biology, and he's the foremost biologist on Canopy, so we're stuck with each other.

"Students, today we're going to focus on the reproductive cycle of the sentient Canopian species commonly referred to as a whale. It's more complicated than anything I have ever studied, due to the whale being a distributed being."

When the professor talks about something that interests the other students, their minds usually stay quiet. But not today. I hear much mental chatter.

After we kill'em all, how they reproduce won't matter.

If I lay my head on the desk, I can see up Julie's skirt.

Why do we want to study their reproduction? We just need to know how to kill them.

All that matters is how high we have to stay to be safe.

He talks like they're interesting. They're just murderous.

"They transform similar to the caterpillar/butterfly metamorphosis on Earth. Don't say it, please. I know you've never seen a butterfly or a caterpillar, but we've studied it, and just for this reason, so we could use it as a basis for comparison in the study of the Canopian life cycle."

I use the trick that helps me cope with the chaos. I try to quit listening to thoughts. It's hard, but I'd learned the trick. The mental chatter fades into a muted jumble of background noise.

Carson drones on for twenty minutes, detailing the bubble-tripod-spidermonkey-raccoon-whale metamorphosis. I'm half asleep when he pisses me off.

"It's the brain of the whale that ties all this together and allows for a distributed being. It's the organ that communicates with the other parts of its body remotely. The whale's brain uses energy waves of altered gravity to communicate as well as to murder humans. They can do this at a distance of …"

"It's not murder when you're just defending yourself!"

"Mr. Miles, please don't interrupt me."

"But you're spouting nonsense. Calling them murderers for self defense misrepresents the truth."

From the seat next to me, Julie says, "Are you out of your mind? They killed my older brother, and he never did anything to them."

I lose focus, and the thought-babble resumes. The only one in the class not wishing me pain or humiliation is

Diego. He's only thinking, *I can't believe he said that. Has he lost his mind?*

Carson's words and thoughts are in perfect union when he says, "Mr. Miles, go to the Dean's office at once. Now!"

As I cool off while rolling my way along the bridge connecting the Science Building to the Administration Building, I realize how stupid I've been. Humanity is at war with the Canopians, and one word I heard other students thinking a lot in the babble was *traitor*. I wish I was in the swimming pool.

I'm passed by a student running fast to the Dean's office. It looks like Ronald from the front row of Carson's class. He's thinking, *this is great, freak-fish-boy is finally going to get what he deserves.*

When I roll into the Dean's waiting room, Ronald is coming out of the Dean's office. He leers at me with a mean grin. Dean Brandt appears in the door behind him. "Mr. Miles, we should talk. Please come in."

I wish I was in the pool.

~~~

"Mom, they didn't really suspend me for being a traitor. They suspended me due to fear of violence by other students."

"Well, that's a fine distinction. I feel so much better. I can't believe you said that in class." [*He is so naive. He thinks they won't attack him. I'm really glad they sent him home.*]

"Mom, you know I'm right. You've talked to more whales than anyone on the planet. They didn't mean us harm until we started killing them."

"They aren't being killed by 'us', Mose. They are being killed by the Republic of Humanity. The whales are smart enough to get that if we can just get through to them." [*Of course, he's right. He's almost always right. Why in the world was he so foolish? He had to know how people at school see things.*]

"Mom, I know you went to talk to Beluga in secret one time. I was too young to remember, but Saoirse told me about it. Let's go talk to Beluga again."

"Are you crazy? They are actively killing humans on sight. No way, young man." [*He's right, we should. But we can't risk it.*]

Saoirse walks into the living room, followed closely by Beasley.

I roll to Saoirse and hug her as she squats down to meet me. I hear her mind taking pleasure in the embrace. I feel her mind accept the love I offer. I feel the bond grow even deeper than I remember it.

Three-year-old Beasley's hand touches my lower torso. He says nothing, but thinks, [*Hi, Uncle Mose.*]

I'm caught off balance. Could it be? I say nothing and think, [*Beasley, can you hear me?*]

"I'm really glad you came back, Uncle Mose." [*Where's his knee? That don't feel like a knee.*]

Beasley, can you hear me?

"Mama, why won't Uncle Mose say hi?"

Saoirse feels my disappointment. Emotions comes through clearly for her. "He's just so surprised, Sweetie. He can't believe how big you are." [*I bet he is trying to get through without words.*]

"Sorry, Squirt. She's right. You're so tall now. Give me a hug why don'tcha."

While I hug Beasley and revel in the innocence of a three-old-mind, Ela walks in.

"Hey, Ela, when did you go off active duty? It's great to see you."

"You know when, silly. Same as all the other twenty-year-olds." [*He's grown up so much.*]

"Sis, when you gonna have a little kid for me to hug?"

"That's a rude question. I forgot how you are, but I miss it." [*If he only knew. I forgot how you are, but I miss it.*]

More than anyone else in the family, Ela's words sync up with her thoughts. I forgot that. I've been gone too long.

Beasley's ability to project thoughts so strongly gives me pause. I need to come clean with Mom about my mind. She should start a project to get pregnant women to spend time around whales like she did when I was in the womb. I bet I wouldn't be alone in my abilities, then. But, not yet. I need to think this through. No, not yet.

Beasley climbs into my lap. "Uncle Mose, your legs feel funny."

Saoirse grabs him and lifts him up into a bear hug. "That's enough of that. Something tells me we interrupted Uncle Mose and his mother. They need to finish their conversation. Ela and I will go fix lunch." [*The tension in here is so thick you could cut it with a knife. Food is always a good excuse.*]

I feel guilty at what I am about to do, but I can't help it.

"Mom, why's Dad not here?"

"He's over at Kejuon and Latesha's." [*He's not here because he is ashamed of you.*]

"That tells me where he is but not why. I asked why."

"I think he and Kejuon are working on some project." [*I'm such a liar. How did we get here?*]

"Did you tell him I got suspended?"

"Yes, he was a little upset." [*Yes. He punched the wall and stormed out of the room.*]

"Is he going to come over and see me?"

"I don't know, Honey." [*It's not just you he's avoiding. He can't stand to be in the same room with me.*]

"Are you and him okay? Are y'all back together?"

"No, he's still staying with them. Can't we talk about something else?" [*I don't think he's ever coming home. He no longer loves me.*]

"We can if I can get an answer to just one more question. Do you still love him?"

~~~

"What the hell happened, General?"

General Otis Cormier was pacing back and forth in President Anwar Pawar's office in the capital building. "I'll tell you what the hell happened, Mr. President. What the hell happened is that these damn whales are smart and we got complacent, that's what happened."

"General, please sit down. Take a deep breath and give it to me piece by piece, in detail. I've heard multiple versions from different people, and I need the truth from the horse's mouth. Please, sit."

There had been a push to make the President's office in the shape of an oval. Anwar had been the one who most objected. His office was a large rectangle with a massive desk carved right out of the same tree as the room. The desk was basically a part of the floor and would never move. There were four "K-chairs" in front of the desk. Kejuon's chairs were so prolific they now had a name. General Cormier pulled one back from the desk and sat down.

He stared up at the green and brown UC flag on the wall behind Anwar's desk. He rubbed his eyes and took a deep breath.

"You want details? How about this detail. We lost eight

soldiers. Eight teenagers that will never become adults. How's that for a detail?"

"Yes, that matches what I heard. I feel their loss as well as you, General. One managed to escape and give warning, right?"

"Yes, Bina Miles was the highest Glider. She hurried to Thicketown and sounded the alarm. If she hadn't we would have lost more people. Three hundred thirty-four, there's another detail for you. That's the number of people we lost in Thicketown. Out of the four hundred fifty-three residents, we lost three hundred thirty-four!"

"I should've known it would be a Miles."

"You think this is a joke or something?"

Anwar leaned forward and fixed the General with a hard stare. "I assure you I do not. General Cormier, I share your anger and your outrage. We can scream at God and punch the walls, or we can analyze what happened to prevent it happening again. I choose the latter. Do not mistake my resolve for lack of empathy. Do not mistake me for someone you would like to have as an enemy."

General Cormier leaned back in his chair and closed his eyes. He took three deep breaths. "I apologize, Mr. President. My daughter and her family lived in Thicketown. None of them made it."

Into the silence that followed, President Pawar spoke softly, "I am so sorry for your loss, Sir."

General Cormier suddenly jumped up from his chair and began pacing again. "We've been going over the area, racking our brains trying to figure out how the creature did it. Apparently, it had its raccoons clear a tunnel through the underwater roots without the whale being a part of it. We listen for signs of whales as they move through the tunnels, but this was a new tunnel, uncharted."

"But didn't the whale have to be present to attack the people? It must have been part of the attack."

"That's the thing we discovered. This tunnel is over twice as wide as any we have encountered before. It appears they took their time — years in fact — to build a very wide tunnel so the creature could approach without touching the roots along the sides of the tunnel. That's normally how we hear them coming."

"And the tunnel ended just underneath Thicketown? They can navigate that well? If we have the areas around the settlements free of Canopians, how do they manage that?"

"You're not asking the right questions, Sir, and you're making an invalid assumption."

"Please, by all means, General. Correct my assumption and tell me the questions I should be asking."

"You assume the tunnel ended under Thicketown. It didn't. You should be asking which settlement it is headed towards. You should be asking how close it is to

Woodstock."

~~~

The apartment 'building' where Myoki and Choop lived in the Overhead near Daylight was a spectacular mess. Each apartment was either attached to or carved into a separate branch. The apartments were connected with an incredible tangle of footbridges. From a distance it looked like a three-dimensional spider web.

Choop arrived early on purpose. He was afraid if Mose knew he was coming to visit, Mose would leave to avoid him.

When he knocked, he was overwhelmed with awkwardness. Why was he knocking on the door to his own apartment? He knew the answer but tried not to think about how he was now a stranger to his family.

Myoki answered the door. When she saw who it was, she immediately became stiff and formal.

"Oh, I didn't know you were coming over."

"Yeah. Sorry to come so early. I was hoping I could see Mose."

"Oh. Of course. That's a good reason to visit me."

"Myoki ..."

Myoki held up her hand, palm out, as she stepped away from the door. "No. No excuses and rational explanations, please. Come on in."

Myoki walked towards the bedrooms without looking

back. "I'll see if he's awake."

For several minutes, Choop paced back and forth in the living room rehearsing what he wanted to say. When Mose rolled his chair into the room, Choop couldn't seem to find words. He tried not to make it obvious he was avoiding looking at Mose's lower torso.

Mose rolled to the open spot unofficially reserved for his chair when he was in the room. He spun around and looked at his dad. He was silent a long time and only spoke when he realized his dad couldn't.

"Don't tell me, let me guess, you came to chew me out for getting suspended."

"No. I just wanted to talk to you. My understanding is you got in trouble for expressing opinions against the war. I would never get upset with you for that."

Mose was caught off guard. His dad's thoughts matched his words.

"Oh. Well, okay, thanks. They were afraid other students would attack me."

"This war is crazy. There's no way we can win it even if it was the right thing to do. More people need to speak out against it."

"So you just came here to talk about the war?"

"No. I, uh, I just wanted to see how you are doing."

Since his thoughts said otherwise, Mose said, "That's not why you're really here. Why don't you be honest with me and tell the truth."

Choop turned and began pacing again. "I think we need to patch things up. I don't like how it's gotten between us."

"You forgot to include the part about thinking I'm a freak."

"What? I don't think that."

"You didn't tell me about how ashamed you are of being the father of the freak-fish-boy."

"What? No. Where are you getting this stuff?"

"You know."

"Damn it, Mose. I came here to apologize. Why are you making it a fight?"

"So, you came to apologize but you can't say the things that you're going to apologize for?"

"I don't think you are a freak. I am not ashamed of you."

"I've got a phrase for you. I've heard you use it before. 'I call bullshit'."

They were shouting at each other. The noise caused Myoki to come and stand in the doorway. Choop looked at her with pleading in his eyes. He saw hardness in return.

Niti slipped under her mother's arm and ran into the room. The teenager stood between Mose and Choop and began to yell.

"Stop it! Stop it! You're driving me crazy. Stop it, please."

Choop whirled and stomped to the door, yanked it open,

and left without another word.

~~~

"Everyone, come to order, please. Let's begin."

Anwar sat in the middle of the dais at the front of the congressional chambers. Each Congressman's aide sat on the wall bench behind the dais. Other than the shorthand reporter, the only other person in the room was Kejuon.

"For the record, this special session of Congress is being held behind closed doors. Everything discussed here will be treated as confidential, top secret information. We will be deposing Mr. Kejuon Washington, resident of Daylight."

Kejuon squirmed on the first-row bench. The summons to attend caught him off guard. The sinking feeling in the pit of his stomach was turning to nausea.

The census on the wall for **Year 23** underlined the seriousness of the times. The numbers for Thicketown had not yet been updated, but the row of zeros for Shade seemed to glare at Kejuon.

City	Adult	Child	Total	Elev.	Year
Knot City	2189	422	2611	4110'	1
Burl City	2237	569	2806	3980'	2
Threshold	489	401	890	4320'	3
Daylight	2678	788	3466	8675'	3
Thickettown	354	99	453	2940'	4
Woodstock	458	121	579	3840'	5
New Frisco	333	98	431	7100'	6
Utopia	255	99	354	6800'	6
Shade	0	0	0	2150'	7
New Venice	1235	378	1613	0	9
Skye	435	114	549	8623'	10
Dawn	421	101	522	8412'	11
Refuge	678	218	896	7893'	12
New Haven	567	289	856	7784'	12
Island City	1014	212	1226	0'	12
Boardwalk	992	245	1237	0'	14
Atoll	878	301	1179	0'	15
UC Total	10646	3190	13836		
R of H Total	6595	1803	8398		
TOTAL	17241	4993	22234		

Anwar slapped the lectern with his palm. It sounded like a gunshot in the mostly empty chamber. "Mr. Washington, are you listening?"

"Oh, yes, Sir. Sorry."

"I was just asking if you understood the confidential nature of this meeting? I need verbal confirmation for the record."

"Yes, Mr. President. Mum' s the word. What happens in Knot City, stays in Knot City."

None of the leaders smiled at his joke. A few frowned.

"Mr. Washington, I have received a request for extradition of Choop Miles. The Republic of Humanity believes he assassinated President, Dedric Krieger. It is my understanding Mr. Miles is separated from his wife and frequently stays at your residence in Daylight. Is that correct?"

"So, you just assume he's guilty because the R of H says so?"

"No such assumption has been made. We are just trying to determine his whereabouts. We also have other questions."

"You don't determine his innocence by determining his location. You've already decided he did it."

"That is not so. You are his best friend. You know him better than anyone. Surely you can understand we would think you can shed some light on these accusations."

"Oh, I understand alright. You think if you approach him directly, he'll run. You want me to help you find him so you can ambush him. Here's what I have to say: I know nothing about the assassination. I'm not going to answer questions about Choop Miles."

"The United Colonies operate under the rule of law. I'm not asking you casual questions. You will answer."

"Is that some kind of threat?"

The representative from New Haven, Shorty Wanstedt, rose halfway from his seat. "You're damn straight it is!"

Anwar jumped to his feet. "Enough, Shorty! This isn't the Wild West. Reporter, please strike representative Wanstedt's outburst from the record."

Kejuon stood and waved his hand in a dismissive motion. His words drifted back as he walked toward the door.

"Strike me from your record, too."

~~~

Mom thinks Dad killed Dedric Kreiger. Uncle K thinks he killed him. Ela thinks he killed him. A part of me wants to go see Dad and ask him so I could see the truth behind whatever he answers, but I don't really need to. I know he did it.

God, I know us teenagers are expected to have issues, but being both freak-fish-boy and son-of-an-assassin seems like piling on. The school isn't going to want me back. My Dad doesn't want me.

What am I doing? I can't believe I'm just sitting around this apartment feeling sorry for myself. That's not what Saoirse would do. She'd take some sort of action even if it was wrong. So would Ela. So would Mom.

So would Dad, but his action might be illegal. What I gotta do is think outside the box. I've got to do something — even if it's wrong — or I'm gonna go crazy.

But what?

It hits me in a flash of insight. The answer is so obvious, I laugh. I don't belong here. I belong with the whales. I might be just the thing needed to help the whales understand humans and know not all of us have it in for them.

I anguish over the note for a long time. I've got to tell the family what I've gone to do. Even Dad needs to know. In the note, I ask Mom to tell the family, but *only* the family and Saoirse.

I probably didn't need to be so specific. If there is anyone who understands being branded a traitor, it's Mom. I used to lay awake at night listening to her dreams of imprisonment on Inception.

I struggle deciding what to take and laugh again when it becomes clear in my mind. Where I'm going, none of my possessions will be of use. I dress in my newest leather jumpsuit and strap my knife in its scabbard to my lower torso through the loops Mom sewed in.

I quickly leave our apartment building and glide down the main trunk of a tree. My hands are the only part of me touching the tree. I move fast, staying on the bottom side of the trunk when possible. I'm pretty sure anyone who sees me will not even recognize what they're seeing. A rapidly gliding freak-fish-boy is not something likely to register on the senses.

I am especially glad to leave that wheelchair.

~~~

They came for him in the morning. Choop stepped onto Kejuon's back porch expecting to enjoy his long morning meditation. Instead, he was face to face with his friend, Sergeant Charles 'Cooter' Holliston.

"This ain't my proudest moment, Choop. But, I'm gonna have to ask you to come with us."

It was obvious who he meant by us. There was a Glider at each end of the porch with an arrow already notched and pointing slightly down at the ready position. He knew the Gliders to be well-trained soldiers. Cooter would accept nothing less.

Choop heard footsteps on the roof. He looked out over the huge porch railing and saw movement in the trees.

"Did you bring a whole Squad?"

"Nope. Two, old friend. I can see you thinking 'bout running. Please don't. These kids are crack shots. I told 'em to shoot for your legs, but shit happens you know. They've heard the legends about you. They think you're Superman and they're kinda nervous. Please just come with us peacefully."

"That was a dirty trick, coming yourself, Cooter. You know I won't fight you."

Cooter sounded a warbling whistle. Two more Gliders swooped in and landed gracefully on the porch railing on either side of him. They jumped down onto the porch and approached Choop from two directions with long leather braids in their hands to use in binding him.

"Choop, just stay real still and put your hands behind your back. I told'em you're kinda tricky and to expect anything."

Choop complied. They bound his hands tightly behind his back. They tied a hobble onto his legs. He would be able to stride eighteen inches at the most. They each took a leash and looped it around an elbow and stepped back. They could control him from several feet away.

"Damn, Cooter. You know I ain't really Superman, right?"

"I know what you can do, Choop. I was thinking bout wrapping you in a net. We brought one. You prefer that?"

Cooter yelled loudly, "Ahoy, the house. Colonial Union soldiers, Sergeant Charles Holliston. Open up!"

Choop was pleased at the look of surprise on Kejuon's face. He was glad to feel certain his old friend had not been the one to tell them where to find him.

"Don't look so surprised, K. You told me this would happen."

As they marched Choop along the footbridge leading from Kejuon's front porch, Kejoun shouted, "Y'all hurt him, Cooter, and you'll regret it."

They walked along Daylight's footbridges for thirty minutes before coming to the jail.

Cooter seemed deflated, almost embarrassed, now that the deed was done. "We'll keep you here for the day. You'll be speaking to Anwar soon. Others, too, I expect."

The jailer was a redhead named Angus Eschew. He roughly shoved Choop into a cell and bellowed orders.

"Woman, get this criminal some breakfast. I promised Cooter we'd treat him better than he deserves."

The woman he addressed did not move. She was just a girl really, twenty-three years old with jet-black hair and olive skin. She just stared at Angus until he left. She then picked up a chair, brought it near the bars of the cell, and sat lightly on the front edge.

"Hello, I'm Tsintah Eschew. Please excuse my husband. He's rude by nature."

"Hello, Tsintah. That's an unusual name."

"Arapaho. I bet you know my mother, Nascha. She's mentioned you before."

"Oh, yeah. I like her. Now that you say that, I can see the resemblance. Hadn't you better get me breakfast? Your husband seemed rather insistent."

"Oh, he just blusters that way for show. Wants everyone

to know he's the man. Don't worry about him."

"If you say so. I ain't really hungry anyway."

"Ela saved my life."

"What?"

"Ela, your daughter. She saved my life."

"Oh, you served with her?"

"Yes. But for her, I'd be dead. My mother has a saying: 'pear seeds grow pears'"

"What does that mean?"

"It means since I know Ela, I know you. You're not a bad man."

"Well, thanks, I appreciate you saying that, but I've done bad things."

"Sometimes bad things need doing. Good and bad are relative, don't you think? I do things all the time Angus thinks are bad. Gonna do one tonight."

"Really."

"Yes. Tonight. Angus is going to come by your cell in about an hour and unlock the door. Then he's going to distract the guards so you can slip away."

"That's not you doing a bad thing, it's Angus doing a bad thing."

"Nah, he's going to do it because I'll tell him to, so it's on me."

"You haven't told him yet? How do you know he'll go along."

"He always does what I tell him. He has no choice because my momma's a medicine woman."

"I know Nascha. She's a doctor. That's why she qualified for crew on Inception."

"Well, of course, a Navajo medicine woman would become a doctor in the white world. What else would she do?"

"I'm having a little trouble following what this has to do with Angus."

"He used to beat me."

"Oh, well that explains everything."

Her tinkling laughter was pleasant and soothed Choop's nerves. "When momma started life on Canopy, she made a point of studying the various plants and their medicinal benefits. What medicine woman wouldn't?"

"Do you always talk in circles?"

"I like circles. Turns out there's a plant that is poisonous if you eat it. If you don't eat some more, you die. If eat just a little each day, you live. You have about a day and a half to get some more into you, or you die horribly. Angus is stubborn. He waited until the cramps started before he believed me."

"You poisoned your husband?"

"I told you. He used to beat me. He quit."

Choop was speechless. Tsintah sat patiently, waiting for his response. He thought about it for many long seconds before replying. "Well, he shouldn't have beat you."

Tsintah's laughter filled the jail cell and caused Choop to smile.

"Get you some rest, Ela's dad, you'll be traveling soon."

8

"Birth is painful. That's true for both babies and ideas."
—From the memoir of Myoki Miles

~~~

I heard Uncle K talking once about moving in the forest
without disturbing the animals. He learned it from Dad.
Apparently, back on Earth, Dad had a native-American
mentor who taught him. Uncle K described moving in short
spurts. I thought the term was funny and it stuck in my
head. Now I'm trying it myself.

I'm moving mostly on the underside of the angled tree
trunks. I move quickly, then hold still for a long time. It
would be an interesting game if I wasn't so afraid of being
seen. It's one thing to run away from home, teenagers do
that. It's a whole different thing to go visit a whale during
war. That's the action of a traitor. I know I'm not a traitor,
but people already think I'm weird, so it's an argument I'd
rather not have.

At first, I can hear noises made by other people, but

eventually, the sound of human activity dies off. I'm now low enough to be in range of a whale's brain. I still move in spurts but with shorter pauses.

It occurs to me that I don't know where I'm going. *Down* is not a destination, it's a direction. I pause for a long time, listening carefully. I can hear occasional sounds of activity to my right. This is probably a small, rural R of H community. I veer to my left.

When I reach the water, it feels like a good time to rest, maybe a relaxing swim. This is the longest time I've ever exercised my ability to defy gravity. It's making me tired. I wish I could just float like a balloon, but keeping myself from scraping on the tree trunk is the best I can manage.

Then, I hear a voice. Someone says, "Did you hear that?"

This is disturbing for two reasons. First, I just made a loud splashing noise, so the sound was me. Second, if someone says "did you hear that?" it means there's more than one person. I freeze and listen.

"It came from that direction."

"It was probably a fish jumping."

"Would've been a damn big fish. Let's go check it out."

I see movement just thirty yards away. I take a big breath and submerge. As they come closer, I sink deeper.

They stop when they're almost on top of me. They're staying still to listen for more sounds. I hold still as well.

I hear them talking. More importantly, they're not

moving. I know I can hold my breath a long time, but not forever. I'm in a pretty thick patch of roots. If I move, they'll hear me for sure.

"I don't see anyone."

"If there's someone here, they could've gone under."

"Well, that's easy enough to check. We'll just wait six minutes. No one can hold their breath that long."

I realize that, even though I've been under a couple of minutes, I'm not desperate for oxygen. How long *can* I hold my breath? Five more minutes pass. I'm still fine. This is amazing.

They give up and swim away. Rather than risk them seeing me, I go deeper. About fifty feet down, I emerge into a large *tunnel* in the roots. This must be a whale's tunnel, and those guys are R of H divers monitoring it.

The tunnel has a lot of new root growth jutting into it. It used to be much wider, but is growing narrower. It must be an abandoned tunnel leading to the Clearing of a dead whale the R of H cowards murdered.

This gives me an idea. To find a whale, I can follow the tunnel away from R of H. Eventually, it will reach another Clearing with a live whale.

I need air after about fifteen minutes. Amazing! I can hold my breath more than fifteen minutes. Maybe one of those unknown organs in my lower torso is a third lung.

I surface and breathe for a few minutes to get my blood

fully oxygenated. I descend back into the tunnel and swim rapidly away from humanity.

~~~

"Good morning, Choop. It's going to be a great day. I brought you some breakfast. If you don't mind, I'm eating with you."

"Good morning, Tsintah. You're in a good mood."

"It's going to be a wonderful day. Good food, good company, an exciting jailbreak. What's not to like?"

"I'm pretty sure things are not that simple."

"No, things are really that simple. I get some good food into you for your travels, I signal Hubby to distract the guards, I unlock your cell, I scream and fall down all hurt, and you run into the forest. I'm told when you hide in the jungle, you become quite invisible."

"Tsintah, you're my kind of people. How about we *do* make it complicated?"

"Why, Choop Miles, are you flirting with me?"

Choop came and stood near the bars and lowered his voice. "No, not that kind of complicated. I'm talking real complications."

Tsintah looked over her shoulder at the guards. "Okay, you have my attention."

Choop spoke in a quiet whisper. "I've done this before. You've probably heard of the first landing party and the nastiness involving our first leader's delusions of grandeur.

What you may not know is that I was in hiding for months and had my wife leading a resistance movement on Inception. I suggest we do it again. You can get in on the ground floor of this fine opportunity to save Canopy. All for the low, low price of total commitment and risk of imprisonment or death."

Tsintah paused for a nanosecond. "And here I thought life was boring. I'm in."

"That spinner sausage looks good. Give me some of that. Do you have a pencil and paper? I've got some things to show you before we play out our little charade."

~~~

"Mom, would you sit down? You're driving me nuts. Back and forth, back and forth. You're gonna wear a hole in the floor."

"Ela, don't tell me to calm down. Your Dad's been arrested, and Mose ran away. I have a right to be upset."

"I didn't say calm down, I said *sit* down. Of course, you're not calm. Who could be calm? But, you're driving me nuts with the pacing. Please, sit down and be upset at the kitchen table like I am."

"How's he gonna get by without his wheelchair? Why in the world didn't he take his wheelchair?"

"Mom, he moves around just fine without his wheelchair. He's gonna be okay."

Myoki spun in place and began walking the short

distance to the other end of her kitchen. Ela moaned and put her head in her hands.

Myoki stopped pacing at the sound of a knock on her front door. Both women turned to look at the door leading into the living room. They turned to look at each other. Myoki bolted towards the living room with Ela close behind.

Myoki threw the door open to greet her prodigal son, only to be face to face with a beautiful woman. Thick, jet-black hair hanging almost to her waist made the woman look stockier than she actually was. She was holding a strange, feathered wooden hoop filled with an intricate webbing. She smiled brightly and said, "Hello."

Myoki stared for a few seconds without speaking. "I'm sorry. I was expecting someone else. May I help you?"

"Yes. You can help not only me but the whole planet. Oh, I forgot my manners. This is a housewarming gift." She stuck out the feathered object. Myoki stared at it without taking it.

"Who are you?"

"Oh, excuse me. You've got me flustered. I'm Tsintah Eschew."

"I'm sorry, Ms. Eschew, but we're having a bit of a crisis."

"Actually, it's Mrs. And I know a little about your problem. Your husband was in my husband's jail until I helped him escape."

"Mom, for crying out loud, let her in."

Myoki stepped aside, and Tsintah stepped into the living room.

Ela said, "Mrs. Eschew, would you like some coffee?"

Tsintah didn't drink coffee. "That would be nice. Please, call me Tsintah."

"Mom, close your mouth and show Tsintah to the kitchen table."

As Ela began boiling the tangerana seeds, Myoki sat at the dining room table with Tsintah. "So, Mrs ... uh ... Tsintah, tell me what you know about my husband."

"Right to the point. I like that. Choop told me you'd be like that."

Myoki just tilted her head slightly and stared.

"Wow. He wasn't exaggerating."

Myoki raised her eyebrows without saying a word.

"Okay, okay, here's the short version. He was arrested by Sergeant Cooter and charged with killing Dedric Krieger. My husband is the jailer. I helped Choop escape from jail yesterday morning."

Myoki held up a finger. "First of all, I don't know you, so I certainly don't trust you." She held up a second finger, prepared to count until she had made her points. "Next, what possible motivation could you have for helping my husband. Are you having an affair with him? Third, why would you then come here and tell me this? Fourth…"

Tsintah's laugh was a light, merry sound. "Whoa, please quit counting. I'm losing track."

"Is this some kind of joke to you?"

"Is that number four?"

Myoki's chair scraped loudly as she stood and towered over Tsintah.

"Mom! Stop it. I'm sorry, Tsintah. Mom, sit down, please."

Myoki slowly lowered herself back into her chair.

"Mrs. Miles, I didn't understand. I thought, since you're separated from your husband, that the flame had died. I see it still burns bright. I'm not having an affair with your husband; I'm going to help him with the resistance." She pulled a small piece of paper from her pocket and slapped it on the table. "He said to tell you, *Inception*."

Myoki stared at a note with text that looked like gibberish. The words were each five characters long. It was the encryption format she and Choop had used to pass notes during her imprisonment on Inception. She had trouble breathing and felt like time had ceased. "That doesn't mean anything. You could have scribbled that yourself."

Tsintah rolled her eyes. "Suspicious much? Ela, do you have a pencil?"

Ela reached into her pocket, pulled out the pencil she used to write in her journal, and handed it to Tsintah.

Tsintah began to draw on the note. She made a grid five-by-five. She then filled in the first six boxes with the letters I, N, C, E, P, T, O. She looked up and waited.

Myoki said, "He showed you our encryption method?"

"Yes, he said if you wouldn't lead the resistance, to ask Sergeant Stallman. But, he made it plain you would be the best choice."

"If you learned the encryption technique, you could have written that note."

"Wow. I guess paranoia is a necessary part of leading a resistance movement."

"Mom, what the hell is she talking about?"

Tsintah looked up at Ela with astonishment. "You never told your children?"

"Told us what? Mom!"

Tsintah pushed the feathered, wooden hoop forward to the middle of the table. "This is a dreamcatcher. If you put it on the wall over your bed, it will prevent the nightmares you're sure to have in the near future. I can see you're going to need some time. I'm going to leave now so you can decrypt the note. I will be back later today."

~~~

The first sign I'm getting close to a whale is that the underwater tunnel opens up and is much wider. As I swim along, no new root growth is evident. The tunnel is well maintained. This lasts for several hours, and each time I surface, I expect I might encounter raccoons, but no.

The second sign is the feeling in my skull. I have heard Mom describe it as itching and I can see why she would say that, but to me, it feels more like the whispering of a foreign language I don't understand. It starts out very faint, but the closer I get to the whale the stronger it gets.

When I see movement ahead in the tunnel, I stop. I can't see it clearly at this distance, but it must be a raccoon clearing new root growth from the side of the tunnel. I surface quietly. I climb onto the trunk of a tree, find a comfortable niche where I can sit, and breathe deeply to replenish my oxygen.

I'm scared. This close to human-occupied territory, the whale should have shared memories with the whales I grew up watching Mom talk to, but it's risky. Seriously life-and-death risky.

When I'm calm, I yell loudly, "I hope you remember me. I'd like to talk with you."

The brain itching grows in intensity. It's painful, but bearable.

I see a wave in the water coming toward me even though I know the whale is fifty feet beneath the surface. It's not a large wave; the numerous small trees prevent it from cresting, but it's moving rapidly. It subsides when the creature is next to the large tree where I perch. The many small trees and tangled underwater roots keep the whale from surfacing.

Four raccoons are moving fast in my direction. They fan out as they approach, so when they stop about thirty yards from me, they are in a one-hundred-eighty-degree defensive arc at varied heights above the water. I hold up my hands to show I am unarmed.

I know my thoughts project most clearly when I speak. "I am Myoki's son, Mose. I hope you remember me. I seek asylum."

The raccoons do not use sign language to respond. They just stare, but the Canopian answers in my head. It is very hard to describe what it's like to hear meaning without words, but that's what happens. I hear no sounds that you would call a voice. I experience no words to translate. I just receive *meaning*. Attempts at translation will fall short, but words are all I have.

[*Asylum from what danger?*]

"I have spoken out against those who attack Canopians."

I have not actually been threatened with harm, so I try not to think of this as misleading, then try to dismiss even that thought.

[*Where is your mother?*]

"She doesn't know I'm here."

I begin to feel a strange *probing* sensation. I find myself rapidly experiencing random memories. I can't control it.

I realize I am being *inspected.*

~~~

"Mom, please quit with that silly note and talk to me."

Myoki continued working to translate the note, concentrating on two letters at a time. "It's not silly, Ela. It's the opposite of silly."

"This is just great. A woman I don't even know tells us you haven't told me something important, and now you don't have time to talk to me. She even said, 'You haven't told her?' Did you see her face? She couldn't believe you wouldn't tell your own daughter. You think that note is more important than me?"

Myoki paused and looked up. Ela thought Myoki seemed a lot older than her fifty-seven years.

"Ela, I heard Saoirse's war story. I saw her pain. I've done terrible things. I can't share things with you that will only cause you more pain."

"How can you not understand that the things I imagine will be so much worse than the reality?"

"I wish that were true, Ela, but it's not. I've done things you would never believe. Things that would make you ashamed of me. Please let it go."

"I bet you're wrong. I'm more grown-up than you think. I've seen terrible things. Tell me just a single thing you've done that you think I can't handle."

"I killed a man with a Bic pen by stabbing him in the jugular a dozen times."

The look on Ela's face broke Myoki's heart. Myoki could hear Ela's breathing in the silence. Myoki could think of nothing to say that would help, so she resumed translating the note.

"I don't believe you."

"Told you. Denial is the best way to *not handle it*."

"I'm not in denial."

Myoki's voice squeaked, "*I'm not in denial*, she denied."

"Mom, if you don't put that damn note aside, I'll … I'll …"

Myoki quit working on the decryption and stared at her oldest daughter. "Ela, I love you. You're my pride and joy. I am so proud of who you've become. I'm ashamed of some of the things I've done. Can't you understand why I would keep those things from you?"

"Okay. Touché. Now, why can't you understand my need to really know my mother? At least tell me it was self defense."

Myoki sat still for several long seconds. She turned the partially decrypted note and pushed it across the table. The encrypted lines were intentionally spaced to allow the translation to be written in between. The first line was in ink, in Choop's handwriting. The second line was Myoki's penciled translation:

```
TKIUF EBPJE XTDRL LWTSC HOCTI NMSCF PTGNN
ITSLI KEDEJ AVUAL LOVER AGAIN IAMHI DINGI
```

Ela stared at the odd writing with the spaces not placed between the words. Her lips moved as she concentrated. Ela said, "It's like deja vu all over again. I am hiding i...?"

"*It's like deja vu all over again.* Choop used to say that a lot when he was a kid. He thought it was funny."

"So you know it's him, then. That's sneaky."

"Yes, I know it's him. If you'll let me finish decrypting it, he's about to tell where he's hiding and probably other useful information."

"Was it self-defense? At least tell me that."

"It wasn't, not really. The short version is I was protecting Choop. A man named Colonel Simon Goetsch was going to have him killed. Choop and I led a coup against the military to stop them forming a dictatorship on Canopy."

"A military coup? Mom, I'm a soldier. There is no way I can accept that."

"Apparently, it's deja vu all over again, so you'd better wrap your head around it."

"Wrap my head around it, hell. I'll put a stop to it."

~~~

The highest Knot Choop could find that was remote from human occupation but close enough for the journey was at 8000 feet elevation. It was twenty-five miles to the east of New Haven, about a two-hour journey for an Earth-born but closer to a full day for native-born.

The Knot was a small one, only about fifty yards in each direction, but it had lush, parasitic plants covering all sides.

Choop put the main door to his hideaway on the underside of the Knot. He cut plants so the path through to the entrance went in a zigzag pattern, which kept the entrance well concealed from casual observation.

For Earth-born, getting to the foliage near the entrance was an easy twenty-foot jump from a branch beneath. For the native-born, Choop wove a rope-ladder which could be lowered to the branch.

He burrowed out a room twelve feet to a side, not worrying about aesthetics or symmetry. He carved benches into all the walls so a group of people would be comfortable for long meetings.

One of the reasons Choop selected the Knot was because it was at the center of a large, open space in the Overhead. It could only be approached — by anyone other than Gliders — from below by climbing up the side of one of the trunks creating the Knot. Even an expert Glider would have trouble landing in the foliage near the entrance due to its location on the underside of the Knot.

He reminisced about hiding with Kejuon when they were the only two humans living on the planet. They hid in raccoon caves. The dramatic difference in those days and the current situation of having to fear for your life near a whale depressed him.

In those days, he and Kejuon had grown close. Both had a purpose. Preventing Goetsch from creating his dictatorship on Canopy had consumed every waking moment. Now, Choop felt the same sense of commitment. He believed that if something was not done to halt the Republic of Humanity's attacks on the Canopians, humans would never survive on Canopy.

He made daily trips to the location he told Tsintah to use as a note-drop. It was near New Haven's last footbridge. He marked it with the agreed upon symbol. Each visit, he would sit and observe the drop spot for at least an hour before going down to check it.

One day, on the way back from visiting the drop spot, he saw movement. It was a tripod several hundred feet below him. He jumped closer, but stayed above it, in what he hoped was out-of-range of the whale's killing radius.

"Hey, tripod, up here."

The tripod stopped moving and tilted its body to look upward.

"I have a message for the Canopians. All of you. My name is Choop Miles. I am the husband of Myoki Miles. I have defected from the human military. I am going to find a way to stop humans from attacking Canopians. Please stop attacking humans. I will find a way to stop other humans from killing whales. Just give me some time."

Choop knew the creature would be unable to respond

since it had no arms with which to sign. But, it surprised him by repeatedly jumping up and down. He thought, *either it's acknowledging my message, or it wants to kill me.*

~~~

The room was crowded. Along one wall sat Choop, Bina, Cooter, Larry, and Sarah. There was a palpable tension. On the opposite wall sat Adam, Danielle, Kejuon, Latesha, and Tsintah. Myoki sat in the middle of one of the side walls. Saoirse sat on the side opposite Myoki. By everyone's body language, Choop could tell that Myoki's side of the room became the *head of the table.* They all waited for her to begin.

"Choop, would you like to start?"

"No."

"But you have experience doing this. You led us before."

"K and I were down here living in raccoon caves. You were the one dealing with high intrigue up on Inception. I was a symbol. You were the real leader. You should lead the way."

Kejuon added, "Well said. I concur."

Choop felt the tension in the room lessen. Sarah visibly relaxed against the wall. Danielle leaned forward, put her elbows on her knees, and exhaled audibly. Choop was relieved and simultaneously felt slightly dissed.

Myoki scooted forward to the edge of the bench. "Okay,

well, we all know why we're here. For those of you who weren't a part of that, maybe I should give you a high-level explanation of what we are referring to. The leader of Inception decided …"

"Decided to fall victim to mutiny?" Ela's head stuck up through the door in the floor. She wore her Glider suit. The folded wings barely fit through the opening. "What's everyone staring at? Was I not invited to participate in my family's delusions of grandeur? Cooter, don't you want help committing treason?"

Everyone sat mute. Finally, Myoki said, "Oh, for God's sake, Ela. Just join us and listen."

Danielle was suddenly on her feet. "Join us, my ass. Ela, you're like family, but you need to leave now, or I'm going to give you a lesson in Earth muscles that are highly trained for hand-to-hand combat."

Ela climbed through the opening, faced Danielle, and squared her shoulders. "Bring it, old lady."

"Danielle, if you hurt her," Choop said, "you answer to me."

Cooter sat up straighter. "Ela, you don't have all the facts."

"Ela, please …" began Myoki.

Saoirse stood and screamed loud enough to cause pain. "Everybody, SHUT UP!"

The room was quiet for a beat, then three voices started

at once. Saoirse screamed again, "NO! Not another word. I'm gonna talk, and everyone else is going to listen. Danielle, Ela, both of you sit."

They both sat, Ela next to Saoirse and Danielle on the very edge of her seat. Choop noticed Danielle's coiled legs and scooted forward on his bench to get his legs under himself.

Saoirse paused long enough to make eye contact with each person in the room. "Ela, you're not the only one here in the military.

"Danielle, you're not the only one here angry about the R of H's tactics and the danger it puts us all in.

"Myoki, you're not the only one that wants to do something about it.

"Now, I want everyone who has seen their soulmate killed by a whale to raise their hand."

No one spoke. Half the people in the room looked at the floor. Danielle relaxed her posture, as did Choop.

"That's what I thought. Ela, I don't have two younger sisters. I have three. You are my little sis as well. I don't believe for a second you will betray me and the rest of your family."

"I can't believe we can't talk about this …" Ela began.

"Hear that, Danielle? She just wants to talk. She just wants to understand why she should risk her life. Why she should act disloyally to the military she has committed her heart to. And Ela, not only would Danielle die defending your parents, but, believe me, you do not want the *old lady* to *bring it*."

Ela made eye contact with Danielle and bowed her head slightly.

Myoki took a deep breath and exhaled. "Saoirse, maybe you need to lead us."

"Now you're just being silly. How about you pick up where you left off. Tell those of us who weren't part of it all about what went down on Inception. Tell us what Goetsch was doing that made you his enemy. Let's talk about it. Let's discuss what you think we need to do about R of H, our roles and our objectives. You and Choop need to lead us. You've done this before." She looked pointedly at Ela. "We need to listen first, then talk."

Choop said, "I won't be leading anyone. I'm gonna go look for my son."

9

"The human race never ceases to amaze me. We are gifted with incredible intelligence and compassion, and we're simultaneously so stupid and selfish it boggles the imagination."

—From the memoir of Myoki Miles

~~~

Jonathon Wilbrand stood out from the other Divers for several reasons. The most obvious was that he was not a Diver. He was in the Republic of Humanity military, but not in the role of Diver. The other reason he stood out was his physique, or maybe lack of it. He was not fit. He was short and pudgy with receding blond hair. He was extremely nearsighted and had lost his glasses three years ago.

Back on Earth, he was a chemistry professor at MIT. On Canopy, he was the Republic of Humanity explosives expert. His nearsightedness made him helpless in many roles, but focusing on the fuse of Canopy's first IED was not a problem.

He had developed Canopy's first useful explosive. It turns out, ironically, the first dead whale provided the best raw materials for an effective bomb. Charcoal was not a problem on a planet covered with forests, and saltpeter could be made from manure and urine, but there was no soil for mining sulfur as was done on Earth. The whale's bones were rich in elemental sulfur. The resulting explosive was much more powerful than gunpowder.

"You need help with that fuse, Jonathon?"

"No, Alfred, I've got it. Have some patience."

Alfred Shenbind was also a scientist. He developed the guncotton used in the fuse and had the flash of insight to use stickypede tendrils to ignite it. Strictly speaking, it wasn't guncotton as made on Earth, but it *was* fabric soaked in an explosive mixture, and it *would* vigorously ignite when the stickypede tendril was pulled through it.

"Okay, it's ready. Be careful moving it. If you pull this string, it explodes."

The Divers took the bomb and began moving toward the chosen location. "I know, I know, old man. Let us do our job."

They put the bomb close to the edge of the tunnel, fifty feet down. The trigger cord was stretched across the tunnel and attached to the opposite side. If it went as planned, when the massive beast swam into the cord, it would die a horrible death.

The Divers escorted Jonathon and Alfred away from the tunnel. They ascended to a safe distance to wait out the day in boring fashion.

It was not until three days later that a whale hit the cord. The explosion threw roots and water two hundred feet into the forest above. The Scouts and Gliders above were able to kill the spidermonkey, raccoon, and tripod traveling with the whale, but the whale didn't die. Instead, it stayed submerged and sporadically pulsed human-killing gravity waves.

For a full day, it killed every Diver that approached within five-hundred feet. The water around the whale was littered with twenty dead Divers before the Canopian finally died.

One of the tricky things about the new tactics employed by the Canopians was that even though the humans had killed a whale, it was roaming and they were unsure of the exact location of its home Clearing. Their victory seemed much less glorious with no Clearing to occupy.

~~~

Choop approached the spidermonkeys' web with caution. He thought he was safe since the tripods had seen him twenty-five-hundred feet higher in the forest. The Canopian could have popped his head already if that was its intent. He approached the web carefully just the same, trying to appear as non-threatening as possible.

The spidermonkeys were waiting for him. Four were at the edges of their web, one was in the center, and one was on a thick branch fifty yards in front of the web. The nearest one signaled for him to stop.

Choop kept both hands in sight. "Hello. I'm Choop Miles. I come in peace and mean you no harm."

[*Remain still.*]

Choop raised his hands higher and said nothing.

[*What is your purpose?*]

"I am looking for my son, Mose. I believe he may have come to visit a Canopian."

[*I cannot help you.*]

"He has been gone for a long time. I'm worried about him."

[*I cannot help you.*]

"I know you are very literal in your speech. 'I cannot help you' is not the same as being ignorant of his whereabouts."

[*I cannot help you.*]

"Would you at least give him a message for me?"

The creature did not sign an answer. All six spidermonkeys stared at Choop without moving.

"Tell him I am looking for him. Tell him I am taking actions designed to stop human aggression against Canopians. He needs to understand that I love him and want him to come home."

[*These are things you should tell him yourself.*]

"That's what I'm trying to do, but I don't know where he is."

[*How can this be? Confusion.*]

"Trust me, we humans can hide from each other. I know you have trouble understanding our separateness, but he can't know these things unless I tell him and I don't know where he went. Please help me."

[*I cannot help you.*] [*Leave now.*]

~~~

Myoki was on the back bench of what had become known as the *war room*. "Okay, it's been three weeks since we last met. Everyone get settled. Cooter has a report."

Ela, Saoirse, Sarah, Danielle, Adam, Larry, Tsintah, Kejuon, and Bina all stayed seated as Cooter rose to speak. "Well, it's worse than we thought. The R of H has developed a powerful explosive. My source tells me they killed a whale with it."

There were nervous glances around the room, but no one else spoke.

"The whale took a long time to die. It killed a score of soldiers in its death throes. They didn't even know where its Clearing was. The intel I have says R of H is going to start a major program of placing explosive booby traps in tunnels as far as they can travel. It seems every time they kill a whale, its body provides the materials to make more bombs."

Cooter sat back down and looked at the floor.

Sarah leaned forward intently, staring at Cooter. "Please tell me that's not all you have to say."

"What more is there to say? I'm just relaying the info I have."

"What more is there to say? What needs to be said is what we plan to do about it. Our plan of trying to talk the whales out of killing humans will never work if humans are booby-trapping their tunnels."

"Sarah, calm down. Of course, you're right." Myoki put her hand on her best friend's shoulder and rubbed. "Cooter, Ela, y'all are our active military. Is there anything we can do? Think. Maybe there's something."

Ela raised her hand. "We should train a team of Divers what to look for and send them out to try and disarm the bombs."

Cooter was shaking his head as he answered. "We haven't recruited any Divers into the resistance yet. That will take time, not to mention the danger of running into R of H Divers. If that happens, it means war between UC and R of H."

Adam nodded. "And we don't know how often they check the bombs that don't detonate. If they check and find they've been disarmed, it might also cause problems."

"But we can't just do nothing!"

Danielle's laughter caught everyone by surprise. "Is this the same Ela that was going to stop us from doing any of this?"

Ela smiled sheepishly. "Hey, when I change my mind, I thoroughly change it, okay?"

Tsintah raised her hand.

Myoki said, "Tsintah, you don't have to raise your hand."

"Ela raised *her* hand."

"Yeah, well, she didn't have to either."

Sarah laughed. "Aren't we the most fearsome resistance ever. Madam, I make a motion we remain civilized."

Ela's giggle joined Sarah's. "I second the motion supporting civil behavior. All in favor."

Everyone except Tsintah was smiling. "You people have no sense of humor." There was laughter all around.

As the laughter subsided, Kejuon spoke. "I'm a good swimmer. Cooter, get me just a single Diver to work with and I'll volunteer as the bomb-sniffer slash bomb-diffuser."

Saoirse said, "I'm a better swimmer than you. I'm in."

Sarah said, "Whoa, there. You're not in."

"Why, Mom, because I would be in danger? You know I'm a soldier now, right? My reserve duty is still six months away. I'm doing it. You can watch little Beasley while I save the world."

"Okay, eldest daughter, you may go and try to save the

human race. There's something I never thought I would hear myself say."

After a pause, Myoki looked at Tsintah. "Tsintah, didn't you have a question?"

"Not anymore."

"Tsintah, you've never been reluctant to speak your mind before. Out with it."

"Well, I was going to ask what I should be doing. But then everyone was suddenly having a good time."

"Haven't you been checking the message drop every day?"

"Yes, but that doesn't seem like it's enough."

Myoki leaned back and ran her hand through her hair. "There'll be more for you to do later, trust me, but that reminds me." She looked straight at Kejuon. "Has anyone heard from Choop?"

"Why you looking at me?"

"You're his best friend."

"You're his wife."

"But, he's been living with you more than me."

"Mom, stop it. We're all worried about Dad, not just you. Uncle K would say something if he heard from him."

"Sorry." Myoki's apology hung in the air.

Tsintah said, "What? Is the fun over?"

~~~

I feel like I've been living my entire life in a glass bubble that's frosted over obscuring the world and now the glass has been cleaned.

At University, I took Calculus — both differential and integral — as well as Differential Equations. We were just starting to study Recursive Function Theory when I got expelled. Being in University seems like child's play to me now.

The Canopians are mathematical geniuses. They teach you by just stuffing the concepts into your head. I *understand* math in a way I never did before. Every day I learn something new.

I know they choose to give me math concepts because of my interest. They can see it both pleases me and is something I can grasp. Other things are not so easy to understand.

I feel honored that they allowed me to go to a Gathering. Trying to explain their group-mind is another of those things that I can't seem to get right. Words just can't quite describe what it's like.

When I meet a Canopian for the first time, he already knows me. We've already *spoken*. See, that's what I mean. Canopians don't have language, but the best I can describe it with words is to say we've already *spoken*. We exchanged ideas, we met, we got to know each other. All different ways to say *we spoke*.

Each Canopian has all the other's memories — at least

since the last *linking* — but they are also individuals that *taste* different in your head.

Canopians not only don't have language, but they also don't have names. I laughed when they showed me how confused they were when Mom kept giving them names and she shared the names of any people she introduced to them. It took them a long time to understand why human names are necessary.

At first, I tried to give a name to each new Canopian, but they objected. I asked why, and the names Moby, Beluga, Bottlenose, Humpback, and Narwhal were listed. It was pointed out to me they all had names, and they are all now dead.

They feel sorry for us. They see our *aloneness* as horrifying and infinitely sad. They probed me about it, trying to understand. They still don't grasp it, not fully, but they know enough to be appalled.

I have been living with the raccoons of a whale I call Bob. I never refer to him that way directly, because it would be rude since he doesn't want a name. I know he can see in my mind that I think of him as Bob, but he lets it slide.

I have been experimenting with my control of gravity. It turns out a better understanding of Recursive Function Theory — they don't call it that, of course, it just *is* — helps me control gravity better. I can float a tangerina for several minutes even twenty feet away from me. That's not very useful, but I can now levitate myself much more easily and for longer periods of time. It's helped make me so mobile I don't mind being legless.

I go on long swims daily. I'm pretty sure my ability to hold my breath so long is due to extra organs in my lower torso. I think being around Canopians while in the womb changed my brain as well as my body. I feel lucky. I've never felt lucky my entire life, until now.

They told me Dad is looking for me and gave me his message. I have hope that humans and Canopians can co-exist peacefully.

I miss Dad and Mom, but especially him. My new understanding of the universe causes me to feel sorry for him. He is so alone. That's how it works with humans. When Dad and Mon are together, even hugging, they are still alone.

It's clear to me now. Am I becoming a Canopian? I don't think so, I'm still human, still alone, and very different from them.

But, many things I never understood are now obvious.

~~~

The pounding on the door woke Niti first. She jumped out of bed and threw on her robe.

"Mom, wake up. Someone's at the door."

"Wha…?"

Niti ran into her mother's bedroom and shook Myoki's shoulder. "Mom, wake up!"

The front and rear doors to the apartment were kicked open simultaneously. They splintered as they slammed back against the walls. Men dressed in Republic of Humanity police uniforms rushed in.

Two of the men hurried into Myoki's bedroom. As Myoki sat up in bed, Niti screamed and jumped onto the bed.

"Myoki Miles, you're under arrest. Miss, get away from your mother."

Niti's face was red and blotchy as she hugged Myoki. "How dare you break down our doors! Get out of our home!"

"Miss, get away from your mother. I won't warn you again."

Myoki pushed Niti gently away. "Niti, do as the man says."

"But, Mom …"

"Officer, you can plainly see I'm not going to resist. Can I please have a moment with my daughter?"

The officer raised his hand palm out to the other policeman.

"Niti, you're almost grown, and I'm so proud of you. Your military service is about to start, but you're going to have to begin facing tough decisions now, I'm afraid. Find

Sarah and tell her what's happened."

"Mom, how can you be so calm?"

"I've walked down this road before, Sweetie."

"What?"

"Tell Sarah I said you deserve the truth, the whole truth. If she is reluctant, insist and tell her it's time I start writing my memoir with a Bic pen."

"What? Is that some kind of code? ..."

The policeman stepped forward and grabbed Niti by the bicep. "That's enough, Miss."

Niti rose and stepped away from the bed as Myoki stood. "Officer I have two questions for you. What are the charges? And, may I please get dressed before our little journey?"

~~~

Sarah and Larry arrived first to the emergency meeting. Adam showed up next.

"Hey, guys. Danielle told me Myoki was arrested. What the hell?"

Sarah's strawberry-blond hair was in disarray. She twirled one of the strands in her fingertips. "Niti came and told me R of H policemen took her this morning."

"What did they charge her with?"

"Treason. Conspiracy to commit treason. Aiding an assassination. Harboring an enemy of the state. That's all Niti could remember, but there was more."

"They know we aren't in the Republic of Humanity, right? How the hell do they think they have the right to arrest her?"

Larry laughed a single harsh bark. "What? You want to call your lawyer?"

Sarah held up her hand, palm toward Larry. "Stop. Enough of that. We have to discuss how to deal with this. Our leader has been captured by the enemy. Think of it as war, not a courtroom. We have to come together and decide what to do. Adam, where's Danielle?"

"She went hunting early this morning. I left a note for her. She should show up soon. I wish Saoirse were here. We all know she's going to lead us in Myoki's absence — no offense, Sarah."

"None taken. A mother couldn't be prouder. She's the obvious choice. We should've formalized that already. I'll just have to stand in until she and K return from their sortie."

A man wearing the uniform of a Republic of Humanity Scout climbed through the floor's opening and rolled to his right. Another followed and rolled to his left. Adam spun and kicked at the second one. A third, half his torso in the room, shot an arrow into Adam's thigh. Adam fell screaming.

The shooter climbed into the room and moved to the side to allow their squad leader to enter. "You are all under arrest for treason. Keep your hands in sight and don't make sudden moves."

Sarah's face was hard as she looked at the shooter while raising her hands. "Danielle's gonna be pissed. You shot her husband. What's your name, soldier? She's gonna want to know."

The squad leader backhanded Sarah in the mouth. Larry lunged forward. The Scout that first entered the room tackled Larry and wrestled him to the floor. The room became quiet except for Adam moaning.

"Now that we have your attention, let me say it again. You are all under arrest for treason. Any backtalk will be severely punished. I suggest you comply quietly or there will be more pain."

Niti saw two Republic of Humanity Scouts guarding the entrance as she was climbing the trunk of the tree leading to the hideout Knot. She paused, moved around the trunk to hide and peeked over a branch to watch.

Sarah, Larry, and Adam were lowered with ropes out of the hideout with wrists bound behind them. When they reached a trunk they could walk on their own. One of the Scouts assisted Adam, who was limping. As they descended the trunk, Niti moved further around it to stay hidden.

The two Scouts guarding the hideout began cutting foliage which concealed the doorway and throwing it into the room. They put enough branches into the room to half fill it. They lit a torch and threw it into the room. They lit other torches and started setting fire to the vegetation near the doorway.

The extremely wet conditions of Canopy had always made fire a minor threat on Canopy. The fire burned out after reducing half of the Knot's covering foliage to ash. Smoke was still pouring from the room as the Scouts left, knowing it would burn itself out without catching the tree afire.

Niti moved out to get a better view as the Scouts were disappearing down the trunk.

Fifteen minutes later Danielle arrived. She saw the fire and jumped to land near Niti. "What happened, Niti? Where is everyone?"

"They arrested Sarah, Larry, and Adam. I think they hurt Adam."

"How long ago? Which way did they go?"

"There were six of them, Danielle. You can't do anything now."

"Which way did they GO?"

The distinctive sound of Ela's wings billowing distracted Danielle. She turned to watch as Ela landed near the doorway of the hideout and immediately jumped again when her feet touched hot ash. Only Ela could make the unplanned jump turn into a graceful, downward glide ending with a soft landing next to Danielle.

"What happened?"

Niti was wringing her hands. "Here comes Cooter and Tsintah. Let's wait for them, so I only have to tell this one more time."

Lower on the trunk, Tsintah stopped fifty yards away and cupped her hands around her mouth. "What happened? Where's Sarah?"

Niti burst into tears.

10

"Sometimes, it's just too much. Too much ugliness. Too much greed. Already powerful power-hungry men ruthlessly seeking more power. It's easy to give up fighting them."

—*From the memoir of Myoki Miles*

~~~

Saoirse was floating on her back with her head resting on a tree root just beneath the surface. She spoke quietly. "The best way to find a bomb is also the most dangerous. We find a tunnel that is still clean, all edges cleared of growth. This indicates a tunnel still traveled by whales, so it's also a good candidate to be booby-trapped with bombs. Then we simply travel down the tunnel until we find a bomb."

Kejuon floated next to her so they could talk without being overheard from more than a few feet away. "The only two tunnels we've found so far are regrowing the roots. We ain't even out of R of H territory yet. This is taking longer than I thought."

"We're getting close. I can feel it."

"Feel what?"

"Every so often my brain gets the whale-itch. Real faint, but I can feel it. Last time was just a couple hours ago. You haven't felt it?"

"Nope, but Myoki always says you and Mose are special. More Canopian than the rest of us."

"Well, duh, we were born here. You're an alien from another planet."

Kejuon squirmed a little to get more comfortable. "We should hush and get some sleep."

"You didn't even get upset that I called you an alien."

"The truth is the truth. Did you hear my suggestion about sleeping?"

"I heard. Several outcomes are likely from following a tunnel. First, we set off a bomb and die. Second, we encounter a whale and die. Third, we're ambushed by R of H divers who kill us. And, last and least likely, we find a bomb and diffuse it. One out of four isn't bad."

"Well, I have two observations about your observations. One, Myoki always counts on her fingers like that. Two, I don't like the odds."

Saoirse's giggle was barely audible. "She's been my teacher my whole life. I guess I picked it up from her. Wait. Shhh. Feel that?"

Kejuon was about to whisper *no* when he stiffened. He

could feel a strong itching in his skull. She put her hand on his and squeezed.

He remained quiet until she let go, then whispered. "That felt pretty strong. We must be really close to a tunnel."

She put her hand back on his. Her return whisper was so faint he almost missed it. "Shhh. The raccoon might still be around."

They lay still for another ten minutes before she moved. "Okay, I think it's clear. Let's go find the tunnel."

They took turns, one submerging to look for the tunnel while the other stayed vigilant. After about thirty minutes of searching, having moved only fifty yards, Kejuon found it.

She stared at the forest as he surfaced quietly. "It's right under us. Runs this direction. Either this whale is a huge one, or the raccoons are clearing roots for wider tunnels than we've seen before. It's at least a hundred feet wide."

"What? No bomb? You were supposed to come back up with a bomb. That's how I imagined it going."

"I'll let you go down and get the bomb."

"Well, we have to decide which direction to search it. I say that way. I'll go down and search the tunnel in that direction. Move along so you stay close to me. Keep your eyes peeled."

Kejuon moved quietly in the direction she indicated. She could hold her breath much longer than he could. He moved seventy-five yards before she came up.

She slicked her hair back out of her eyes. "I found it. The bomb is right under us. It's placed in the roof of the tunnel. Looks like a small cord is stretched straight down vertically to the bottom of the tunnel. Probably a tripwire. I don't know how the whale missed it."

"Maybe this bomb's a dud. I'll go down and look at it."

As Saoirse watched and listened, she felt oddly at peace. She thought about joking with K earlier about him being an alien, but this being her home. She knew her home was in trouble, torn by vicious war, but she loved it anyway. She'd never been on one of the continents Myoki talked about, and she didn't want to. She belonged here.

Kejuon surfaced and held up the end of a hemp cord. He began coiling it. "The cord was loose on the other end. I think the whale did hit it, but it came loose on the lower end rather than triggering the bomb. There's what looks like a strip of stickypede tendril this was attached to. That must be the trigger that sets the bomb off. I cut the cord with about a foot left attached to the tendril and tied it off so the bomb should be safe for us to move."

"How do we know movement won't set it off?"

"We don't, but we'll be going slowly to stay quiet. We probably won't jostle it too much."

"Where we going to take it?"

"We're going to hide it far from this tunnel. No sense

taking it back home. If we ever use it, most likely it will be here in R of H territory. We need to make a good map as we return so we can find the bomb again."

"You want to use it to blow up humans?"

Kejuon stared at Saoirse solemnly. "This is war, Saoirse."

~~~

Choop was tired. He was feeling his years. It took two days to make his way back from talking to the whale. He was frustrated that the whale refused to help. He was afraid he would never see Mose again. He was so tired he frequently traveled without jumping, instead walking and climbing the sloping trunks like the weaker Canopy-born.

He thought his eyes were playing tricks on him when he came into sight of the hideout. It was burned! He jumped the remaining distance in four huge leaps, landing just short of the ash.

The smell was horrible and filled his senses. He thought he might throw up.

He didn't want to go into the hideout, but he had to know. He was afraid it would be full of dead bodies. He took a deep breath, put his hand over his mouth and nose, and went in.

Every wall and the ceiling was charred. The ash in the room was several inches deep. Choop trudged around long enough to confirm there were no bodies, puked in the far corner, and left.

He began to jump long jumps, rapidly heading for Myoki's apartment building on the outskirts of Daylight. He realized he would pass Tsintah's house on the way and detoured to see her.

"You don't have to bang so hard! I can hear you … Oh, Choop it's you …"

"What the hell happened to the hideout? I was afraid y'all got burned up. I searched for bodies. The smell made me so sick I threw up …"

"Choop! Stop. Stop. Come in. Let's go sit and talk. I have a lot to tell you."

"I don't wanna sit."

Tsintah walked into her kitchen."Don't be pigheaded. Come in the kitchen and sit."

Choop entered the kitchen, walked to the far end, spun on his heel, walked back to the door, spun, and headed for the far end again. "I don't wanna sit."

"Alright then. At ease."

Choop stopped pacing and stared at Tsintah. "What?"

"Isn't that what an officer tells a soldier when he wants him to shut up and listen?"

"You're not an officer. If you don't start talking, I'm gonna do more than pace."

"There's the Choop I know and love. Threatening people. Aggressively throwing his weight around."

"Tsintah!"

"Okay, Okay. The R of H sent policeman and arrested Myoki. They took her right outa her bed in front of Niti."

"Where's Niti?"

"She's with Danielle, who's also alone because after Sarah called an emergency meeting, they sent Scouts and arrested Sarah, Larry, and Adam."

"What?"

"I think Adam fought back because they hurt him. Then they set fire to the hideout and left." She looked at Choop's boots which were covered in soot. "But I'm guessing you knew that last part."

"Do you know where they took them?"

"We don't know where they are. You'll notice I said we. I said we because there's a lot of us in this together. You don't need to go off on your own to save them. I know how you are. I can hear you thinking."

"Have Saoirse and Kejuon made it back? Were they successful diffusing the bombs?"

"They have not come back. Let's go to Danielle's. I think Ella may be there, too. We need to get everyone together before R of H knows who we all are."

"Yes, we probably don't have much time. All four of them are going to be undergoing interrogation. No one can hold up to that forever. They'll have all our names before long."

~~~

Moving quietly made progress slow. After marking the tree where they hid the confiscated bomb, they traveled three days before they found another tunnel. They were no more than fifteen miles from where they found the first bomb.

"Saoirse, are you sure this ain't the same tunnel?"

"Yes, for the tenth time. We moved at right angles to the first tunnel for miles before stashing the bomb. Is your sense of direction broken?"

"All you had to do was say yes. You didn't have to give me a hard time. You didn't sleep much last night, I noticed."

"Sorry. Sleeping is wasted time. You can make me lay still, but I can't sleep. Too much to do."

"Trust the advice of an old soldier. Exhaustion will lead to mistakes."

"So, can I go down and examine this tunnel you say we've found or are we just going to talk about it?"

"Go, please, it will give me a break."

Two minutes later, Saoirse surfaced twenty yards away. "Found one!"

"Shhh."

"Oh, sorry. The bomb's at the top of the tunnel about twenty feet below me. It's live, the cord is still attached. Let me borrow your knife."

"I'll go cut it." Kejuon submerged.

Saoirse heard voices in the distance. She sank until her

nose was barely above the water and froze. Two different voices were laughing, joking, and the people splashed loudly as they made their way closer. She was astonished at how loud they were.

Kejuon surfaced close to her, and held up the end of the cord. "Got it."

She put her hand on his arm. "Shhh."

The laughing and joking stopped. "Did you hear that?"

"Hear what?"

"I heard a voice."

"No way."

"Be quiet. Listen."

Kejuon moved close to Saoirse and whispered. "Count to twenty, then make some noises to attract their attention."

As Saoirse started counting under her breath, Kejuon climbed onto a large root near the surface, tied the cord around a smaller root next to it, squatted, then leapt out of her sight straight up. She was so surprised by his action, she squealed lightly.

"There, did you hear that? That's no animal I ever heard."

So much for counting to twenty, she thought. She began to lightly slap the water with her palms.

"Hear that? Something splashing around over this way."

She could see them, less than a hundred feet away, when Kejuon flew from the trees on her right. He smashed into the leading Republic of Humanity Diver, crushing his skull against a tree. Blood spurted from the Diver's head, and Kejuon gained his footing on the side of the tree and jumped out of sight back the way he had come.

The speed and power with which Kejuon moved amazed Saoirse. She had seen her mom and dad jump around a lot when she was little, so she knew about how strong the Earth-born were, but she had never seen the violence such power could generate. She stared open-mouthed.

The other Diver, a hapless teenager, screamed, turned, and began swimming back the way he had come. Kejuon flew from the right, smashing into his back and driving him under the water. The two thrashed around briefly, the kid screeched, and then there was silence. The water around them was red as Kejuon cleaned his knife on the kid's uniform.

Kejuon looked over at Saoirse and spoke softly. "Bring that cord and help me tie them together. We need to hide the bodies. ... Saoirse? ... Saoirse?"

"Why did you do that?"

"I had to. Bring the cord over here. ... Saoirse?"

Kejuon pulled himself rapidly over the tops of near-surface roots, splashing in the open water in between until he was beside her.

"Why did you do that?"

"Saoirse? What the hell? You know that was necessary."

He reached out to touch her shoulder.

"You gave them no chance."

Seeing the revulsion in her eyes tore at Kejuon's heart. He pulled back, giving her distance. "Saoirse, think it through. I had to."

"But, you gave them no chance."

Kejuon's voice became firm and demanding. "Chance to do what? Surrender?"

"Yes!"

"And then what?"

"I don't know. Anything but that."

"That's right. You don't know. If we took them hostage, could we get back home without them giving us away?"

"No, but …"

"Right, we take them hostage and we die. How about we tie them up and leave them here? Then what?"

"Then you didn't murder them right in front of me."

"Then either they starve out here — that's a nice way to die — or they're found and the R of H knows about us. The R of H sends Divers looking for us on our two-week journey back home, and we never make it. Again, we die. Or, maybe we get lucky and just get imprisoned and tortured."

"Those can't be the only possibilities."

"Saoirse, listen to me. You saw Beasley die in front of you, so you think you're not naive about war. But, believe me, you're naive about what's going on if you think this isn't all-out war. Your survival, my survival, Little Beasley's survival, and the survival of the entire human race is at stake. I'm sorry you had to see that, but I'm not sorry I did it. It's gonna get worse before it gets better. Now suck it up and help me hide these bodies."

~~~

I didn't think to bring an extra pencil for my journal. This is a problem because I can't seem to be succinct when I write about Canopians. My pencil is already half gone, and still my writing remains wordy.

For example, Canopians are colorblind. Three words sum it up, but don't come close to telling the truth. So, with apologies to my short little pencil, here's MY truth about colors on Canopy.

I associate colors in my head with Canopian emotions. As Bob communicates, if he's angry I see red in my head. It's darker the madder he is. I've not seen really dark red and hope I never do. I don't see the color with my eyes at all. It's in my head. Hard to explain, but I see yellows and light greens when he's happy, orange when he's curious, lavender when he pities me, and blues when he's laughing.

Yes, Canopians have a sense of humor, but they laugh at things that aren't funny and don't laugh at my jokes. But still, they do have a sense of humor.

When I asked Bob if he sends the colors as part of his

transmission, he was confused. He wanted me to explain colors. I tried, but he couldn't get it. So, I asked him about the colors of the forest as he sees them through the eyes of his various creatures. I was thinking maybe raccoons, spidermonkeys, and tripods see different colors. Long story short, I'm pretty sure they all see greyscale.

See what I mean? Way more than three words.

As far as words go, when I talk to Canopians, I still whisper. Maybe you could call it sub-vocalize. It seems to help a lot for them to understand me. I still think in words, and I don't think this whole brain-to-brain thing will ever get past that.

When I exercise my gravity control, Bob thinks it's funny. As the raccoon hangs around in the underwater lair watching me bounce the log up and down in the air, I feel light blue bubbles in my brain as he laughs. I think Bob doesn't understand that by bouncing the log my control gets better and stronger. Or, maybe he does understand, but just thinks it's funny.

The raccoon hangs around so Bob can see me. Sometimes, when I'm in the lair alone, Bob swims up into the Clearing and talks to me without being able to see me with any of his eyes. He needs to see me to focus his transmissions, but the general vicinity of the small cave is close enough.

I'm thinking of going for a swim when he comes up close

enough to the lair that a wave comes up the entrance ramp. In his usual abrupt fashion, he gets right to the point. [*I have a message from your father.*]

I'm so surprised I speak loudly. "What?"

[*I have a message from your father.*]

"So, what are you waiting for? Tell me."

[*You are upset.*]

"No, I'm just impatient. What did he say?"

[*You are upset. This emotion is curious. Why does information about your father cause this?*]

"Okay, now I'm upset, and it's because you're studying me rather than giving me the message. I'm frustrated and a little pissed, and it's because of you. Happy?"

[*Interesting.*]

I dive into the water. He is no more than thirty feet away. I swim as fast as I can toward his eye.

Suddenly the water around me seems to thicken. I come to a stop, held in the powerful grip of a crushing force. My mind is filled with a blood-red color which quickly becomes lighter shades until it fades into orange.

[*You would cause me harm?*]

"Apparently not."

[*You wish me harm?*]

If I wasn't underwater, I'd scream, but I can only sub-vocalize. [*Would you just tell me the damn MESSAGE?*]

[*This constant emotional condition of humans. I am*

amazed you evolved beyond animals. Canopians must learn to understand it if we are to allow you to live on our world.]

The force holding me dissipates.

[*Your father is looking for you. He said he wants you to come home. He wants you to know he is trying to take action to stop the evil humans who attack us. The message you will most want to know is that he said he loves you.*]

I swim up and hit the surface fast enough I jump from the water several feet. When I land, I spin to face Bob. He rolls so one of his eyes is just above the water, staring at me.

[*You still wish me harm?*]

"I didn't wish you harm. I was just mad. I wanted to poke you in the eye."

[*Your definition of harm is inaccurate.*]

"You can't tell me you've got a message from Dad and then withhold it and expect me not to get upset."

[*This emotional connection humans have in place of a real connection puzzles me. I admit I do not fully understand.*]

"It *is* a real connection. We just connect differently."

[*The word love seems to be important to humans. I discussed this with Myoki, but have difficulty understanding.*]

"It's not the word that's important, it's the love itself. Canopians will probably never fully understand unless they can feel it. Since you are all just a single entity, that will probably never happen."

[*Why do you assert that we are all a single entity?*]

"Because of the Gathering. The way you all merge your memories. And you say things like 'I spoke with Myoki' when I know for a fact you've never met her."

[*You have only been to a local Gathering. Your understanding is incomplete.*]

"What? Wait, if there are local Gatherings, then that means there are larger ones. Tell me about them."

[*Once every one-thousand days, we gather near the equator. All Canopians send a representative. There are also regional Gatherings every one-hundred days.*]

"Whoa. You're freaking me out. Are you telling me, when you go to this big Gathering, you meet other Canopians with which you don't merge in the same way as the local Gathering?"

[*I did not specifically tell you that, but you deduced it. There is hope for humans yet.*] This statement is accompanied by blue bubbles flashing in my head.

"Quit laughing and focus. Tell me this. If you Gather with these other Canopians but don't merge memories, do they have names?"

[*No.*]

"Then how do you tell them apart?"

[*Because they are different. Just when I thought there*

was hope.] More blue flashes.

"If you don't merge, what do y'all do?"

[*At the last several Gatherings, we talk about humans. It is very hard to explain humans. I am hoping you will accompany me to the next major Gathering to meet them. Maybe then they can understand fully.*]

"But, you keep saying that you don't understand completely when I explain things to you. Yet you think they will understand fully when I explain it to them. That makes no sense."

Many different shades of blue in my head. I think Bob is having a laughing fit.

~~~

Choop was impressed with the meeting location Kejuon chose. It was impossible to approach without being observed.

They met high in the Overhead, so high that the branches above them swayed with the winds above Canopy's forest. There was no way to approach from above. The air was so thin Choop felt lightheaded. The tree branches in the canopy above the group were less than two feet in diameter, mere twigs by Canopian standards, and widely spaced enough that two of Canopy's suns were visible.

They were gathered in what Kejuon called a *mini-knot*. It was a branching point where five branches ascended at forty-five-degree angles. The small knot was covered in light-green foliage no more than two feet thick. Each ascending trunk was about four feet thick.

The team assembled with each member facing inward. Because they were tilted downward due to the angle of the trunks, they could easily observe anyone approaching by looking past each other. This defensive observation technique was something Choop and Kejuon used when they were the only two humans on Canopy, living in hiding after abandoning Inception.

Kejoun and Latesha shared a trunk. Saoirse and Bina were together on another. Danielle and Tsintah were on a third branch. Cooter and Ela were each sitting alone. Ela was in the highest position of all, wearing Glider wings.

Ela saw him first. "There's Dad. I knew he would make it."

Choop whistled the bird call he and Kejuon used as a recognition signal so long ago. Kejuon whistled a response.

Tsintah snorted. "You guys know there's no birds on Canopy, right?"

Choop made a big entrance by jumping the last fifty feet to land in the foliage of the mini-knot.

Ela spoke quietly while looking out and down. "The prodigal father returns."

Bina turned to look at Ela as she spoke to Choop. "Did you find Mose?"

"No, but I found a Canopian that I think he's living with.

I sent a message."

Saoirse smiled. "That's good news. I'm sure he's okay if he's with them. And I'm glad you're back so you can resume duties as our leader. How are we going to get everyone out of prison?"

Danielle grunted and twisted to look at Saoirse. "Wait just a minute. Choop said he didn't want to lead, and we all agreed you should do it. You can't back out now."

"Both Mom and Dad are prisoners. I'm not very objective. Uncle Choop said he wouldn't lead us because he was going to look for Mose. Now he's back." She briefly glanced at Kejuon and away. "Plus, I don't think I'm cut out for this."

As Danielle drew breath to respond, Choop held up both hands, palms out, to stop her. He watched Saoirse and Kejuon as they both avoided eye contact. Kejuon did it more effectively by scanning beyond Choop's shoulder to watch for others approaching. Saoirse just looked down at the bark in front of her.

"K, I think we need to hear a report about your sortie looking for bombs." Choop's eyes bore into Kejuon. "Leave nothing out."

Kejuon sighed and squirmed around on the branch. "Well, we found two bombs. On the first one, the tripwire had become unattached. We moved that bomb to a hidden location. While we were disarming the second bomb, R of

H Divers showed up. I, uh, dispatched them and then we took that bomb to the same location. The bombs are concealed deep in R of H territory nowhere near whale tunnels or any human settlements."

"Okay, thanks." Choop stared at Saoirse until she raised her eyes. "Saoirse, you have anything to add?"

"No, it happened like he said."

Choop looked at Kejuon for few seconds, then back at Saoirse. "I would like more detail. He said he *dispatched* the Divers. Could you clarify that for me? It's kinda vague."

"Why don't you ask him?"

"Because I'm asking you. I've seen K in action before. It was the first time for you. Tell us what happened."

Danielle sat up straighter. "Oh crap. Choop, not in front of Latesha."

"Not do what in front of me? I'm no shrinking violet. I think I'm feeling insulted."

"Latesha, Choop and I are the only two here who have seen it when he, uh, dispatches. You don't need to hear this." Danielle turned to Choop. "Why are you doing this?"

"Because the person who the group looks to for leadership seems to be having a moral crisis. Please, everyone be quiet while Saoirse gives her report."

Saoirse suddenly stood on her branch with one leg bent to balance herself on its slope. "A moral crisis? Is that how you describe it?"

"Describe what, Saoirse? You haven't given your report."

"Okay. It was just like he said except the word dispatched could be replaced by crushing a man's skull like an appleberry and slitting another man's throat like it's an afterthought and then, then, then calmly asking me to help hide the bodies like we were doing our daily chores."

Saoirse collapsed back into a sitting position like the air had gone out of her. Choop noticed that Danielle, Kejuon, and Ela kept watching the perimeter while everyone else looked down.

Kejuon cleared his throat. "Saoirse, I'm sorry you think I was too brutal. I assure you nothing I did felt like an afterthought. Soldiers learn to objectify to stay sane. We use words like dispatch, target, and subject to keep our emotional distance because there's no other way to do the job and come out the other side intact. As it is, I will have nightmares about what I did for a long time. Ask Latesha if you don't believe me. She's the one beside me when I wake up with the cold sweats."

Everyone stayed quiet. Saoirse's rapid breathing could be heard over the background noise of the forest creaking as it swayed. Ela, Kejuon, Choop, and Danielle continued scanning the perimeter.

Kejuon leaned forward and put his elbows on his knees. "Saoirse, this is exactly why *you* need to lead us. You're a soldier, but you haven't become jaded. The fact that taking a life is so abhorrent to you means you should be making decisions, not avoiding them."

Saoirse looked up with tears hanging on her lower eyelashes. She slowly looked around the group, making eye contact with each person. "Okay. … We have bombs that I pray we never use. We can discuss those later. Let's talk about how we can get Myoki, Adam, and my parents out of prison."

~~~

Myoki was drowning. Her mind knew better, but her body disagreed. When she could no longer hold her breath, she sucked water into her lungs through the towel over her face. Not enough to kill her. Just enough for her body to refuse her conscious mind's message that she wasn't drowning.

The two men holding her chair in a reclined position pulled it back vertical and removed the wet towel from her face. Myoki spat water and coughed while the man with the bucket dipped it in the barrel for the next round. The others checked her bonds to make sure her thrashing hadn't loosened them, while their leader began repeating his questions.

"You can make this stop. We just need the names of everyone in your group of traitors. Be careful and give us all of the names. We know some of them. If those names aren't included, this will only get worse. If you tell us, you can quit drowning. We might even let you put your clothes back on."

Myoki finally cleared her lungs enough to take a deep breath. She drew several deep breaths, looked at the wet towel in her lap, and spit in the questioner's face.

~~~

Sarah was drowning. Her mind knew better, but her body disagreed.

When they removed the wet towel from her face, she spat water and coughed. When she caught her breath, she saw the man with all the questions leering at her breasts. She had always been body shy. The humiliation was worse than drowning.

"You can make this stop. Just tell us where Choop Miles is hiding."

"Go north from the hideout where you caught me about ten miles …"

Spittle flew from the man's mouth as he screamed at her six inches from her face. "Do you think I can't tell a lie when I hear one!" He looked at the two men holding her chair. "Again."

She couldn't remember how many times he said that horrible word. She thought she might be losing her mind. Over and over she drowned, was leered at, told a lie, and then drowned again.

When she could breathe again, he repeated his question.

"Look, mister. You can do this as long as you want, but I don't know where he is. He has only one weakness and it's not me. There's no way…"

He didn't scream at her, he didn't say *again*. He interrupted her to say something much more alarming. "*You* are not his weakness. An interesting way to say it. *You*. But another *person* must be …"

"What? No! I just meant no one knows where he is, that's all. …"

"Take her back to her cell. Leave her naked in front of the other prisoners."

"NO! You can't do that to me! NO!"

~~~

Tsintah enjoyed the sway of the footbridge as she approached Daylight Square. She was lost in thought and didn't notice them at first. Daylight Square was the largest platform in Daylight, and the Republic of Humanity soldiers were on the opposite side of the hundred-yard-wide Square, between the fruit-stand and the blacksmith. Their green and brown mottled uniforms stood out like beacons because of the bright yellow lacing on the collars.

Tsintah put her hand on Latesha's arm and pulled her into a U-turn on the footbridge.

"Whoa, what are you doing? It's almost lunchtime. I want to get a good seat at the restaurant. Where are we going?"

"Don't look back. … Latesha! What did I just say?"

"You can't say don't look back and expect someone not to look. That's like saying don't think about a lavender panther. I bet you just thought about a lavender panther, right?"

"No, I'm thinking about R of H soldiers."

"That's not something I like to think about."

"Then be glad I turned us around. There's three of them by the fruit-stand."

"Crap. That's not good. We're over eight thousand feet high. Aren't they a little out of their territory? Just three of them? You sure?"

"No, I'm not sure, but I know there's at least three. It looked like they were nailing a piece of paper on the lamp post."

"You don't think they know us do you?"

"Why don't you go ask them? I'll stay here and watch what happens."

"Aren't you clever. So what's the plan?"

"My plan is we get to the next square and blend in like regular shoppers while we watch to see what they do."

To the immediate right of the entrance to the smaller square, was a jewelry shop. Necklaces made of panther claws, intricately woven belts, and bracelets made from tangerina seeds, hung on racks on each side of the shop's counter.

Tsintah and Latesha stood looking through the racks toward the larger square one hundred yards away.

The shopkeeper was a plump woman who wore a bright red scarf over her tied-back hair. "Hi, I'm Glenda. See anything you like?"

Tsintah's attention never wavered from the soldiers, but Latesha glanced the shopkeeper's way. "Just browsing, Glenda, thanks. We'll holler if something strikes our fancy."

"These belts are woven from strips of panther hide and strips of hemp. I made them myself. Feel the panther skin. It's so soft."

Latesha ignored the belt and fingered a bracelet of panther teeth. She wasn't even looking at the bracelet, but past it to the distant platform. "No thanks. Don't need a belt. I'll let you know if I find something."

The three soldiers were crossing the footbridge, heading toward the smaller square.

Tsintah tapped Latesha's arm and walked to the next shop, farther from the footbridge. She touched a blue shirt hanging by the walkway. "Do you have a changing room back there? I would like to try this on?"

"Yes ma'am, back on the right."

The two women disappeared into the store and peeked through the gap in the curtain as the soldiers nailed a piece of paper on the post separating the jewelry shop from the clothing store.

Glenda folded her arms across her ample bosom. "Hey mister, you can't just be nailing posters up. Does this look like a post office to you?"

"Do we look like you can stop us from doing whatever we want? You need to read this and tell all your hick friends."

Latesha and Tsintah didn't come out of the changing room until the soldiers finished nailing notices on several more posts and left. They told the lady the shirt didn't fit and went to read the notice.

LET IT BE KNOWN TO ALL : The terrorist known as Choop Miles has thirty(30) days to turn himself in to the Republic of Humanity to be prosecuted for the crime of political assassination. He was assisted in the heinous crime by his wife, Myoki Miles, who has been arrested and confessed to being his co-conspirator. Should Mr. Miles surrender within this time-frame, the life of Myoki Miles will be spared. Otherwise, she will be executed by public hanging at noon on May 17. Mr. Miles may turn himself in to any member of the Republic of Humanity military.

Tsintah ripped the notice off the post. "Latesha, go get Saoirse. I'll find Choop. We'll meet up at the mini-knot."

"That's not going to do any good. We don't have the manpower to stop this."

The two friends shared a long, sad, forlorn look into each other's wet eyes.

Tsintah's voice was barely audible as she looked down. "I know. Go get her anyway."

11

"You can only impact the world by going all-in. It's humbling to have a part in it."
—*From the memoir Myoki Miles*

~~~

They met at the high location again. Danielle, Ela, Kejuon, Bina, and Cooter all perched in the mini-knot as Saoirse and Latesha approached.

Saoirse stopped short of the mini-knot, turned, and looked over her shoulder. "Where's Choop and Tsintah? I thought we would be the last ones here."

"Why don't we go ahead and start discussing options. I assume everyone has seen those damn signs the R of H is putting up," said Danielle.

Saoirse settled onto the last unoccupied trunk. "This really doesn't change things much if you think about it. We were always going to try and get them out. It just puts a deadline on it. We've got thirty days to figure out how."

"I think it might be time to use one of the bombs, but we

need to decide quick. The trip to get it and bring it back will take over a week," said Kejuon.

Cooter shook his head. "Use the bomb how? Threaten to blow something up if they don't release the prisoners? They wouldn't believe us. We would have to detonate one to prove we could then use the other as the threat. That means we have to move two bombs, not one. And, we would need to put it somewhere in heavily populated R of H territory, or it's not much of a threat."

"New Venice. Right under that disgusting fiber carbon island in the main Clearing."

Ela turned to stare. "Danielle, there are over five hundred people that live on that island!"

"Right. That makes it a serious threat."

Saoirse held up her hands. "Hold it. Let's think this over. If we have to detonate a bomb to make them know we can, then we're wasting it. Plus, since when did we decide it's okay to kill civilians? We're not terrorists. If we take action, it'll be against military targets. It's better if we can just figure out where they're holding the prisoners and break them out."

"I'd bet my buck knife they've got'em in Burl City. Right in the middle of R of H's most populated city. There's no way a handful of us could break them out."

"Uncle K, I learned a long time ago not to bet with you." Ela spread her hands, palms up. "This is hopeless."

"Here they come," said Bina.

As they waited on Tsintah and Choop to join them, Ela patted Bina on the knee. "Good eye, Sis. At least someone was watching the perimeter."

Bina blushed. "I don't know military tactics like you. Can't help with all this strategy talk."

"Don't sell yourself short. You're a Miles. You'll do what it takes when it's necessary. Like I said, good eye."

Saoirse scooted up the trunk to make room for Choop and Tsintah. "What took you guys so long?"

"We've been arguing. This idiot wants to turn himself in. He thinks they'll honor their word and spare Myoki. I think they'll hang him right next to her."

"Choop, I've got to side with Tsintah on that one."

"K, don't start. My mind's made up. I killed Dedric, and I'm willing to pay for it if it saves Myoki."

"Daddy! That's suicide. They'll kill you."

"Bina, I can't let your mom die for something I did. I'm doing it. You'll understand when you find the love of your life."

Following an awkward silence, Kejuon spoke quietly. "Tsintah's right, though. You can't trust these bastards. We need to make it a prisoner exchange. Some footbridge in neutral territory somewhere. You only surrender when they send her across the bridge."

"I like that idea, but there's no way to arrange it. That

requires a negotiation. A negotiation means someone has to expose themselves as a member of the resistance. That's not acceptable."

"I'll do it."

"Tsintah, no. I won't let you sacrifice yourself for me."

"I didn't ask for you're permission. You're not the boss of me. I'll do it."

Danielle cleared her throat. "If we find a way to let them know we want to talk, we arrange the negotiation to happen on a rural footbridge. Me, Kejuon, and Choop are in hiding close enough to help if things go south. At the risk of seeming cocky, Earth-born muscles can make a big difference."

"I can help, too."

"No, Cooter. You're what, seventy? No offense, but let us youngsters handle it."

Ela laughed. "Youngsters? You've all got grey in your hair!"

"It doesn't matter. I'm not lettin' Tsintah sacrifice her freedom for me."

"I thought I made it clear you're not the boss of me? Everybody might as well get comfortable. Choop is pig-headed. This is going to be a long argument, and I'm going to win it."

~~~

"Tsintah, are you sure you wanna do this? You're putting a

target on your chest. I'm a warrior, always will be, but you're just a civilian at heart. I should go out there."

"Danielle, what gives you the right to tell me what I can or cannot risk? Just because the Army decided to make me a clerk after I was injured doesn't mean I don't believe in what we're doing. This is my planet and these R of H bastards continue to attack aliens that could sneeze and wipe us out."

"Keep your voice down. They're not supposed to know I'm here. I wasn't questioning your resolve. I'm just worried about you. I've grown kinda fond of you."

The footbridge chosen for the negotiation was halfway between Threshold and Utopia. It was high enough in the Overhead to be mostly open but low enough to have ample foliage in the surrounding trees for the others to hide. Danielle was in the bushes ten feet behind Tsintah, and Kejuon and Choop were in hiding high on either side of the bridge with the advantage of high ground. They could ambush with great force if necessary. Tsintah was standing in plain sight at the end of the bridge as agreed. The time of the meet was still ten minutes away.

"Sorry, I didn't mean to snap at you, Danielle."

"Well, they agreed to send just one person, so you might not be in any danger."

"We said we'd only send one and there are four of us, so that doesn't reassure me much. My mouth is really dry for some reason."

"Remember, make sure they agree the prisoner exchange happens on the bridge between New Haven and Refuge at the spot I told you about. It's a lot better than this one."

"How could I forget? That's the tenth time you've told me."

"Shhh. I see movement."

A man came into sight on the bridge. He was still hundreds of yards away, in the middle of the next open span of the bridge. Tsintah started to walk.

"Tsintah, wait! Remember? Don't go until he reaches the other end of this span."

Tsintah wiped the back of her neck with her palm. "Just checking to see if you're paying attention."

"My ass. While we're waiting on that asshole to amble his way here, why don't you take a few deep breaths?"

Duncan Heath wore a Republic of Humanity uniform with insignia indicating he was a Sergeant. In reality, he was a sniper in the Republic of Humanity's clandestine service known only as WSA. No one in the United Colonies even knew what the acronym stood for, much less the identity of its members, but the horror stories were legendary. He strolled casually with his head on a swivel. His eyes missed nothing. To Tsintah, he appeared to be unarmed.

They stopped fifty feet apart in the middle of the open

span. Tsintah heeded Danielle's coaching and waited for Duncan to speak first. It didn't happen.

As the seconds passed in silence, Tsintah could take it no longer. "It looks like you came alone. That's a good start. I'm Jane. What should I call you?"

"John."

"Well, John, first of all, when the prisoner exchange happens, it won't be on this God-forsaken bridge. I don't like it."

"The exchange will be in Burl City."

"No, the exchange will absolutely be in neutral territory. In a location I choose with no cover for any of you murdering bastards to hide."

"Jane, surely you realize I can see that there are five good spots to have soldiers hidden above us. I know we're not alone."

"You don't seem upset by the thought of being surrounded."

"Not my first rodeo. The exchange will be in Burl City."

"No it won't. You don't listen well."

"I listen fine. You must not be very fond of Myoki Miles. I've heard that hanging an Earth-born in this thirty percent gravity is inhumane. She'll choke to death slowly. Takes several minutes, I understand."

"Okay. Hang her." Tsintah turned and walked away.

Duncan didn't yell until she had walked over a hundred

feet. "Wait! You're bluffing, or you wouldn't have come."

Tsintah turned and stared, but did not move back toward him. "Choop is worth ten Myoki's to us. I bet you know about a few of your fancy bombs disappearing? Who you think killed your guys? That'd be Choop, all by his little self. He's a one-man army. You're confused if you think we'll trade him for her even-up. We need all four of the prisoners back in exchange for him, and it'll happen at the location of our choice. Take it or leave it." She turned and resumed walking.

"Okay, okay. You win. One of these four must be really special to your cause. What's your last name, Jane?"

Tsintah stopped walking and looked over her shoulder. "The bridge that goes from Refuge to New Haven. The longest open span, right smack halfway. Bring all four prisoners, only two guards go out on the bridge with them. We'll send only two to escort Choop, and if you send more than that, we disappear. Choop will start walking when the four prisoners make it halfway across the span. Three days from now at noon. What's *your* last name, John?"

Tsintah was still close enough to see the smile that spread across his face didn't reach his eyes.

~~~

There was two-hundred-fifty feet of open space above the middle of the bridge. Saoirse, Bina, Cooter, and Tsintah were all concealed in the forest above the bridge, spaced widely. Ela, wearing her camouflaged Glider uniform, hung motionless with her legs curled around a small branch directly above the center of the span.

Twenty-five Republic of Humanity soldiers stood on the platform at the east end of the bridge as the four prisoners walked onto the bridge, accompanied by two guards. Four soldiers were widely spaced on the platform with arrows already notched and drawn. Forty more soldiers were making their way down the sloped trunk of the tree supporting the platform.

Six people walked onto the bridge from the east. The first was a teenage Republic of Humanity Scout, thin and pimple-faced. He was leading the prisoners with a leash in his left hand. Each prisoner had their hands tied with rope, and a three-foot length of rope lead from their tied hands to a rope collar around the neck of the prisoner in front of them. The prisoners were followed by an older Scout, stocky with receding hair.

Myoki was leading the prisoners. Her long black hair, normally kept tied back, was dirty and disheveled. She had a black eye, swollen lips, and scratches on the side of her face. Sarah was next. Her strawberry-blond hair was a tangled mess. She looked down as she walked and the hair hid her face. Adam had a bloody bandage around his thigh and limped unevenly. His eyes, nose and mouth were blue-black and so swollen he could not see clearly. Larry's face was an unrecognizable mass of bloody black bruises. Neither of the men appeared to be able to stand up straight but walked hunched over.

Choop led Kejuon and Danielle to the middle of the bridge. When he was within four feet of the young Scout, he raised a hand vertically and clenched it. Danielle and Kejoun each quickly mounted the railing on each side of the bridge, curling their legs around the rails and raising their bows, notching an arrow, but not drawing it.

The teenager said, "I have been instructed to tie your wrists …"

"Shut up!" Choop clenched his fists at his thighs so hard the tendons popped. "What's your name?"

"Uh, Clarence."

"Clarence, listen carefully. I know y'all want me alive, but you need to understand I don't care if I live or die. You are about to make a very important decision. I am going to ask you to do two things. If you do those two things, you get to live. If you do anything other than what I tell you …"

The older Scout yelled, "We're not here to take orders from you."

Choop pointed at the speaker with his left hand. "K, if he makes another sound, kill him."

Kejuon drew his arrow, pointing it at the man's chest. The man quit talking.

Choop lowered his hand. "Clarence, as I was saying, if

you do anything other than what I say for you to do, you have maybe two-tenths of a second to live after that. Have I made myself clear?" Choop's eyes were pinpoints. He could hear his own teeth grinding as he waited.

Clarence's Adam apple bobbed twice. He wiped sweat out of his eye with the back of his sleeve. "Y-yes."

"First thing. What is the name of the man responsible for the treatment of these prisoners? Don't look at him! He can't help you, look at me. Answer me. Five. Four. Three …"

"D-Duncan Heath."

"Second thing. You will take that bone-knife out of your sheath, turn around, and cut the ropes from around the prisoner's wrists and necks so they can stand tall with dignity as they finish their walk across this bridge. Five. Four …"

Clarence wiped sweat from his forehead, drew the knife, dropped it on the wooden floor plates, picked it up, and turned to do as told.

As the Scout sawed on the ropes around Myoki's wrists, she and Choop made eye contact. Her eyes were like wet green marbles. His eyes, now fully dilated, were soft and brown. Neither spoke.

When her ropes were cut, she shuffled forward and put her forehead on Choop's chest. He bowed his head and tilted it to lay his cheek on her head. "Tell Mose I'm sorry."

Her voice was muffled by his chest. "We'll come get you."

"No, you won't. Don't try to bullshit a bullshitter."

Choop put his hands on her shoulders and moved her past him, pushing her between Danielle and Kejuon.

Myoki spun and grabbed his elbow. "So the last word you ever say to me turns out to be *bullshitter*?"

"No." Their eyes locked again. "Forever."

He spun and stepped past a flinching Clarence to put his arm on Sarah's shoulder. She did not look up. He walked past Adam and Larry, putting his hand on their shoulders and squeezing as he passed. He crossed his wrists and extended his arms toward the older Scout.

~~~

"Bob, oh crap, I called you Bob before I realized I was gonna. Sorry, I know you don't like us giving Canopians names."

[*Do not worry. I hear you when you think my name, but don't say it. I do not mind. The intolerance for names is based on the killings that followed. I know you will not kill me. I have grown to like being Bob.*]

"Wow. I think I'm flattered. But, what I've got to say, you might not like so much."

[*I am aware.*]

It confuses me a little when Bob does that. He makes statements that can be interpreted multiple ways. Does he mean he's aware that I'm flattered? Does he mean he's aware that I know he doesn't like some of my views on things? Does he mean he already knows what I'm about to say? I may never get used to how his mind works.

"I have to return to human territory. My dad said he is going to try and stop the humans killing Canopians. That is very dangerous, and he might need my help. Plus, I miss him. I said things I regret. I need to see him."

[*Human interaction with other humans is very complex. We have been observing humans living in Threshold to better understand. It is important that you return in time for the next regional Gathering. Decisions will be made at the Gathering. You must be there to represent your species.*]

"You make it sound like a trial."

[*That is an accurate assessment.*]

"That's in, what, three weeks? I should be back by then."

[*It is in seventeen of the arbitrary time units you refer to as days.*]

"I will return, I promise. But I believe the effort to stop the humans who attack Canopians is important, and I believe I can help. Surely my presence at the Gathering will be better received if I can say the attacks have stopped."

[*That is a valid conclusion. You will find that your abilities to communicate directly with other humans is much stronger due the time you have spent with me. Your chances of success are high.*]

"My abilities will be stronger? Stronger how?"

[*Clearer communication. Better control of gravity. Stronger in all ways. Your connection to others born on Canopy will be very strong. The one who protected you as an infant is very connected, for example.*]

The one who protected me as an infant? "You mean Myoki, my mother?"

[*No. The one who protected you. The one connected to you.*]

Connected to me? Bob's at it again. I feel like he knows things he isn't telling me. Or maybe he thinks he's telling me and I'm just too dense to get it.

"You mean Saoirse? I can't believe you even remember her."

[*And I do not understand how your mind fails to remember things.*]

So, I guess Bob never forgets anything. He says he's hundreds of years old. It seems like his mind would get full.

"About the Gathering. You say it's gonna be a kind of trial? Am I going to be on trial?"

[*Decisions will be made about the future of your species.*]

"Wait a minute. I don't like the sound of that."

My brain sees blue bubbles. Tiny, light blue ones. I think that's Canopian chuckling.

[*There is no sound.*]

"This isn't funny. Are you saying Canopians are going to decide whether to attack humans based on my testimony?"

[*We have learned to respect the tenacity and willfulness of humans. Attack is too strong a word. A better word would be quarantine.*]

"And just how might that work?"

[*One proposal that has been suggested is we kill all humans we can, knowing many will flee to live in the Overhead, out of reach. We would send our largest and most powerful underneath the surviving humans to drive them as high as possible. Such an approach planet-wide would deprive humans of most water and much food.*]

"Wait! That's not a quarantine. That's just genocide in slow motion."

[*I am not in favor of that approach, but I am influenced by my fondness for you. Other Canopians are focused on the fact that humans are killing us. Your attendance at the Gathering is critical. My advice is that you do not miss it. Be back here in seventeen days.*]

He's so fond of me it would bother him to quarantine my whole species. I'm glad he's not annoyed with me.

[*Be back here in seventeen days.*]

"I get it. Seventeen days. Don't want to miss my trial."

[*Now it's sixteen days and twenty-three hours. Hurry.*]

~~~

Kejuon volunteered his large house to be used as a field hospital for the recovery and recuperation of the prisoners. Sarah and Myoki stayed in Sentell's room, as he was on active duty. Larry and Adam used the twin beds in Jayden's room while Jayden slept on the couch in the den.

Saoirse cracked her knuckles as she sat at the kitchen table. "Danielle, Mom won't talk. Not at all. She hasn't said a single word since she got here."

Danielle stood at the window over the sink, staring out. "Sarah doesn't have many physical injuries like the others. They messed with her mind somehow. It's going to take time."

"I know that. I just don't know how I can help her."

"I think you should hug her a lot and just talk to her about pleasant things, like Beasley." Danielle pulled the curtain aside with her finger. "Did Cooter tell you he was going to assign protection to this house? There's at least a squad out there. Looks like two men on each side of the house. They're pretty good. I didn't even notice them at first."

Tsintah walked into the kitchen and sat at the table. "They're all sound asleep. Apparently being tortured by scumbags makes you tired."

Saoirse lightly slapped her palm on the table. "Is that supposed to be funny?"

Danielle turned from the window and leaned against the

counter. "Sarcasm is just her way of dealing with stress. Didn't you figure that out yet? Tsintah, why don't you just sit and pout like the rest of us?"

"I'm sorry, Sirsh, that was a stupid thing to say."

Latesha came into the kitchen from the porch. "Did y'all see that guy? A Scout just showed up in the tree next to the porch and gave me a message from Cooter."

Danielle turned and leaned over the sink to look sideways out the window. "He didn't just now show up. They been out there a while."

Saoirse rose halfway out of her chair. "What's the message?"

"He said Cooter's on his way here with some new information."

"So, we got a message that we're about to get a message?" Danielle stared at Saoirse. "That gives us something else to pout about."

"Danielle, why are you giving me such a hard time? My mother is in the next room with a broken mind. I'm having trouble dealing with it, so get off my back!"

Kejuon stepped into the doorway and looked over Latesha's shoulder. "It looks like I got here just in time for the fireworks."

Myoki entered the room. "K, I hate that beard. You used to look like Denzel Washington. Now you just look like a huge black Q-tip," Myoki's voice was faint and scratchy.

Everyone stared at Myoki with surprise.

Danielle said, "You're up. How you feeling?"

"I feel beat up. Danielle, it appears you have an issue with Saoirse." Myoki sat gingerly in the chair next to Saoirse.

"Who's Denzel?" asked Tsintah.

Kejuon, Latesha, and Danielle all smiled.

"It's one of those things that, if you ask about it, you get tall tales about a planet fifty light-years away that's a burnt rock." Saoirse paused and looked around the room. "Maybe I'm not doing a good job as a leader. At least the emotional part, anyway."

"I wasn't saying that," Danielle said.

"You didn't have to say it. You're just tired of sitting around when you want to do something about R of H." Saoirse stood and began to pace as she talked. "And, my attitude — pouting you call it — isn't helping. But, here's the thing that keeps eating at me. We're an army of twelve people — fifteen if you count Niti, Ben, and Sentell — against a whole nation. When we take action, it has to be big and it has to be decisive. We have to have the citizens of the United Colonies behind us when it happens. We ..."

A loud knock interrupted Saoirse. Kejuon stepped aside to let Cooter into the room.

"Sorry to barge in, Saoirse. Before you go much further with that train of thought, I have information everyone needs to hear.

"I don't want to bury the lead, so I'll start with the big part. R of H is going to declare war on the United Colonies."

Everyone in the room reacted. They drew deep breaths, shuffled their feet, and murmured.

Saoirse sat back down at the table. "What do you mean '*is* going to'? How do you know what they're going to do before they do it?"

"Well, that's the other part. We had a mole inside R of H Command. I say *had* because he felt he was compromised and had to get out. They finally broke … Myoki, you look really tired. Maybe you should go lay down."

Myoki sat straighter. "So you could tell everyone your news about Choop while I pretend like it's not happening?"

Cooter looked at the floor. "I don't doubt your grit, but you've been through a lot. It'll be hard for you to hear."

Cooter paused for a response. He got none. Myoki just stared at him with raised eyebrows.

"Uh, okay, Choop finally broke."

Cooter could not meet her eyes, but stared at the floor as he spoke.

"According to my source, they started with waterboarding. That lasted for about twelve hours. They got nothing. It seems he kept spitting on the interrogator. Then they tried the physical. Broke a bunch of his fingers and just plain beat him for two days. He began to give names, but they only got the six they already knew. You know, the prisoners they gave up and, of course, they saw Danielle and Kejuon at the exchange. So, then they started with psychological stuff. It turns out keeping a guy awake for four days by poking him with a stick and throwing water on him will cause hallucinations and loss of any connection to reality. He gave'em everything. All our names, the fact of the bombs — thank God he didn't know where they're hidden."

Myoki's voice was so soft it was hard to hear. She smiled a sad smile. "It took them seven days."

Cooter finally looked up. "It was my name that got'em really riled up. They see my involvement as an indication the United Colonies sanctioned the assassination of Dedric Krieger. Runners should be on their way to Knot City to make a formal declaration of war."

A voice came from the back door. "Well, that solves the problem of getting UC on our side."

Everyone turned and stared in astonishment.

Saoirse squealed in delight. "Mose, you're back!"

~~~

I think I'm prepared for what Bob called *clearer communication*, but I'm not. The power of the thoughts and emotions flooding my mind overwhelms me. Even though only Saoirse spoke while everyone else stares, I hear a cacophony in my mind. All I can do is partially mute the flood of information.

I lock eyes with Mom. I am aware that levitating will freak everyone out, and it's a struggle to stay near the floor as I drag myself hand over hand toward her. She takes me into her arms and I hug her.

Her mind is not as I remember. At first I think it's the *clearer communication* causing me to see her more or differently. Then I realize it's because her mind is *bruised*. I turn to Saoirse as I try to block the thoughts of the others from my mind.

"What happened to her?"

I don't mean to project thoughts at Saoirse, but I can hear in her mind the equivalent of a gasp. She says nothing out loud, but her mind speaks clearly. [*Mose? What's happening? You're scaring me.*]

I think, [*Use your voice, the others don't need to know.*] I repeat, "What happened to her?"

She thinks, [*I've got to be imagining this.*] She says, "She was captured by R of H. They tortured her."

During this exchange, Mom's mind is murmuring in the background, [*He's back. He's back.*] Her face is buried in my chest.

I say, "Everyone, please be quiet."

They all stare at one another with quizzical expressions. No one was talking. The noise was just their thoughts in my mind. The pain in Mom is making me emotional. I need to pull it together.

I glance around. "Where's Dad?"

More nervous glances at one another, but they've all told me, with their minds, before Saoirse speaks.

"That's how we got your mom back. Your dad turned himself in as a trade. They had Larry, Sarah, and Adam, too. He gave himself up for them."

I descend into depression. I lose my ability to block out the noise. It's like being at a sporting event full of the relentless din of a crowd. I feel Saoirse's powerful presence in my mind. I can tell she senses my pain.

Saoirse says, "Let's all go into the living room and give these two some privacy."

Mom cries into my chest. Big, convulsive sobs rack her body. I cry, too.

Finally, I manage to control myself. I take several deep breaths to calm down. I pick her up and float toward the bedrooms. I don't think any of the others see this, but I don't care if they do.

I lay her next to Sarah. Sarah's mind is jumbled. It makes no sense. What did those bastards do to her?

I sit with Mom hoping she will fall asleep and get some rest, but she wants to talk.

"I can't believe you ran away." [*What did I do to make him want to leave?*]

"I'm back, Mom, I'm back now. You should rest."

"I know you think you're grown, but you're still a teenager. Don't you ever run away again." [*Just look at him. He's not a kid anymore. Who am I kidding?*]

"I'm staying, Mom. I had to leave because I grew up, but I'm back now. I'm here to help out. You should sleep now."

[*He grew up. He grew up. He's back. He's back...*]

Her mind murmurs for a few minutes and she finally closes her eyes. I sit with her a little longer to make sure she's asleep.

I steel myself for what I'm about to do. This will be hard for everyone, but I'm through messing around. I take more deep breaths to calm my rage.

I don't have time for long explanations, so I decide shock is best. I float into the living room four feet off the ground and stare back at the astonished faces. I have better self-control now, the noise of their thoughts is muted.

"I apologize for not easing into this, but time is of the essence. As you can see, I can control gravity. Not with the power of a whale, but I don't need a wheelchair anymore. I know you're all full of questions, but there's no time, so here's a quick summary of what's important. I can control gravity in a limited way and sense your emotions in a limited way."

To Saoirse I think, [*Okay, that last part was a little white lie, but they don't need to know more. Keep my secret, please.*]

"More importantly, the Canopian I have been living with — I call him Bob — has invited me to a meeting of Canopians from all over. He says the fate of humans are on the agenda. The Gathering is in less than three weeks, so forgive me if I'm brisk."

"Saoirse, What's happening?"

"Shhh, Tsintah, be quiet. Let him talk."

"First, Kejuon, how quickly could you move the bombs from where they're hidden to here?"

"Who told him about the bombs?"

"Tsintah, please." Saoirse puts her hand on Tsintah's arm. "We'll talk later."

Kejuon says, "Maybe four days if we don't get ambushed."

"What if you took out the explosive matter and just brought it and the detonators?"

"That would cut out at least half the weight. If I had three other Earth-born, we could do it in a day."

"Make it happen. Start now."

Cooter says, "So, we're taking orders from him now?"

Kejuon, Danielle, and Saoirse all speak at once. "Yes!"

"While K is doing that, I will spend time here answering your many questions and getting up to speed on everything."

While speaking, I send thoughts to Saoirse. [*Saoirse,*

gather *Ela, Ben, Bina, Niti, Sentell, Andrew, Alana, Samuel, Haley, and Jaden. Bring them all here. We need to talk.*]

[*That's all the third-generation in our families.*]

[*Yes, but that's not what's critical. What matters is it's all the humans born on Canopy who developed in the womb while living near whales.*]

[*Surely you don't mean what I think you mean?*]

[*Can't you see what I mean? Just look deep into me.*]

I meant it to be funny, but she doesn't laugh. I wonder if she sees blue bubbles?

12

"Humans are good at a lot of things, but there's nothing like a good fight."

—From the memoir of Myoki Miles

~~~

I look around the room at the people I grew up with, seeing each of them as though for the first time. It's amazing how knowledge has changed my perception of reality. I don't see just friends and family, I see hope for humanity's future.

I keep my mind quiet as I watch them. They are all curious since Saoirse was vague about the reason for the meeting, but no one seems eager to get to that. They seem content visiting with one another. Just a big family reunion.

They naturally sit in groups by family. Across from me, the Miller girls. Saoirse, at twenty-six, is the oldest and most dominant personality, but twenty-two-year-old Alana and eighteen-year-old Haley are both the type of people who brighten a room when they enter. They all have Sarah's curly strawberry-blond hair, which shines from light streaming through the window of K's large living room.

To my right are the Samara boys. Twenty-five-year-old Ben is stocky like Adam with the same dark-brown ringlets. Andrew, twenty-four, and Samuel, twenty, both look more like Danielle with her prominent nose and piercing brown eyes. Especially Samuel. He is looking around the room, taking stock. My memories of him include watching him kick ass in karate class. So much like his mother.

To my left are K's kids. Twenty-one-year-old Sentell and seventeen-year-old Jayden are both lighter skinned than their dad. But, they both look so much like him it's amazing. Two K replicas.

My sisters flank me. Bina, just turned twenty-two, and Niti, twenty, are on my left. Ela, now a beautiful twenty-five-year-old spitting-image of Mom, sits brooding on my right. Her mind is in turmoil. She is torn up about Mom's mental condition and keeps thinking about what Dad is going through.

Haley, Niti, Sentell, and Sam all had to get leave from their units, but Cooter helped with that. Alana was also on active reserve duty, but Saoirse managed to get them all here.

It's time to start. I need to get their attention in a dramatic way, or we'll spend the first thirty minutes with a lot of repetitive questions.

I brought Mom's dream-catcher. I throw it out into the middle of the room and grab it with my mind. I float it in the center of us all, turning it slowly right and left. The voices in the room gradually grow quiet as people notice it.

Alana murmurs, "What the hell?"

"Excuse the dramatic demonstration, but I wanted to get the ball rolling quickly. I figured a picture is worth a thousand words."

I spin the catcher and then stop it. I bounce it up and down gently. I move it around the circle of amazed faces.

"I can control gravity, but that ability is just the tip of the iceberg. I can also communicate directly, brain-to-brain, with Canopians."

I lower the dream-catcher and lay it on the coffee table in the center of the room. When I look up, all eyes are on me. Nobody is blabbing questions. No one looks overly alarmed, although Alana's expression of incredulity is almost comical. Such self-control and reserve in the face of the unexpected make me proud to call these people family.

"Now for the other shoe. I can do this because I grew up living in close proximity to whales."

I wait as calmly as I can while these humans — who all grew up in close proximity to whales — do the math. Slowly, they turn their stares from me to each other. Still, no one talks.

"I spent the last several weeks living with a Canopian.

Not only did I communicate with him every day, but I also spent time exercising my ability. Whatever physical changes in me caused this ability, it seems to grow stronger with use."

[*Saoirse, tell them what you're experiencing.*]

"He's in my mind right now. We can talk without words." She begins crying suddenly. Big tears roll down her face as she continues. "I can't explain what it feels like. I get meaning without the actual words. I can even send thoughts back to him, at least a little."

Ben says, "Why are you crying? Does it hurt?"

"No, these are happy tears. It's wonderful."

I feel Ela probing at my mind, trying to touch me. I put my hand on hers and squeeze. [*Patience, Big Sis.*]

Niti's eyes are closed. Her communication is weak but clear. [*Mose? Can you hear me?*]

My throat explodes with joyous laughter. "Everyone chill! We have the rest of our lives to learn this."

[*Yes, Niti, I can hear you. Quit trying to hog my mind, I'm busy.*]

Niti giggles and doubles over, hugging her knees.

"Okay, everyone. I know this is amazing and it's new and exciting. But, listen carefully to what I say next. The people in the rest of this house, our parents, love us unconditionally and would sacrifice themselves for us. But, even they, if they knew what I just revealed, would be *concerned.* They would worry about us. Are we freaks? Will we be harmed by this? Will we be outcasts? You can imagine.

"So, think about the others in our society. Some of them attack whales. Few of them love us enough to put us first. People are suspicious of what they don't understand. Some old-timers witnessed gravity control being used to kill people."

Their minds gradually calm as I speak. Their expressions match their thoughts. No one is smiling.

"Trust me when I say I know what it's like to be different. We MUST not share this with others. Eventually, sure, but not now. Not a word of this to others, even parents. Our lives depend on it."

~~~

My new and improved gravity control is coming in handy. This wheelchair weighs as much as I do when it's stuffed with explosives. My increased strength makes it easier to push, but I don't overdo it. I only help with my mind enough to keep my arms from getting fatigued because I can hear in the thoughts of each guard or soldier I pass how weak I look to them. I'm just a poor cripple in a wheelchair.

My story was convincing at the border to Burl City. I just want to see my dad to say goodbye.

The first guard at the nets is just a kid a couple of years older than me. He pities me. He knows there is an important prisoner in the city but doesn't know where.

His Sergeant knows more. He knows what my dad did and where he's being held. I hear him think, [*Crap. I guess I should send him to Duncan.*]

That's good news. Locating the man named Duncan Heath is a top priority. My sessions sitting with Mom, Sarah, Larry, and Adam give me a strong desire to meet Mr. Heath. He is going to pay, especially for what he did to Sarah's mind.

Apparently, Duncan Heath is quite the mystery even to his own people. It seems odd that the Sergeant only thinks of him as Duncan with no rank. *Exactly* what he is must be a mystery even to the common Republic of Humanity soldier. The two Scouts assigned to escort me are terrified at the thought of having to meet him.

We follow a wide bridge that looks like it might traverse the entire city. The other end of it seems to fade into infinity as it winds through the trees. Burl City is beautiful and the thoughts of the people I pass are not evil. They are just normal folks living normal lives, even those in the military.

At one of the large shopping platforms we branch off onto a narrower bridge that descends at a steep angle. We are moving slower and slower as we descend and when I probe the minds of the Scouts I know why. Each of them wants the other to be the one to explain to Duncan Heath why I'm here and is trying to let the other Scout take the lead.

Burl City's official elevation at the Capital is three thousand nine hundred and eighty feet. As we descend it gets murky and darker. We must be close to two thousand feet elevation when we come to a control point. A large platform has a guardhouse big enough for an entire squad and there's a barrier arm lowered across the bridge. There is another set of nets like the ones around the city's borders. I realize I am entering a major facility, either a prison or maybe the main Republic of Humanity military base.

A Scout comes out of the guardhouse and approaches the gate. "State your business, Scout." [*What's with the cripple?*]

My increased control and strength really helps with the whole *words not matching thoughts* thing. I can understand both without confusion much easier than when I was in school.

The smaller Scout loses the battle to be in the background. "I was told to bring him here and ask for Duncan Heath." [*Maybe this guy will take the kid off my hands and I can head back now. I won't need to meet Duncan Heath.*]

The bored guard is no longer bored the instant he hears the name. [*I've been told not to bother Duncan. There's no way I'm calling him. But, this weakling says he is the son of the traitor, so Duncan might be really pissed if I don't bother him.*]

The guard tells another guard to escort me to the brig. His mouth says *brig* but his mind says *dungeon*. The fear that fills the escort's mind is so intense I block his thoughts. It's scaring me a little and I don't have time for fear.

The bridge from the rear of the guardhouse platform leads to a large opening in the side of a huge trunk. As we go into the tree, I resume monitoring the guard's thoughts. I'm thinking he might reveal useful information, but all I get is massive fear of having to explain to Duncan Heath why there is an interruption.

This tree must be two hundred yards wide. After we go in forty feet, the four-foot-wide tunnel turns to the left sharply and then has a gradual bend to the right as it follows the perimeter of the massive trunk. It descends at a more gentle slope than the bridge to the guardhouse.

Lamp plants are growing on the walls and the ceiling. It looks like they were planted every thirty feet as there are larger plants evenly spaced at the juncture of wall and roof, but younger ones have grown randomly on both walls and ceiling. It is really quite beautiful.

We come to an intersection. The beautiful tunnel continues ahead and I can faintly hear multiple voices barking orders and other sounds of yelling, but we take a right turn into a short tunnel leading to an ante-room. This outer room is a thirty-foot-wide oval with five openings leading to three-foot-wide tunnels. A desk in the middle of the room is manned by a bored-looking Scout.

The Scout looks less bored when he sees me. Someone in a wheelchair is a new experience for him.

My escort says, "I have a visitor for Duncan Heath."

The Scout is now totally alert. I swear I can hear his heart hammering. His voice squeaks as he mutters, "Wait here."

He turns and walks into the middle tunnel. While we wait, I decide to dig through the escort's thought for clues.

"Wow, what is this place?"

He doesn't answer, but he thinks about it. I learn this place is informally known as the dungeon. When prisoners come here, they never leave alive. Other than those that work here, only corpses exit these five tunnels. The escort is clenching his thighs to keep from pissing himself.

~~~

All the members of the original resistance group plus their families numbered twenty-four adults. All but Choop and Mose were gathered.

The only place which could hold them comfortably was the huge back porch of Kejuon's house on the outskirts of Daylight. Two of Canopy's suns were in the sky, one high and one low. The light streaming through the widely spaced branches of the Overhead illuminated the porch brightly.

They positioned themselves subconsciously in family groups. Myoki had a chair, as did all the recovering prisoners. Larry sat in a chair with Sarah curled in a ball in his lap with her head against his chest.

Alana and Haley sat cross-legged on the porch by the blanket on which Amanda, Alana's daughter, crawled back and forth. She was trying hard to escape the blanket, but Saoirse's son, six-year-old Beasley, and Ben's son, five-year-old Abraham, took their assignment of keeping her on the blanket seriously.

Cooter addressed the group.

"War has been declared by R of H as we thought it would. I will be leaving shortly to report to headquarters at Knot-City. My guess is that everyone will be called to active duty with few exceptions. I expect our generals to focus on defensive tactics rather than attacking R of H."

Bina barely heard Cooter's words. She was focused on a small wood chip she had dug from the porch rail with her fingernail. She was pushing the chip around on the railing using her mind. Ever since Mose made her aware of her abilities she couldn't stop experimenting. She and Ela worked to try and communicate without words, but it was hard. Compared to the clearness and power of thoughts from Mose, communication was weak, but they kept trying.

Ela felt Bina in her mind. It was faint and fuzzy. [*Ela? ... hear me? ... afraid Mose ... die ... Burl-City.*]

Ela whispered, "shhh," and put her hand on Bina's.

Cooter continued, "Divers may avoid active duty since we'll be defending cities at elevation. I'm sorry I don't have more information. Are there questions?"

Danielle leaned forward in her chair. "Hell yes, I've got a question. Why are we being defensive? That's not how you win wars. We need to attack."

"Damn straight." Kejuon punched the air with his fist.

"Don't shoot the messenger. I agree with you, but I'm just telling you what I expect based on what I know so far."

"I think we all need to stick together as a unit," said Saoirse.

Everyone except Bina turned to stare at Saoirse.

"Don't look so surprised. We're all outlaws already and we have unique talents in this group that make it a formidable fighting unit."

Ben stood up from his perch on the porch rail. "Saoirse, don't."

There was a pause while no one spoke for several seconds. Most of the Canopian-born were looking at the floor, except Bina, who continued pushing the wood chip around with a slight smile on her lips.

Finally, Tsintah said, "Don't what?"

~~~

The man that emerges from the tunnel doesn't look like the monster I expect. At five-nine he is not physically imposing, although he appears quite fit. His eyes are cold and expressionless, but the thing that stands out is his mind is quiet. I get nothing. Apparently, he doesn't mentally sub-vocalize his thoughts like normal people. Not until he speaks do I get any thoughts.

"What do we have here?" [*Billy says this is Choop's son. This must be my lucky day.*]

"My name is Mose Miles. My father is being held prisoner here. I would like to talk to him."

"You say prisoner as if we are doing something wrong. He is, in fact, a political assassin we have arrested." [*This freak has no legs. He couldn't be more unable to defend himself. I hope Choop loves him. What a bargaining chip.*]

"I understand. I'm told you plan to execute him. I just want to say goodbye."

"Isn't that sweet? Follow me and I'll let you talk to him." [*This kid's a fool. His mind must be as damaged as his body.*]

This narrow tunnel is long and imposing. The lamp plants no longer appear beautiful to me, but instead seem threatening. We finally emerge into a large room with cells along the back wall. Instead of bars, they have thick posts of hard wood. The lock is simply a rope tie that can't be reached from the other side because of a big wooden panel. There are large openings at each end of the room that appear to lead to similar rooms.

Dad is in the middle cell, sitting on the floor leaning against the back wall. His left hand is covered with bloody bandages. He has lost a lot of weight and his face is bruised. When he looks up and sees me, there is immediate joy on his face followed quickly by panic.

"Mose! Duncan, you bastard, this is low even for you."

"I didn't bring him here. He came on his own. He wants to say goodbye. Isn't that sweet?" [*This is great. He obviously loves his son. Watching his son's pain will break him. I'll get everything he knows.*]

"Will you give me and my dad some time alone?"

"Of course, I'll be in the next room." [*It'll give them a chance to bond, the closer they are the better.*]

Duncan walks into the next room. I roll next to the cell and motion for Dad to move closer. He struggles to get up, is obviously stiff. But, he manages to move fairly well as he crosses the cell.

"Mose, what the hell are you thinking? You need to try and leave now, if he'll let you." [*Why did I say that first? I should've said I love you.*]

"Dad, keep your voice down. You know he's listening."

Dad can barely hear my whisper, so he leans close to the bars.

"Dad, I love you, but we'll talk about that later. Are your legs injured? Can you move well? If so, we're getting out of here."

"My legs are fine, so far, but, Son, there no way I'm leaving this place alive." [*I love you, too. Why the hell can't I tell him?*]

"Dad, stay quiet and just watch."

I levitate from my wheelchair and float down to the floor near the bars. The expression on his face is priceless, but he makes no sound. As for his thoughts, I learn a new cuss word.

"I'll explain in detail later, but just accept I can control gravity. I can read minds. If you can move, we can get out of here. Duncan just sees a helpless cripple. He posted no extra guards or put anyone on alert. If your magnificent earth muscles can jump distances, I can amplify that with my mind. Trust me and we can get out of here."

I float to the rope keeping the cell locked and untie it, push the cell door open a couple of feet, float back to my wheelchair, and pull a foot-long cord out from under the butt pad. I tie the cord to the wheel with no slack.

Dad steps though the door. "Are you booby-trapping that chair?" [*How did this happen?*]

My answer is to float around to his back, loosen my belt, re-buckle it after slipping it under his belt, and wrap my arms tightly around his chest.

"It will take a couple of jumps for us to get in sync. When we run, I will amplify your jumps. No one will be able to catch us. Trust me. When Duncan collapses, you need to get his knife. We'll need it for the nets."

"Collapses?" [*This must be a dream.*]

"Duncan! We're finished. Come meet your fate."

A smug Duncan walks into the room. I waste no time. I'm not sure how much damage I can do since I've never tried this. I concentrate and try to crush his brain — not his head, his brain — with gravity waves. He screams and falls to the floor. He's unconscious if not dead.

"Get his knife. We'll need it for the nets. Let's go."

Dad grabs the knife and runs to the door. He pauses.

"To the left. Jump a long, flat jump down the tunnel. I need to practice."

The training of a soldier shows. I know his heart is hammering and the adrenaline is pumping, but he doesn't hesitate. I try to enhance the power of the jump. It works except for the part where we bounce back and forth off the walls as we go.

Dad needs no instructions in the ante-room. He slices the guard's throat without slowing and goes out the door and through the short tunnel into the main tunnel.

"Wait. We're going that way, but before we do you should cut all the lamp plant vines."

"Good idea." [*My son's a genius.*]

To the left of the door, Dad cuts every vine he can reach. By the time he gets them all, the light leaking from all the slices bathes us in sunshine. The lamp plants continuing into the depths of the tree dim, but still glow enough to barely light the tunnel..

"Yank on them. Separate the cuts."

Dad complies, yanking repeatedly. The tunnel heading into the tree grows dark. There is a lot of yelling coming from that direction.

"Okay, Dad, we still have the element of surprise. Let's go."

"I got this, Son. Hang on tight."

~~~

Duncan awoke with a massive headache. He moaned and held his head as he stood. The cell door was standing open and Choop and his son were gone. He saw the empty wheelchair. He screamed and kicked the chair.

The explosion cracked the massive tree. Since the trunk was one of the four that wrapped around each other to make the main Knot on which Burl City was built, the residents of Burl City experienced their first Canopian *earthquake* as the Knot abruptly sank two feet before sagging into a stable position.

~~~

Kejuon hugged Choop and clapped his back. "I can't believe an old man like you could escape. Thought I'd never see you again."

"It was Mose. I wish you coulda seen him in action."

Kejuon's puzzled look was lost on Choop, because all

Choop could see was Myoki. She stood behind the others. He waded through hugs from Ela, Bina, and Niti, never lowering his gaze from Myoki. Latesha didn't even try to hug him, but just stepped aside.

Ela was the first to understand. "Let's all go in the kitchen and give Mom and Dad some privacy."

As everyone left the room, Choop gently folded his arms around his wife. "I'm sorry."

"Sorry? For what?"

"Being me."

For the first time since her capture, Myoki smiled. She leaned forward as he leaned down to put his forehead against hers. They looked into each other's eyes from two inches.

Her voice was soft. "Other men are boring."

~~~

Before we even get to the kitchen, Bina has started in on me. [*Why are you sliding on the floor?*]

[*You know why. K and Latesha don't know about me yet. It's not time for them to know.*]

[*I disagree.*]

Kejuon sat at the kitchen table and pulled out a chair for Mose. "Mose, you have to tell us your tale. How the hell did you get him out of there? In fact, where exactly was *there*. Come on, Son, spill."

I have to focus to filter out the chatter between Ela, Bina, and Niti. They have been improving their brain-to-brain communication. Their thoughts are clear and concise. My effort to filter fails. I don't answer Kejuon as I listen to them.

[*Ela, tell him. It's time to let K and the others know. We need to start planning how we can help.*]

[*Bina, be patient. He just saved Dad. It looks to me like he knows what he's doing.*]

[*Aww! Niti, help me out here. Tell him your idea.*]

"Mose? Son, are you okay? Hello?"

"Sorry, Uncle K, it's been a long day."

[*Come on, Niti, tell him. It was your idea. You should tell him.*]

[*Bina, it can wait. After what he's been through, let him settle in. You're so impatient.*]

Uncle K just thinks I don't respond because I'm tired.

"That's okay, Mose. I'm just glad y'all made it back. The war stories can wait until later. You want anything? Coffee? Water?"

It occurs to me that, as far as informing the parents about our abilities, the cat is out of the bag. Dad is probably telling Mom about it right now.

[*Niti, I'll get your idea in a minute. Let me get Uncle K up to speed first.*]

I float up from my chair to above the level of the table top and then settle back down.

"Uncle K, as you can see, I can control gravity. I can also communicate with Canopians brain-to-brain."

His mouth is wide open; his eyes are big and round.

"Don't freak out on me, Uncle K. How else do you think a cripple in a wheelchair could help Dad escape? The wheelchair bomb worked by the way. We were at least a half mile away, but still heard the explosion."

Ela waved her hand in front of Uncle K's face. [*Is he okay, Mose? He's just staring at nothing.*]

[*He's fine. It's just a lot to absorb.*] "Uncle K? I'm guessing you might have some questions?"

He suddenly shakes his head and wipes his hand across his forehead. "How long have you been this way?"

"I'm pretty sure I was born this way, but living with Bob seems to have strengthened me."

I had forgotten about Latesha. Suddenly, she giggles hysterically and sags a little. Ela puts her arm around Latesha's shoulders to support her

[*Dad! We should tell him my idea!*]

"Niti, give me a minute for crying out loud. This is a lot for him to take in. We'll get to that, okay?"

Uncle K looks from me to Niti and back. "Can she do it, too?"

"Yes, but she's not very strong yet."

He looks to his right at Ela and Bina then back at me. I just nod and shrug.

Latesha finds her voice. "Sentell and Jayden?"

I look at Ela. All three girls nod their heads. The room is quiet for a few seconds as Kejuon and Latesha absorb this.

"Niti, tell us your idea." [*Use your mouth.*]

"Okay, well here's the thing. While you were away, we been practicing. We can cross-think, that's what we call it cause it's not words, really, you know? Anyway, we can do it over a pretty long distance. We didn't measure it, I guess, but really far, and the more we practice, the farther it gets. It seems like Ben is the strongest. Anyway, it occurred to me that if we used it in the army, it would be, you know, like those phones or radios you like to talk about that you had back on Earth. If there's a battle and our side could communicate quicker and clearer than the other side, wouldn't that be, like, you know, a big advantage?"

By the time she's through rambling, Uncle K's smile is ear-to-ear.

<p style="text-align:center">~~~</p>

Saoirse, Ben, Ela, Bina, Sentell, and Haley accompany me on the trip to Bob's Clearing. I try to prepare them for what it's like to be *inspected*. Bob did it to me; I'm pretty sure he'll do it to them.

Saoirse has taken the lead in trying to get me to make it clearer. [*I'm still not sure what you mean by inspected, exactly.*]

[*Well, it's hard to explain it. It feels a little like dreaming, sort of. You see, hear and feel things from your memories.*]

Ben stops climbing the tree we're on and looks back at me. [*Wait. You mean it will take control of us? I don't think I'm up for that.*]

[*Don't stop walking. Can't you climb and think at the same time?*]

[*I'm not joking. Giving up control is a problem for me.*]

[*No, Ben, he will not take control of you. You just won't have any secrets. He'll see you for who you are.*]

Haley grabs Ben's hand and pulls to get him started moving again. [*Don't be paranoid, Ben. I like you, she'll like you, too.*]

Bina giggles. [*I wish y'all would decide to call Bob either him or her. It's confusing.*]

I send a focused [*thank you.*] to Bina for changing the subject. We have developed our own channel, sort of. We can cross-think, and the others don't receive it. I make a mental note to ask Bob about gravity-wave frequencies.

[*You're welcome, Little Bro.*] [*Y'all should have seen how pissed Niti was. She really wanted to come meet Bob.*]

Ben huffs. [*If you'd of told me I was gonna be inspected, I would've swapped places with her.*]

[*Ben, it ain't gonna be that bad, man. She understood we had to split and some would stay to work with neurotypical UC soldiers to work out procedures for using us as radios. She knows the six of you were picked because of the strength of your communication. She'll get over it.*]

I feel Bob in my head before the others do. It's weak, but I sense his presence.

[*You are not alone.*]

"Everyone stop. Please stay quiet. Let's take a break. Bob's calling out to me."

[*What? I can't hear anything.*]

"Ben, what don't you understand about stay quiet?"

[*I didn't say anything. So, be quiet means don't cross-think? And, suddenly you're talking out loud? This is confusing.*]

"Ben, please!"

[*Many have accompanied you. Explain yourself.*]

[*Bob, you know it was my intent to return to you with the good news that the humans who attack Canopians have been stopped. That is not possible as they continue their activities. But, I do have some good news. It turns out I am not alone in my ability to communicate with you. Many of my childhood friends also have the ability. I think this shows hope for the future of our species' coexistence. It is my desire that either we take them with me to the Gathering or they stay with another Canopian to be trained and grow stronger in their abilities.*]

[*This is indeed good news. Our efforts appear to have worked. I am pleased.*]

~~~

Bob decided the others would stay behind with one of his Canopian neighbors while he and I go to the Gathering. He seems concerned that the other whales at the Gathering might be confused by the extreme differences between individual humans.

He inspected Saoirse first, and everything seemed okay. But, when he inspected Ben, it did not go well. Ben was scared and defensive during the process. His screams were so loud I took the others for a swim.

"Can Bob hear us if we talk rather than cross-think?"

"Yes, Bina, you might wanna give up on the idea of privacy where Bob is concerned."

Haley quits swimming and paddles slowly toward a large root close to the surface. She climbs up on the root and wipes wet, blond hair out of her eyes. "I'm scared. I don't want to be inspected."

I float up and settle next to her. "Haley, Ben was screaming not because of Bob, but because of his own fears. Bob isn't doing anything but looking. Ben's own fear and paranoia is the problem." [*Take deep, slow breaths, Haley.*]

"What if I'm paranoid, too?" [*Is scared shitless the same as paranoid?*]

"All I can tell you is Bob doesn't mean you harm. In fact, my time with him has made him pro-human. We have a Canopian ally. Just relax when he inspects you. You'll be fine." [*Breathe. Just breathe.*]

When I feel Bob in my brain, the difference in the strength and clarity of the signal reminds me how weak our abilities are compared to his. [*Your friend Ben is fine. We must leave soon. Please return.*]

On the return swim, no one says anything.

Bob is in the middle of his Clearing rolling slowly as he likes to do when he concentrates. His six Raccoons are all inactive on their shelves.

Ben is sitting on a huge root on the edge of the Clearing, looking sheepish. It's a new look for him. [*Hey, guys.*]

Haley is the first to swim over to him. [*Are you all right?*]

[*I might have overreacted a little.*]

Haley turns to look at Bob. [*Do me next.*]

[*Your bravery and eagerness please me, but we are out of time. Mose and I will now leave for the Gathering. My neighbor will arrive shortly. He will spend time with all of you and help you strengthen your brains.*]

Haley seems relieved. [*What do we call him?*]

[*He and I have shared our memories. Call him Bob.*]

Ben moans and rubs his forehead. [*This is hard to get my mind around.*]

~~~

Five of Bob's Raccoons wake up and swim to him and, as he rolls, appear to insert a hand into him. This is something new.

Bob moves closer to my edge of the Clearing. [*Swim to me and I'll give you a ride.*]

I swim toward him as he stops rolling with one of his huge eyes just above the water. It takes a lot of concentration to filter out the excited cross-think of the others. Especially when it's combined with a lot of blue bubbles in my head. I don't know why Bob thinks this is funny.

[*Insert your hand in my blowhole.*]

I can't believe I haven't seen it before. About two feet from his eye is a blowhole eighteen inches in diameter. Maybe I never noticed because it's closed as it emerges from the water and not fully open until it's on top.

I hesitate, but comply. Before I can get a grip or really feel any kind of edge to grab, it closes on my wrist.

[*Take several deep breaths. When you feel yourself running low on oxygen, let me know and I'll stop for a breather.*]

I get three deep breaths before Bob submerges and drags me on the ride of my life. We are going fast. At least that's what I think until he turns into a much larger tunnel and accelerates. The pull of the passing water is extreme. I flatten myself against his side to lessen resistance and discover the pressure holds me in place securely. I shift around a little to get completely face down against his soft, rough skin and the ride is comfortable.

I can hold my breath for almost thirty minutes. When we stop, he lets me suck wind for about five minutes before we resume.

I don't know exactly how fast Bob can swim, so it's hard to estimate the distance we travel. We stop for me to breathe three times before he turns into a huge tunnel several times as wide as any I've ever seen. We stop to breathe a dozen times while in this super-tunnel before I tell him something he doesn't want to hear.

[*Bob, I've got some bad news and some worse news.*]

[*Is this going to be one of those things you call a joke?*]

[*Nope. The bad news is I've got to stop and take a dump. The worse news is I'm about to fall asleep. I think if I do, I'll drown.*]

Bob immediately slows down. [*What is the shortest time span that will provide you adequate rest?*]

[*Give me three hours, and I can last another day.*]

[*While you dump, my Raccoons will gather some fruit. Eat, then sleep.*]

Even with the amazing speed Bob swims, I sleep twice more before we arrive at the mother of all Clearings. Bob's Raccoons jump off at the Clearing's edge, so I get off as well.

My mind is overwhelmed with sensations.

The roof of the Clearing is at least a thousand feet

overhead. The width of the Clearing has to be a half a mile. I imagine it's what one of Earth's oceans looked like.

The strong charcoal smell of whales permeates the atmosphere. There are so many Raccoons crawling around on the branches of the Clearing's roof that it looks alive, pulsing with movement.

I see many whales rolling. Many are side-by-side. Others travel in small groups. I try to count them, but most are moving around. There must be a hundred.

The tree roots must be cleared deep under the water as there are large rolling waves created by all the huge creatures cavorting.

I climb one of the trees at the edge of the Clearing. As I ascend the slope of the tree and get a better view, it becomes obvious I have under-estimated the number of whales. For as far as I can see there are whales swimming. Many are gliding in groups in various kinds of dances. That's right, dancing is what comes to mind. One group of three in the mid-distance are *braiding* through the water. Whale One goes over whale Two, then whale Three over whale One followed by whale Two over whale Three. It's hypnotic.

Out in the middle of the Clearing, whales can be seen leaping from the water. They don't fully clear the surface, but a hundred feet of whale falling back creates a huge geyser of water. The splashing sounds are constant and loud enough that I doubt I could hold a normal conversation even if I had someone to talk to. The water is choppy over the entire visible surface.

The cross-think is ubiquitous. It merges into a feeling in my brain not unlike what Mom describes she feels when a whale is broadcasting, a kind of static. But it's not unpleasant. I can pick out no individual thoughts, but I sense a common theme of *joy*. This is a celebration.

There are a thousand Raccoons on the lowest branches of the Clearing's ceiling. It is so high they look tiny. They are all in motion, wiggling around. When I look closer, it appears large groups are also involved in what can only be called a dance.

I realize my mouth is hanging open. I shut it, but it doesn't quench the feeling of awe. I feel joy, too, in a way that's hard to explain.

I can't make out where Bob is, so I call out to him. [*Bob? This is incredible!*]

The split-second I broadcast my thought, a stunning thing occurs. It is a wave of stillness. Across the surface of the water, the whales become still as the wave reaches them, like the Panther-bone dominoes Dad would line up and knock over. As they quit dancing, each whale assumes the arched pose at right angles to me, staring at me with their big eyes.

The wave also progresses across the top of the Clearing.

As it reaches them, each Raccoon stops his dance, turns four of his eyestalks in my direction, and freezes in place. Some of them are hanging upside down, so I can see all six eyes.

Thousands of eyes are staring.

Focused on me.

13

"When Mose was little, he asked me whether it's better to deserve what you get or get what you deserve. I told him I thought they were the same. I was wrong."

—From the memoir of Myoki Miles

~~~

I would like to say the simultaneous attention of hundreds of whales doesn't unnerve me, but that would be a lie. Time seems to stand still as they stare. The silence extends to my brain. No cross-think, no static, just me all alone. I have never experienced this level of solitude before. I don't like it.

A large whale swims my way through the crowd of whales. He's moving fast and leaving a massive wake. The other whales move out of his way as he makes a beeline straight for me.

He looks to be at least twice as thick as Bob, maybe more. I name him Kingfish in my mind, then panic at the thought of naming a creature I know will hate being named.

Don't think of the name Kingfish. Don't think of the name Kingfish.

He stops fifty yards from the tree I'm in and ascends. He doesn't make the arch Bob normally does, although it starts that way. He rises farther making a huge horseshoe shape a hundred feet above the surface, towering over me. One of his eyes is three feet in diameter.

It's obvious he's not just big. He's strong. He's powerful. He's in charge.

Don't think of the name Kingfish. Don't think of the name Kingfish.

I feel a bass rumbling and not just in my head. It resonates in my bones. I'm certain if I try to move I will be unable to do so. I've never seen concrete, but I imagine this is what it feels like to be stuck in it.

Don't think of the name Kingfish. Don't think of the name Kingfish.

[*This is the creature you say threatens us?*]

Bob swims between me and Kingfish. [*Not as a single entity. It's complicated.*]

I can feel the fear that fills Bob. His willingness to insert himself between us is impressive. I will thank him later. For now, I resist pissing myself. So far so good.

[*What is a Kingfish?*]

Bob tries to save me. [*It is a label. Humans label each other.*]

The pressure surrounding me increases. [*I did not ask you. You have informed us it can communicate. Let it speak for itself.*]

I'm glad I'm not speaking aloud. I'm sure my voice would squeak. [*Kingfish means powerful leader. It seemed like a good name for you.*]

[*Its thoughts are puny. I doubt the veracity of your claims for the need to co-exist with these creatures.*]

[*It's not that simple. As a group ...*]

[*Let me speak for myself, Bob, as he requested.*]

There is a spike in the general level of gravity waves. I think many of the whales gasped, for lack of a better description.

My chest feels the same pressure it feels when I'm fifty feet under water. I force myself to breathe deeply anyway.

Now I'm pissed off. Rage is burning inside me. I remember Dad talking about some general or politician back on Earth who had a saying Dad liked. It went something like, 'Diplomacy is the art of carrying the biggest gun.' I'm probably not remembering it right, but the principle Dad was teaching me flashes through my mind as I respond.

[*Kingfish, are you implying co-existence is only necessary if humans are a danger to Canopians? Are you saying if we're not dangerous, there is no need to co-exist?*]

[*I am saying co-existence implies a level of equal*

standing.]

[*Equal standing in what aspect? Intelligence? Power? Ability to survive? Some other measure? If you're going to say things like that, you should be specific.*]

The pressure increases to the point I see spots and feel like I might pass out. Bob suddenly leaps from the water and splashes back violently. [*STOP!*]

The pressure on my chest abates. Kingfish slowly lowers back into the water to the normal arched posture. The noise in my brain dissipates.

Bob continues. [*I have spent much time with Mose. We have studied math and philosophy. Mose, share your view of humanity as a network.*]

[Sure. *The discussion he is talking about grew from Bob's difficulty in understanding what he calls humanity's separateness. Humans are not connected directly brain-to-brain as Canopians are. We communicate through audible speech combined with visual signals we call body language. We are never inside each other's brains. This leads to many concepts we think of as normal — but Canopians find alien — such as secrets. A human can see or feel something and never tell a soul and no one knows it happened.*]

At this last statement, I could feel cross-think activity as whales reacted. I interpret this as a collective muttering of amazement.

I find this encouraging and continue. [*But, the concept Bob found most elusive is how humans can act collectively. How can we work toward a common goal if we don't share thoughts and memories? If we are each isolated from all other humans, how is it we act in concert? My way of explaining it is to think of humanity as a network. A fault-tolerant network of nodes where each node acts based on internal assumptions and beliefs. It gets a little deep and would take too long to really get into here, but the bottom line is this. Humans are adaptable. Humans — collectively — are almost impossible to kill. On our home planet, we lived in deserts, in oceans, in jungles, and on a continent covered in ice. We killed animals many times our size and ate them for breakfast. We thrived in caves, in trees, underground, underwater, anywhere on the planet. If you kill half of us, the other half just keep going and adapt to what you've done. It's a little hard for Canopians to understand, but it helps explain how humans have killed seven whales at last count. More may have died on my trip here.*]

Another burst of brain waves. This one is stronger.

[*And make no mistake about it, my family knows I'm here. If I don't return, you will find yourself at war with the fiercest foe you've ever faced. Thus far, only a portion of our populace has been attacking you. If I am harmed, you will galvanize them all. You will find that any fancy plans you have to drive us into the trees and starve us will only work temporarily. We will adapt to whatever you do and thrive. You've kind of pissed me off with your lack of hospitality, so maybe I'm acting out of emotion rather than logic, but what I'm saying to you is our two species are not on a level standing.* Your *species is the one at risk. Humans have been at war our entire existence. We have learned to co-exist with each other only with treaties and agreements of non-aggression. I suggest we work on figuring out how our two species can work to live together non-aggressively. I like Bob and enjoy his company, so I know it's possible. But, if a fight is what you want a fight is what you'll get, and you'll regret it. Feel free to inspect me and see for yourself.*]

When I finish, I expect a comeback, perhaps a rebuke. There is none. There is no splashing, no cross-think, no movement.

Then, quite suddenly, there is so much cross-think I hear only loud static.

~~~

Sergeant Eldon Emsworth arrived first east of Knot City's wood mill. He waited patiently for the other Republic of Humanity squads. His squad traveled only at night for seventy-two hours to get into position three hundred feet to the east and one hundred feet higher than the mill's loading platform.

Scout Osmond Brent settled onto the branch next to Eldon. "How much longer do you think they'll be?"

"Lower your voice, Scout."

"Yes Sergeant, I just can't wait," whispered Osmond.

"Soldiers wait, Brent. It's what we do. And when we're waiting to ambush, we do it quietly."

Osmond could barely hear Sergeant Emsworth's soft voice. He decided not to say any more.

Thirty-five minutes later the west squad arrived. Fifteen minutes later the south and north squads arrived within two minutes of each other. Each squad of eight archers set-up three hundred feet away and slightly above the platform.

"Okay, Brent, all squads have signaled. We'll be here a while waiting for the main force to come up the trunk. Move down the line and make sure each Archer has an arrow notched but not drawn, and stays comfortable. No talking. Make sure the men know it's silence for however long it takes. Then return and confirm readiness."

The main force of eight squads arrived five hours later. They signaled readiness and prepared to swarm the platform to clean up whatever the arrows missed.

United Colonies only had one squad on the platform for night duty, so clean-up was unnecessary. All sixty-four arrows struck within a two-second time span. The squads swarming from below found only dead United Colonies' Scouts.

Lieutenant Burnet Thorpe was pleased, but cautious. His whisper carried only as far as the Squad leaders. "We've been over this many times. Execute."

It took fifteen minutes to place the explosives on bridges and elevator.

The sixteen bombs created the damage expected.

All four commercial bridges no longer connected to the platform.

As the Republic of Humanity squads fled down the trunks, the open-air elevator rising toward Knot City was a shambles.

~~~

I find it hard to describe the Gathering. I have no trouble telling them how scared I was when Kingfish was squeezing me, but relating the feelings of the joyous celebration is difficult.

We are all on Uncle K's porch. It seems to have become our headquarters. It's nice for our abilities to be out in the open with our parents. They hang around watching us have animated conversations with no words. Their expressions shift between awe, fear, and humorous smiles. A part of me feels sorry for them.

Ela furrows her forehead as she keeps digging for details. [*You keep comparing it to a dance. You mean the whales couple up? Is the Gathering about procreation?*]

Niti giggles. [*Eeew.*]

It's weird to have my big sisters talking about whale sex. [*No. I think procreation is accomplished by some sort of group sharing of genetic material.*]

It's Ben's turn to laugh. [*Cool.*]

Saoirse claps her hands, making a sharp, loud sound. [*Children, please! I can't believe how old y'all make me feel. Let him continue.*]

[*Ela, think of the dancing more like the Texas line dancing Dad taught us. Small groups of three, four, or five move in patterns. It's amazing to watch, but the emotions their brains broadcast are what's compelling. It's joyous.*]

Ben leans forward in his chair and puts his elbows on his knees. [*Enough about dancing. Tell us more about this Kingfish asshole.*]

[*Once I threatened his whole race, he calmed down a lot. He seemed to respect the whole 'we can kick your ass' approach to diplomacy.*]

Alana coughs, one of those 'I'd like to have the floor' kinda coughs. [*So is he now what we would consider an ally? Is he some kind of official leader? Is he in charge of the Canopian society? Does this mean ...*]

[*Whoa, Alana, too many questions at once. Three is my limit. One, he is not what I would consider an ally in the way Bob is, he's just not an enemy. Two, he's not an official leader, he's just very old, big, and powerful. Three, it doesn't appear to me Canopian society has leaders in the way we think of them. They just cross-think to a decision and all abide by it.*]

Sentell steps forward. [*Wait a minute. When Bob shared himself with the new Bob, it was like the exact same being. Are you saying that at the Gathering they all become a single entity?*]

[*No, that's not what happens. You know how the local whales keep their Clearings far enough apart so they have privacy and only share memories when they want? In the global sense, each local tribe that melds to a single mind — each Bob — stays separate when they get together. They don't meld, only cross-think, which they do much deeper than we do. By that I mean they share not just concepts in word-like chunks, but also images and other senses. If we could do it, I would show y'all the dancing.*]

[*How do you know all this?*] asks Haley.

[*I spent the final two days with them asking a lot of questions. Also, Bob explained much of it on the return trip.*]

[*Did you name any of the other whales?*]

[*Hell no, Ben, Kingfish didn't appreciate his name much. The other Canopians kept mocking him. Bottom line, they all agreed to quit going on walkabouts trying to kill humans. That's a big win for us. But, enough about the Gathering. I want to hear how your training with Bob Prime went. And what did Cooter think of it?*]

Saoirse scoots forward in her seat. [*It went great. We all got much stronger and clearer in our cross-think. We can all do it for over a half mile. Ben, Sentell, and I for over a mile. With Cooter, we developed this technique where the two radiomen — can you believe that? Cooter insisted we be called Radiomen. Anyway, we learned a complex set of hand signals we can use to communicate with the officer to which you're attached. That way, the officer can ask questions or give orders which are relayed to the distant radioman and when you get a response, you can signal the officer. It allows two remote officers to communicate with no sounds at all.*]

[*Of course, if you're close to your officer, you can whisper.*] Niti adds.

Ben gets excited and speaks aloud. "I just thought of something. The whales ceasing to roam and attack means all the bombs R of H are placing will remain un-exploded. We can gather and use them ourselves."

"That's a really good idea, Ben." Everyone turns toward the new voice coming from the doorway.

"Dad! I thought you went to see Cooter."

"I did. I'm back. Remember, us Earthborn supermen move pretty fast even when we don't have our hero-sons amplifying our jumps." [*I know you can hear my thoughts. So, there, now everyone else knows you're a hero.*]

"Dad, everyone else can hear your thoughts, too." [*I can

feel y'all laughing. Cut it out.]

[*Ooh, Little brother's a hero.*]

[*Look, Ela, I think he's blushing.*]

[*Bina, cut him some slack. He is a hero in my book.*]

[*Thanks, Niti. I refuse to feel guilty. For years he would hardly speak to me.*] "So, what did Cooter have to say about it?"

"He is understandably skeptical, but accepts my view that you know whales and we don't. He is willing to move forward on his strategic planning with the assumption we no longer need the whale monitoring activity."

"That's good, Uncle Choop. Do we have an idea what those strategic plans might be?" Saoirse asked.

"Yep. We discussed how to use our secret weapons." [*I know y'all are snooping on my brain. Secret weapons mean you kids, of course.*]

Ben throws his arms up. "This is weird." [*This is weird.*]

Sentell isn't as amused as everyone else. "Are you going to share these plans with us?"

"Yes, I am. It involves using half of you as radiomen and the other half as spies."

"Spies?"

"Well, maybe listening posts is a better term. You guys are gonna love it. We use our superior communication not to kill R of H soldiers, but to manipulate their troop movements so they go past areas where some of you are deeply concealed. If you can read the thoughts of some of their officers, we're liable to get some valuable intel. Y'all should get a good night's sleep. We're traveling to Knot City for briefings tomorrow morning."

~~~

Choop settled in with just his head sticking out of the leaves, looking straight down. "Niti, are you still in contact with Sam and Jayden?"

"Yes. Uncle K and Jayden are in place. Danielle and Sam are almost in position."

"Be sure Sam tells Danielle I made it before her."

"Why do you do that? You always goad her."

"It's like a hobby."

"Jayden says Uncle K wants to know what's been keeping you. That's funny. He has a hobby, too."

"Niti, you know this is a military operation, right?"

"I'm not the one doing all the teasing. Yes, I know all us youngest had to be the ones you supermen lugged around as radios to use on a mission."

"It's not because you're the youngest. It's because y'all are the lightest. I'm not as young as I once was. And why do y'all insist on calling the Earthborn supermen?"

"Well, you can jump through the forest carrying a whole nuther person. Duh."

"Okay, lets get settled in. You stay up in this foliage. You do not raise your head. You stay hidden, no exception. Got it?"

"Got it. I'm just a really heavy radio."

"Cute. But, you have another function. You get to hand me grenades. I'll be hanging out where I can see straight down, so I'll have no place to put'em."

Niti began placing the hand grenades among some branches where they could sit undisturbed. "So as long as these wooden pins stay in, I'm safe, right? I can't believe how good Sam can carve. All three pins are intertwined."

"You gotta give him credit. He came up with the idea for that. Otherwise these grenades would be dangerous just to carry around. We had to put firing pins covered with stickypede all over the grenades so they explode no matter which side it lands on."

"But you didn't like them, I thought."

"Well, I don't like having to pull three pins to arm it, but beggars can't be choosers. It'll do for our purposes."

"Sam says Danielle is in position."

"Have her and K check in when they have all grenades safely stashed and are all set up."

"Done. Tell me again why we are doing this between Boardwalk and Atoll rather than closer to Burl City?"

"Two reasons. We have great three-dee maps of this region made by Myoki, and staying away from Burl City is just safer. Fewer R of H troops available."

"Mom mapped this area?"

"Yep. Before you were even born, we taught sign language to a whale named Humpback. R of H killed him to use his Clearing. It's now Boardwalk."

"Ooh, Sam and Jayden say they're ready."

"Good. You and them check with all the listeners."

"Okay." [*Alana, Bina, Sentell, Haley, can y'all hear me?*]

[*Here.*] [*I'm settled in.*] [*Good to go.*] [*Ready.*]

[*Remember, this is only gonna work if you identify yourselves.*]

[*Alana in position.*] [*Bina settled in.*] [*Sentell here. Good to go.*] [*Haley. Ready.*]

[*Thanks. Sam, Jayden, are you in touch with all your listeners?*]

[*Sam here. Everyone says they're ready.*]

[*This is Jayden. Everyone but Andrew is ready. Andrew has a problem.*]

[*What kind of problem?*]

[*The place he was supposed to hide is home to a Panther.*]

[*Hold on a sec.*]

"Dad, Andrew's hideout is a Panther's home."

"Crap. Any other places he could use that are close to the same spot?"

"I'll check." [*This is Niti. Jayden, are there other acceptable hiding spots nearby Andrew can use?*]

[*Jayden here. Hang on, I'll check.*] ... [*He says there's*] one down on the water and another up at almost a thousand feet. He says that's too high for him to listen effectively, wants to go down to the water.]

[*Stand by.*] "Dad, Andrew says there's a good place on the water and another at a thousand feet, which he thinks is too high."

"No way he should go down to water level. Losing a life is by far the greater evil when compared to having a hole in our net. Tell him to go up. He still might get intel, and can relay visuals if he sees movement."

[*Niti here. Jayden, tell him to go to the higher position.*]

[*I'll tell him.*] … [*Andrew is pissed. He wants to go down.*]

[*Niti, this is Samuel. I can't hear Jayden, but I can hear you and I shared with Mom. She says tell Andrew if he doesn't follow orders without further question, she's coming over there.*]

[*Thanks, Samuel, I got this.*] [*Jayden, Niti here. Tell Andrew to quit whining and follow orders. Say it that way. Use the word whining.*] "It's done, Dad. Andrew's position will be too high, but everyone else is in place."

"What about Mose?"

[*Tell Dad I'm in position, Niti. I'm exactly where we planned it. I can hear all three of you. You did great, Sis.*]

~~~

I'm the only CT in the water.

Niti came up with that label and it stuck. We were discussing whether R of H would have people who can cross-think. We've never seen an Earthborn who can do it. We believe it's because we grew up near whales, but that's just a theory. Many R of H citizens live on the water, so we were thinking maybe they have cross-thinkers. The discussion was awkward because we've never made a word for us. Niti said CT and it stuck.

All the other CTs acting as listeners are hidden anywhere from two hundred to three hundred feet above the water, so they can get strong signals from any R of H soldiers we can lure close. But, since I can hold my breath so long, I'm hiding in the water. I'm in some heavy roots right smack in the middle of the territory we mapped for our mission. I just have to move a couple of feet up to take breaths every thirty minutes or so, and since I have the farthest listening range of the CTs, the risk is worth it.

At least that's what I told Dad. He didn't like it, but wouldn't argue with me. He must think of me as a man now. I just turned eighteen, so I guess I am, but I don't think that matters to him. He believes in me.

Dad, Uncle K, and Danielle are all hidden at around fifteen hundred feet in locations where they can see straight down clearly. They have grenades they can throw to cause a lot of noise and attract R of H troops.

I cross-think to Niti on our private channel. [*Niti, how's it going? You enjoying the boredom of combat?*]

[*Dad keeps having me check with everyone about every five minutes. He's driving me nuts. He keeps asking about you. I keep telling him you're fine.*]

[*Tell him I think we should drop another hand grenade. Apparently they didn't hear the first one.*]

As I'm making this request, I hear thoughts that don't come from a CT. [*Niti, wait. Tell him I hear R of H thoughts. Faint, but I'm getting something.*]

[*Niti, This is Alana. There are R of H soldiers sneaking through the jungle below me. It looks like mostly Divers and just a few Scouts. There looks to be one squad of Archers.*]

[*Copy, Alana.*] [*Sam, Dad wants your mom to drop a grenade to draw R of H closer to the center of the area.*]

I hear an explosion from my right. The thoughts I'm picking up gradually grow stronger.

[*Niti, Alana here. It appears to be working. The thoughts are getting clearer. But none of them are thinking about anything strategic. There's a lot of nonsense, a lot of sex thoughts.*]

[*Copy, Alana.*] [*Mose, is your signal getting stronger?*]

[*Yes. Tell Dad it worked. If we drop no more grenades, maybe we'll get lucky and they pause, so we can listen a while. How many CTs are getting their thoughts?*]

[*You, Alana, and Haley. Start your recorders.*]

[*That's funny; I wish we had some. I'm going silent, so I can concentrate on what they're saying.*]

The R of H soldiers are now so close I can hear splashing. I raise my mouth above the water, take three deep breaths to replenish, submerge, and freeze.

"Halt. Everyone silent and still."

"Yes, Lieutenant."

"Silent, I said."

The voices help. I've identify the Lieutenant's thoughts. His are most likely to have strategic value. He breaks his own command and whispers.

"Sergeant Adler, how far away do you think the explosion was?" [*I can't believe they decide to attack now. Just when we're getting close. That last whale's remains probably gave us enough explosive.*]

"Sir, it's hard to say without knowing how large the bomb was. But, it definitely came from that direction." [*I can't believe I have to explain something so basic.*]

"Sergeant, we'll just stay here until we hear more." [*We'll take care of whatever puny attack this is and march to glory next week, maybe two at the most.*]

It takes another fifteen minutes listening to his delusions of grandeur before I hear what I need. Oh my God. How stupid can they be?

[*Niti, Tell Dad we got all we need. Have everyone start the exfill procedure. Get everyone on the edges out, so y'all can draw these guys away with more grenades.*]

[*Dad says he doesn't mean to be cold-blooded, but wants to know what you heard in case you don't make it out.*]

[*Of course. Tell him R of H plans to blow apart all four main trunks that support the Knot of Knot City. They plan to try and collapse a large portion of the jungle with enough damage to bring sunlight all the way to the water. If it works, they think the entire South Pole region of Canopy should be cleared.*]

~~~

We can't let R of H level a whole section of Canopy's forest, so Dad is going to meet with Cooter and the Generals to discuss possible actions.

Speed is critical. We don't have much time. Since Dad's busy, I asked Uncle K to take me to Bob's Clearing. He can get us there much quicker with his jumping ability.

When I suggested we share R of H's plans with the Canopians and get their help, Dad didn't blink.

He said, "What are you waiting for? Why are you still here?"

But, he was thinking, [*Why didn't I think of that?*]

Bob picks up my broadcast while we're still a mile away, so he knows I'm coming. He is at the surface and waiting in his Clearing as Uncle K makes the last jump.

[*Hello, Bob. Sorry to be so frantic.*]

[*What is wrong? You are agitated. Your friend has never*

seen a Canopian up close. Tell him to close his mouth.]

In my head, light blue bubbles come with Bob's attempt at humor.

[*No time for levity, Bob. This is serious.*]

[*Speak, then.*]

[*The Republic of Humanity plans to blow up the main tree trunks supporting our largest city. They want to level a large section of forest to let sunlight all the way to the water.*]

So much for blue bubbles. Along with pain in my head comes a dark red color I've never seen. Uncle K groans and grabs his head.

[*Bob! Cool it, will you? We're the good guys.*]

The pressure dissipates. [*I apologize. This is distressing news.*]

[*Yes it is. We can't allow it to happen. I think Dad wants our army to descend to the water below Knot City and try to create a protected barrier around the trees. The problem is, due to the way the trees come up at angles from the water, the four trunks cover a large area at the water's surface. It's over a square mile. We don't have the manpower to protect it. We need your help.*]

[*Does one of our tunnels run through the area?*]

[*Yes.*]

[*Is the tunnel a large one?*]

[*Yes.*]

[*Then I have an idea.*]

~~~

All twelve of us meet Bob halfway. He comes part way to us because time is of the essence and those of us born on Canopy move slower than Earthborn. It takes ten hours to get to the meeting point. It's over one of the tunnels leading to Bob's Clearing.

[*We're here, Bob. Say hello everyone.*]

A chorus of cross-think hellos assault Bob. I'm wondering how he'll react to it until the blue bubbles. These are big, strong bubbles in my head. I think it's a Bob-guffaw.

[*Wow!*]

[*Am I the only one with bubbles in my head?*]

[*What's with the bubbles?*]

[*Beautiful.*]

I float in front of the group and spin to face them. [*That's Bob laughing. You know because of the blue color. Everyone settle on a root or get comfortable in the water. We'll be here a while.*]

A wave swells the water as Bob moves directly below us. The roots are too thick for Bob to surface. [*Hello back, humans. Normally, I start association with a human by scanning, but Mose assures me there is no time.*]

Ben slaps the water with his hand. [*What? That ain't fair. I wanna watch Sentell squirm.*]

Bob's response is enlightening. Apparently, he's picking up human trash talk. [*No one will ever squirm as deliciously as you, Ben.*]

As the others laugh at Ben's expense and in appreciation of Bob's cleverness, six Raccoons emerge from the water and float over to join us. The laughter subsides as everyone realizes it's class time.

I locate a large, dead branch that has fallen from the forest above.

I begin trying to levitate the branch toward the group only to discover I am not strong enough. [*Bob, can you help me with this branch? I'm trying to get it over by us.*]

Two of the Raccoons go fetch the branch and bring it to us. They gnaw smaller limbs from the branch making it more log than branch. The CTs watch intently. They have never seen a Raccoon's teeth in action.

When they're done, the Raccoons back away.

Bob starts with Ben. [*Ben, attempt to lift the log with your mind.*]

The log wiggles slightly, but does not rise from the water.

[*Saoirse, help Ben. Both of you try to levitate the log.*]

The log wiggles more than before, but stays in the water.

[*Stop. Rest and concentrate on what I say. You are modifying gravity around the log with your minds. You are doing it with what can best be described as waves. Mose has the math to explain it, but understanding the math is unnecessary. You must learn each other's rhythm and get your waves in the same phase.*]

Ben and Saoirse both grimace. Ben is actually grunting. The log rises for just a second and splashes back down.

[*Good. Better. Wave coordination applies not only to levitating objects, but also broadcasting thoughts. Cooperative communication is harder because agreement on content is required, but the synchronization principal is similar. I will gather logs of various sizes for you to practice. In pairs, in threes, in large groups. You will learn each other's rhythms with my help.*]

As the Raccoons fan out to gather logs, it occurs to me how I can help. [*Bob, I think I know a way to make this go faster. As you know, we are a competitive species. I will design games to play. Teams will compete to see who can move logs the highest, fastest, farthest, or move the same log in different directions.*]

Everyone is immediately enthused, especially Bina. [*Are we going to choose up sides?*]

Even though this is serious, I laugh, but quit when a sobering thought occurs to me. [*Bob, please gather a lot of fruit as well. We are going to need to learn to crush skull-sized objects.*]

~~~

Ben's impatience annoys me, but I cut him some slack because I feel it, too. We are moving at a snail's pace through the water; submerging and moving under roots when encountered rather than crawling over them. We move a few yards, then stop and listen. Move, stop, listen, repeat.

[*Mose, you're killing me. At least let us move farther each time if you won't let us move faster.*]

[*No, Ben. Quit asking. We get one chance at this.*]

Ben, Sentell, Alana, and I grow quiet. No conversation with mouths or minds.

Two Raccoons pace us overhead, one from Bob and one from Kingfish. They are not in sight, spaced a mile apart to extend our eyes as much as possible since we don't know the location of the team transporting the bombs.

Alana and I are moving together, and Ben and Sentell are about four hundred yards away. We need to work in pairs to have the strength to attack R of H soldiers if necessary.

In our planning sessions, Dad called the Raccoons Daryl and his other brother Daryl, which made Uncle K laugh, but confused the rest of us.

It scares me how little we know about Canopians. When Bob explained his plan to bring Kingfish to help, I told him I was pretty sure Kingfish would fit in the tunnel running under Knot City, but I was certain he would be unable to turn around in it to go back. Heading on into R of H territory would be suicide for Kingfish, so I was skeptical of Bob's plan.

Then Bob throws me some blue bubbles as he explains that whales can swim in either direction. They have no front or back. Spending my whole life around Raccoons, who also have no front, you would think I might have thought of that.

The extreme range of Kingfish's ability to communicate with his Raccoons is critical to our plan.

The helpful lieutenant I spied on had shared that each tree would be destroyed by multiple bombs connected on a rope wrapped around the trunk. Thirty-two powerful bombs spaced fifty feet apart meant sixteen hundred feet of explosives that would wrap around the huge trunk three times in a spiral. Pulling the detonator on one would start a chain reaction they believed would completely sever the trunk.

But Bob was more helpful. He reminded me that his Raccoons are just an extremity to him. He could sacrifice one, and it would be, to him, just like me losing an arm with the significant exception that he could breed another Raccoon. His idea: if we can locate the string of bombs as they are transported, a Raccoon could just go pull the cord to detonate. It would kill all the R of H soldiers near it as well as the Raccoon, but war is hell.

When I found out that Kingfish was also willing to sacrifice Raccoons to help, I decided he wasn't such a bad guy after all.

Alana breaks the mental silence first. [*Could you believe how Cooter just matter-of-factly explained to us that no siblings could be on the same squad, so a family would lose only one member if things went wrong. Made my blood run cold.*]

My response is probably not comforting. [*He's assuming we just lose one squad. Each of my sisters is on one of the other squads, and Saoirse and Haley are still at risk in your family. This could go south for more than one squad.*]

[*Aren't you just a ray of sunshine?*]

[*I don't think Cooter realized he sent the only two CTs with children, you and Ben, on the same squad.*]

[*You are just a bundle of positive energy.*]

[*I'm just a realist. I think the real risk is to the last squad to find bombs. Surely after hearing the other three squads detonate bombs, the last squad will be facing guards on high alert.*]

[*I don't mean to sound ruthless, but I hope we find ours first.*]

[*Mose, this is Sentell. Our Daryl says he sees R of H Divers, Scouts, and Archers. Lots of them. We are heading to our right, the northeast, to take a look.*]

[*You know that's really Kingfish, right? Let's dispense with the Daryls. Okay, Sentell, you and Bob continue to move quietly. We'll head north-northeast to flank you.*]

I move close to Alana. [*Alana, we need to hurry to catch*

up. I wanna try something. I'm gonna pick you up and float us. We'll make less noise as we advance and can maintain a steady pace. You can help by trying your best to levitate yourself. Just try to make yourself as light as possible.]

[*We should have practiced this during our Bob-games. We could have had races.*]

[*I wish I had thought of it and we would've.*]

I pick Alana up in my arms and start floating as fast as I can to the north-northeast. She feels light; we are making good time.

Alana sees them first. [*Mose, stop. I see something ahead.*]

I settle into the water as quietly as possible. After a few seconds, I see movement. There are two R of H Divers. One of them points and whispers. "You see that? Straight ahead. I saw someone moving." [*There shouldn't be any of us that far ahead.*]

The other Diver appears to be the one in charge. "Shh. Idiot, not so loud, they'll hear you. I see them. Two of them. They're not R of H, that's for certain." [*I should probably whistle the warning sign. I think I'll wait and see for sure how many of them there are.*]

[*Mose, this is Ben. We can see the main force. It's huge.*]

[*Ben, Sentell, freeze. Two R of H Divers have spotted you.*]

I touch Alana on the arm to reassure her. [*You ready,*

Alana? We gotta do it.]

[*We going to kill them?*]

[*No, we're gonna squeeze their brains as hard as we can, so they can't signal. Maybe they die, maybe they don't. We've never done this before. We can't let them sound the alert. The one closest to us is the one thinking of doing it. Ready? Like we practiced. One, two, three, squeeze!*]

His head does not pop like Dad describes from the war, but he moans loudly, grabs his temples, and blood pours from his nose.

[*Quick. The other one. One, two, three, squeeze!*]

The second guy collapses into the water and screams on the way down.

The signal from Ben feels loud in my head. It must be the adrenaline. [*Crap, they heard him. They see us. Archers are drawing their bows. Sentell, get down!*]

Everything seems to happen at once.

Sentell screams.

Ben yells in my head. [*Sentell's hit. An arrow in the gut.*]

I hear far off explosions. A string of explosions — many of them — vibrate the water around me. One of the other squads has detonated their target's bombs.

They are far from me, but I can hear the R of H officers begin yelling commands, telling their Archers to attack.

Ben signals Kingfish. [*Kingfish, can you see that orange cord hanging from the bomb closest to you?*]

[*Yes.*]

[*Can you get to it to pull it?*]

[*I can pull it from here.*]

More explosions. These come from the other direction. Another squad has accomplished its mission.

Ben takes charge. [*Kingfish, don't pull it till Mose and Alana get clear. Mose, you guys run.*]

[*We can't leave y'all.*]

[*I think Sentell may already be dead. Kingfish can you pop the heads of all the Archers before they get to me?*]

[*Doubtful. Too many.*]

[*Mose, run! Now! You might be far enough away to survive. Tell Kathryn and Abraham I love'em. Go! Now! Kingfish, try to get'em all before they get me. If they get me, pull that cord.*]

I pick up Alana and flee. I am only three feet above the water. She is helping, and the water is a blur, but it feels like I am moving in slow motion. I hear the explosion before the shock wave hits us. As we drop, I see a large root in our path. I have time to turn my body so my back will hit it and Alana might be …

14

"The future is, by definition, undefined. I like undefined."
—*From the memoir of Mose Miles*

~~~

I love the view from Uncle K's back porch. I can see two suns on most days, and the forest is sparse for a thousand feet below us, which makes for a beautiful view. Most of the people in attendance at this unofficial wake are inside Uncle K's house. I notice Alana out of the corner of my eye.

[*Hey, Mose. Still in the wheelchair, I see. Back not any better?*]

[*Hi, Alana. I wondered if you were gonna make it. My back still gets stiff sometimes, but I'm okay. To be honest, I'm just kinda fond of my wheelchair.*]

[*That's good. I still feel guilty about what you did, shielding me like that.*]

[*I just didn't want to mess up my beautiful face on that root.*]

She shifts Amanda to a more comfortable position on her hip. [*Yeah, right.*]

[*Alana, this was a good idea, a separate wake for Ben and Sentell. Kathryn, Andrew, and Samuel really kept their emotions bottled up in front of all the adults.*]

[*Mose, you know we're adults, right?*]

[*You know what I mean.*]

[*Yes, I know what you mean. It's one of the reasons I suggested this get-together.*]

[*One of the reasons?*]

[*Yes, one of the reasons. I also ... Oh, hi, Haley.*]

Haley skids to a stop by us. [*You guys know when you use that private channel trick, I hear static right? It's kinda like speaking a foreign language in front of people so you can talk about 'em behind their backs. Rude really. What we talking about?*]

Alana and I both laugh which causes Amanda to squeal, wave her arms, and release a burst of static that makes us laugh more. The laughter feels good.

Alana shoves Amanda into Haley's waiting arms and picks up where she left off. [*Haley, if you must know, Mose was asking me about my reasons for wanting all the CTs to get together. One is to get Kathryn and Ben's brothers to let it out. They all need to quit holding it in and mourn.*]

Haley sits cross-legged on the floor and begins bouncing her niece in her lap. [*It's working. I saw all of them crying in the living room.*]

[*Good. Another reason was to get Mose to talk more about his vision for us. He's talked about it a little, but I want to know more.*]

I sit on the porch next to Haley and tickle Amanda. [*Alana, I don't think we're ready yet.*]

Alana sits by us. [*But, Mose, we still need to plan it, right?*]

Hayley hands Amanda to me and asks, [*Plan what?*]

Amanda begins to purr a steady and gentle cross-think static.

Haley cross-thinks, [*I wish she would do that with me. She only does that with Mose. You didn't answer me. Plan what?*]

I rock Amanda gently back and forth and mimic her cross-think waves. I use words so I don't interrupt my soothing static. "Haley, she's talking about my plan for us CTs to explore Canopy and introduce Canopians to the human race."

[*Oh, I know about that.*]

Alana leans back on her palms and locks her elbows to get comfortable. [*But I want details. I know you've been planning this for a long time.*]

"Well, basically, we would be extending the work my mom and dad did. They thought they were teaching the Canopians sign language, but they were really teaching them English. Canopians don't even have a language. They transmit thoughts but not words, per se. It's not how their minds work. Humans need words to communicate even if we're cross-thinking."

[*But they can just share memories and teach other English. They don't need us for that.*]

"They need us as ambassadors. When they meet second and third-generation humans who can cross-think, it makes it easier for them to accept us. Plus, we need to understand them better. Our future on this planet is intertwined with theirs."

Haley shifts to sit like Alana, leaning back on her palms. [*Speaking of third-generation, when are you gonna get you a girlfriend, Mose? Saoirse told me that's a part of the hold-up to us leaving. Everyone has a partner but you, and she thinks it's only going to work if you've got you a lady. Any hot prospects?*]

"That is not why we've been waiting. We just need to make sure the tear in the fabric of human society has healed. UC and R of H have to be getting along before we go. They lost ninety percent of their soldiers in that final battle. We might just be getting along because they're vulnerable. It might not help things to take much of the second-generation on a walkabout."

Niti seems to appear from nowhere. [*Mose, why you out here talking to yourself?*]

"I'm busy humming to Amanda, so I'm exercising my vocal cords to keep Haley entertained."

Haley moves over and pats the floor to allow Niti to sit. [*He's explaining how we're going to walk-around.*]

I laugh, and Amanda quits CT-humming. [*I said walkabout. I just meant that we will be gone a long time. We'll need to attend a lot of the Canopian Gatherings.*]

Alana laughs. [*Mose, you're really good at changing the subject. We were talking about how he needs to find a woman to give him some babies.*]

I begin CT-humming to Amanda, and she responds in kind.

Niti CT-hums, too. "Ooh, that reminds me. Did you see Kathryn flirting with Andrew? She's shameless.*"*

[*You know in their religion that a man takes his dead brother's widow as a wife, right?*] responds Alana.

Haley wiggles and stomps her foot on the floor. [*He really was talking about the walking-around. Let's stick to what's important. Mose, why do you say we need to attend a lot of Gatherings. How many do they have?*]

"A bunch. You know how I said I spent a lot of time learning Canopian math? Well, their number system is not decimal based like ours, it's based on twelve digits. So, one-zero is not ten, it's twelve, and one-zero-zero is not one hundred, it's one-hundred-and-forty-four.

Turns out they share their local memories — at the Bob

level I guess you'd call it — every twelve days. The Gathering I attended — more like a regional level — happens every one-hundred-forty-four days. But there is a big global Gathering every one-thousand-seven-hundred-and-twenty-eight days. We need to go to that one for sure."

Haley groans. [*Let me guess. That's one thousand in their weird math. So we need to go in, uh, about three years.*]

"Nice guess. Not that simple. It turns out there are places on Canopy that the Tripods can see the sky clearly enough that Canopians do in fact know how long their day is and it ain't the twenty-four hours we arbitrarily use. It's more like twenty-five-and-a-half hours. Don't hurt your brains doing the math. We got time."

Haley smiles and cross-thinks, [*So, the future of Human-Canopian relations just depend upon you finding a woman that'll put up with you. Better get cracking.*]

Alana laughes.

Haley chuckles.

Niti giggles.

Amanda squeals, waves her arms, and releases a powerful blast of high-pitched static.

~~~

Following the Earthborn isn't easy. I can control gravity enough to float, but not fast. Dad's sixty-two now and gray-haired, but he still jumps far and fast.

I get up early to talk to him. I'm not sure why.

I see him leap from the back porch and again off a tree fifty feet away. He jumps three times before I lose sight of him.

I float along on the path I think he took. I might have lost him. I'm high in the Overhead on one of the rare days with all three suns in the sky. The distant one Mom calls star C is low on the horizon, peeking through the trees.

I might as well turn back. I think I lost him.

Then, I see him. He's on a branch ten feet in diameter that is almost level as it branches from the leaning trunk of the tree. The huge trunk of the leaning tree covers him like a ceiling. He's sitting cross-legged, leaning against the trunk, and staring at his forearm.

I hover over the branch a few feet in front of him and lower gently to make no noise. He is tracing the tree branch tattoo on his forearm. Oddly, I get nothing from his mind. No internal dialog at all. Total silence. That's unusual.

"Dad?"

"Hello."

He obviously knows I'm here, but doesn't look at me. Still no thoughts coming from him.

"You okay, Dad?"

His voice is so soft I barely hear him. "Bipin didn't tell me about you."

His tattoo has the word 'Bipin' in it. The tattoo is a silhouette of a complex tree branch with a bird perched in it. There's also a spiderweb between the branches that has the word 'Bipin' entwined in the webbing. I asked Mom about the tattoo when I was a kid. She just said it wasn't her story to tell.

"You never told me about your tattoo. I was always curious. I looked up the word 'Bipin' at school. It's the Apache word for forest."

"Bipin was the closest thing to a father I had. Maybe a grandfather, I guess. He was already so old when I met him that his skin was turning to leather."

Dad finally looks up at me. His thoughts are still silent.

"What are you doing up here, Dad?"

"Meditating. Connecting with the forest like Bipin taught me. That old Indian could see things. He told me about Canopy before I even knew I had a berth on Inception. Told me about a world all forest. Told me about six-legged spiders as big as dogs. Told me about being able to jump like a cricket in low gravity. But, he didn't tell me about you."

His mind still offers nothing. I have only his words. I want more.

"What about me?"

"You're the future of Canopy. Hell, I guess the future of mankind. The Chinese had another colonization ship under construction when we left. Maybe they made it. I hope so."

"You never told me that."

"I never told you a lot of things. I haven't been a very good father. You turned out great in spite of me."

"Thanks for the compliment, Dad, but it's all because of you. Except for little things like having no legs, being able to read minds, and, of course, the whole control gravity thing. Other than that, I'm just like you."

He doesn't laugh as I'd hoped. His voice gets even quieter. "You're nothing like me."

"That's not what Mom says. She says it all the time. 'That boy is just like his father.'"

"She does not."

"Well, okay, she thinks it. And, normally it's when I'm disagreeing with her. But, still."

At last, he laughs.

"Okay, Dad, if you won't talk, let me. Eventually — don't know when exactly — we are going to continue the work you and Mom were doing. A bunch of us cross-thinkers will be leaving, and be gone a really long time. We're going to meet whales, attend their Gatherings, let them scan us, and do all we can to make sure humans are welcome on this planet. I thought you'd like that. You started it, I'm gonna finish it."

"You do me proud, Son. Just promise me you'll come back occasionally and let me play with my grandkids."

"You and Mom can come if you want."

"Nah, our society is bruised. The war has left a lot of

scars. I think I might run for Congress. Ain't that what old gray-haired soldiers have done for centuries? Become politicians?"

"I don't know. The one time you explained your view of diplomacy to me, it didn't seem like something the other politicians would enjoy so much."

He laughs again. It's great to hear.

~~~

I can't believe Dad made me come to this thing. I'm glad United Colonies and the Republic of Humanity decided to quit trying to kill each other, but that doesn't mean I want to party with'em.

Dad leans close to my ear as he pushes my wheelchair. "You could at least *try* to look like you're glad to be here."

"I'm trying."

Ela is wearing a beautiful dress, so unlike her normal attire. [*I heard that, Little Brother. You aren't trying very hard.*]

[*Quit eavesdropping.*]

[*I can't. You're an open book.*]

Bina giggles. [*I'm listening too, Mose. Just so ya know.*]

[*Me three.*] Niti piles on.

Mom turns and scowls at us, whispers, "Don't y'all think smiling and giggling at each other for no reason is a little conspicuous? Can't we try to act like a normal family?"

I see her point. Our abilities make the neurotypicals

nervous. Keeping a low profile is a good idea.

A beautiful, older woman with Asian features steps in front of me. "That wheelchair is beautiful. Is it hand carved?"

"Yes, ma'am. Thanks. My friend Samuel carved every bit of it, wheels and all."

"I'm Tomi Yamashita. My husband teaches psychology at the university here in Burl City. You may have heard of him? His name is Shino Yamashita."

"Yes, ma'am, I have heard of him."

"Please, call me Tomi. Ma'am makes me feel old. He's certainly heard of you. He is so excited he might get an opportunity to study the Canopians, and you've lived with them. Oh, here he is. Shino, come meet Mose Miles."

[*My brother is a celebrity.*]

[*Zip it, Ela. Mom said to cool it. You're gonna make me laugh.*]

[*It's not hard to figure out who Mose is. He's the only person in the room with no legs.*]

[*Damn it, Niti. Did you hear what I just said?*]

Niti giggles. [*You mean just thought?*]

Mom glares at us both as Dr. Yamashita makes his way over.

"Mr. Miles. I have been looking forward to meeting you and your family."

As our families are going through introductions,

suddenly I feel my world shift.

Her eyes are dark brown. Her long, straight hair is jet black. Her skin is alabaster. She's a five-foot-three, younger version of her mother, Tomi.

Her mother is signing with both hands as introductions are made. "And, this is my daughter, Yuki."

Yuki's eyes are locked on mine. They are wide with surprise. Her dress is green, I think. I'm not sure because I can't look away from her eyes. She nods at me, puts her curled hands together palms down, makes a kind of breaking motion, and points at me. She is signing as though I can understand. I hear her in my head. [*Can you hear me?*]

I hear mental gasps from my sisters, but they wisely keep quiet.

"Hello, Yuki. It's nice to meet you." [*Yes, I can hear you. You look surprised. But, I don't know your sign language.*]

[*Pretend you know Sign, please. Am I surprised? You think? I've spent my entire life signing. This is my first non-signed conversation. Ever. I feel faint.*]

[*I'm sorry. It must be a shock. Is there no one else with whom you cross-think?*]

[*Do me a favor. Hold your right hand open by your temple and make a very slight chopping motion.*]

I do as she asks. [*Like this?*]

[*Yes. Next, point at me, then put your fist in front of your*] *face and shove it forward two inches.*]

I comply. [*Oh, I get it. I'm pretending to know sign language.*]

[*And last, put your hand by your ear slightly open as though you're going to grab your ear. Pull your hand forward six inches as you bring all your fingers together.*]

I feel clumsy but do it. [*What did I just sign?*]

[*You asked me if I'd like to get some air. I'm signing yes and indicating enthusiasm. Do you mind if I push you, handsome?*]

My sisters are smirking.

Mrs. Yamashita is open-mouthed.

Both of our fathers just look at each other and shrug with slight smiles.

I only notice all that because Yuki has moved behind my chair and I can't see those beautiful eyes.

I feel dizzy.